Observing Theatre

Consciousness Literature the &Arts 36

General Editor:
Daniel Meyer-Dinkgräfe

Editorial Board:
Anna Bonshek, Per Brask, John Danvers,
William S. Haney II, Amy Ione,
Michael Mangan, Arthur Versluis,
Christopher Webster, Ralph Yarrow
Jade Rosina McCutcheon

Observing Theatre
Spirituality and Subjectivity in the Performing Arts

Daniel Meyer-Dinkgräfe

Amsterdam - New York, NY 2013

Cover illustration: © Pakhnyushchyy, licenced by fotolia.

Cover design by Aart Jan Bergshoeff.

The paper on which this book is printed meets the requirements of "ISO 9706:1994, Information and documentation - Paper for documents - Requirements for permanence".

ISBN: 978-90-420-3780-9
ISSN: 1573-2193
E-Book ISBN: 978-94-012-1029-4
E-book ISSN: 1879-6044
© Editions Rodopi B.V., Amsterdam - New York, NY 2013
Printed in the Netherlands

Contents

Acknowledgments

I would like to thank all contributors to this book for being so open both to the unusual form of collaboration (in the form of discussions in person or via Skype), and the pioneering nature of the material against which we discussed issues of theatre practice and theory—the philosophy of Hans Binder, here presented in an academic context for the first time. I am particularly grateful to Hans Binder for his permission to use his material in this book, and to comment on the discussion resulting from relating his thinking to drama and theatre. The sections in this book headed "principles" and attributed to Binder represent my efforts at presenting Binder's material as accurately as possible in English, based on his writing in German and his personal communication—these sections are thus not directly written by him even if they are attributed to him.

Introduction

Consciousness Studies

The referred web journal *Consciousness, Literature and the Arts*, was launched in 2000 and has since published more than 170 original articles that relate aspects of theatre, literature and the arts to aspects researched in consciousness studies. In 2005, three book series were launched, *Theatre and Consciousness* with Intellect (3 titles published so far) and *Consciousness, Literature and the Arts* with Rodopi (34 titles published so far), and proceedings of the biannual *International Conference on Consciousness, Theatre, Literature and the Arts* since 2005 with Cambridge Scholars Publishing. The conferences have attracted 250 different delegates from more than 30 countries across the world so far.

Consciousness studies as a discipline was launched in 1994 by the Center for Consciousness Studies at the University of Arizona in Tucson, USA, funded by the Fetzer Institute. The *Journal for Consciousness Studies* was founded in 1994, the *Association for the Scientific Study of Consciousness* in 1996, with its journal *Consciousness and Cognition*. The British Psychological Society approved two consciousness-related sections to form in 1997: *Consciousness and Experiential Psychology* and *Transpersonal Psychology*. The discipline of consciousness studies provides an umbrella for a range of individual disciplines that have studied, in their own ways, how we think, feel and act, why we think, feel and act as we do, and what it feels like to think, feel and act as we do. The contributing disciplines are philosophy, neuroscience, cognitive sciences and psychology, and physical and biological sciences. Thus it is likely that a large percentage of departments, institutes or schools representing these disciplines in many universities world-wide will have some contribution to consciousness studies to offer. In some cases such contribution is implicit, for example when departments of philosophy emphasise the research interest of one or more staff members in *philosophy of mind*. In other cases such contribution is explicit, for example in the case of the Sackler Centre for Consciousness Science at the University of Sussex, UK. In the context of those disciplines, consciousness studies cannot be anything else than mainstream: well-established in academia across the world.

The list of constituent disciplines that make up consciousness studies is complemented by two further lists of academic fields that contribute to it: one focuses on *experiential approaches* to consciousness studies not covered explicitly within the disciplines mentioned so far, and encompassing the following: meditation, contemplation and mysticism; hypnosis; other altered states of consciousness; transpersonal and humanistic psychology; psycho-analysis and psychotherapy; lucid dreaming; anomalous experiences; and parapsychology. From this list, psychoanalysis and psychotherapy are without doubt mainstream, whereas the remaining ones could be classified as either niche (transpersonal and humanistic psychology, altered states of consciousness, parapsychology, hypnosis), or emerging (meditation, contemplation and mysticism, lucid dreaming, and anomalous experiences).

The second list, under the heading of *culture and humanities* encompasses the fields that may also contribute to the understanding of consciousness, but which predominantly benefit from the findings of consciousness studies in the understanding of the contents specific to them. The sub-headings here are: literature and hermeneutics; art and aesthetics; music; religion; mythology; sociology; anthropology; information technology; ethics and legal studies; and education. From this list, only mythology might be placed into the niche category, while the others are squarely mainstream.

Consciousness studies, then, can be understood as a useful umbrella for predominantly mainstream disciplines, with some niche and some emerging contributions, that study consciousness, defined as how we think, feel and act, why we think, feel and act as we do, and what it feels like to think, feel and act as we do. The arts and humanities disciplines contribute to this understanding to some extent, but to a larger extent the arts and humanities benefit from the insights of other disciplines under the umbrella of consciousness studies in developing the understanding and knowledge specific to their own disciplines.

In my most recent book (2013) I presented a survey of research published since 1994 that relates the arts, in particular theatre, to findings in consciousness studies. It is interesting to note, by way of conclusion derived from this data, the correlation between the kind and amount of work done within the *Consciousness, Literature and the Arts* context predominantly written or edited by myself, and the development of the two lines of research, broadly speaking, that have become independent of the *CLA* field: on the one hand there is the scientific approach focusing on cognitive science as a framework for enhancing our understanding of the arts; on the other, there is a more recent development towards embracing philosophy (and within it in particular spirituality as a cogent concept) to achieve a similar aim. This latter development is evidenced in the formation of the working groups *Theatre, Performance and Philosophy* within the *Theatre and Performance Research Association* (TaPRA) in 2006, a similar working group in *Performance Studies International* (Psi), the research network *Performance Philosophy*, and the Performance and Religion working group within the *International Federation for Theatre Research* (IFTR) and the *Institute for the Study of Spirituality and Performance* with its associated e-journal *Performance and Spirituality.*

Contents and scope
This book takes up this trajectory and takes it further in the direction of spirituality in the sense of opening up for discussion, to the contributors of the book and its readership, material not hitherto presented, at least in this form and cohesion. In this book are collected the results of a number of discussions that bring together the expertise of colleagues in their respective research fields within theatre and performance studies and practice, and expertise on the relation between theatre and performance, in theory and practice, and consciousness studies. Three self-contained chapters present the status quo of research within a specific field. In the first chapter, I discuss with Yana Meerzon (Canada) and Benjamin Poore (UK), how the phenomenon of *nostalgia* has been taken up in drama. The second chapter moves from the text to the performance: with Gayathri Ganapathy (India and UK) and Shrikant Subramaniam (India and UK) I reflect critically the theory and practice of intercultural theatre. In Chapter Three I illuminate the role of theatre criticism in conversation with Per Brask (Canada) and Harry Youtt (USA).

In Chapter Four, I briefly introduce the model of consciousness I have used in my research so far to contextualise phenomena of theatre and opera. At the centre of Chapter Five, however, is a further dimension to this model of consciousness that I have not fully presented so far, and that allows an even more radical, innovative approach to the discussion of the issues raised in chapters one to three of the book. This further dimension is based on, and presented in conjunction with, the work of hitherto unpublished German geobiologist Hans Binder[1]. I introduce this new dimension in Chapter Four, and discuss the issues raised in chapters one to three , and others not featuring in those chapters, in the context of that new dimension. In Chapter Five, my communication with Binder is central; in addition, however, I present material based on discussions Steve Dixon (Singapore) and Kate Sicchio (UK) on digital performance, with actress Nicola Tiggeler (Germany) on the actor coping with tough roles over an extended period of time, and with Aylwyn Walsh's (South Africa and the UK) about her practice of applied theatre.

In Chapter Six, finally, I present feedback from the contributors to the preceding chapters to our argument in Chapter Five, together with the response to that feedback by Binder and myself.

---

[1] Binder has got a website in German, http://www.naturgesetze.info/, he does not speak any English, all his material exists only in German and it is published to his clients but not in the public domain.

Chapter One

Benjamin Poore, Yana Meerzon, Daniel Meyer-Dinkgräfe

Nostalgia

Introduction

Sporadically, countries or larger geographical areas in broadly speaking the West appear to find themselves engulfed in waves of *nostalgia*. In this chapter, we discuss the role and nature of *nostalgia* as it is reflected in drama and theatre. While we have edited the material to form a cohesive sequence, the way in which this material came into existence, by discussion from two places in the UK and Canada, respectively, via Skype, is reflected in the material as well, predominantly in its free flow of associations. The discussion starts with the term *nostalgia* and its origins, and related terms, moves on to agency and power (Foucault), addresses the relationship of past, present and future, the constellations of characters in plays dealing with *nostalgia,* the nostalgic implications of revivals and re-enactment in the context of drama and theatre, and the role of *nostalgia* in popular culture. We then focus on critical positions towards *nostalgia*, and discuss in particular the context of *nostalgia* and exile. The chapter ends with a survey of plays about *nostalgia* found in the pays database at dollee.com.

Statistic evidence suggests that most people think they know what *nostalgia* is and have encountered experiences of it on a regular basis. The authors of this article are no exception : sitting in his attic surrounded by boxes from moving house, Poore knows that in one of the boxes is a collection of letters, and it gives him a pleasant, warm, fuzzy feeling to know those letters are there, what they are about, and who they are from. However, he is also aware that if he were to find those letters now, and actually read them for the first time in 20 or 30 years, he would get a jolt of a shock because of the direct engagement, and because of discovering things that he was not expecting, and because of the encounter with memories or feelings he had displaced or completely forgotten about. There is thus a distinction between knowing that they are there, which is the aspect of *nostalgia*, and the jolt or shock of the direct engagement of reading them as if for the first time. This example suggests that *nostalgia* could be compared to slipping on a comfortable pair of shoes, as something that has been worn into a certain shape through use. The re-remembering a memory takes on contours, takes on the shape of that act of re-remembrance. It is no longer the brand new pair of shoes, but something that is comfortable and familiar, because we are always already re-engaging with it.

For Poore, *Consuming Histories* by Jerome de Groot (2008) represents a book that puts into perspective his own experiences in the context of *nostalgia*. This book discusses the ways in which many levels of culture are obsessed with history, and provides as examples of this post-*nostalgia* references to British comedy shows from the 1990s, such as *'allo 'allo* and *Blackadder*. Here the detachment from history and the irony and playfulness, and a refusal to engage deeply and to be all about surfaces are highlighted. For Poore, thinking back to that time when he saw those programmes on TV triggers memories of details of film stock, studio audience, colours, and fashions. All this together creates, almost against itself, a *nostalgia* that could be labelled *post-nostalgic*. Time does its work and *nostalgia* seems to come relentlessly in waves, and waves pile on top of previous waves, or supersede previous waves. Often it is not the historical period itself that is being evoked in pure form, as a direct line to history, but it is as filtered through the interpretations of that history of previous generations and decades. This is where the manipulation comes in.

André Aciman's writing on exile and returns (2000, 2001, 2007, 2012) has been important for Meerzon's thinking on exilic experiences[1]: *nostalgia* feeds into the sense of the impossibility of return. There is longing to go back, to remember, but those who do go back tend to be in a total state of shock because nothing is as one has imagined. This addresses mechanisms of engagement and

---

[1] See in particular the section on *Nostalgia*, exile and choice, starting on page 36.

disengagement with one's past and present, and thus the exile's sense of estrangement. In the reading of exilic experience, *nostalgia* would often instigate an émigré desire to come back, to re-connect with one's past and thus to fix the time that is out of joint. However, as many know and as Aciman would write, the return is impossible, the memory betrays the traveller—what seemed to be the genuine longing for home turns into emotional stupor. When finally meeting with one's past, an exilic person experiences the shock of not-feeling. It is only in the aftermath of writing about this experience of return when the creative forces give the exile a new voice and dictate the artistic take on this incomprehensible experience. The act of writing, as Aciman explains (2012), becomes the real experience of return, the gesture of letting go of one's *nostalgia* for the lost past and the lost home. In the exilic theatre practice, it is the process of writing a play or staging a performance that can be considered as an act of return, a possibility for an exilic artist to re-connect with home through the channels of his/her professional engagement. *Nostalgia* can be a dangerous but a welcome guide in such process.

Meyer-Dinkgräfe recalls how in a 2012 stage production of Strindberg's *Miss Julie* with French actress Juliette Binoche in the title role, *nostalgia* took the shape of projecting a younger Binoche as known from older films on to the actress who is now in her late 40s so as to create a match of a younger character as suggested by the script. Friends' and colleagues' responses to his invitation to provide him with their spontaneous thoughts about *nostalgia* led, among other contributions, to this poem,

> *Jeder Augenblick*
> Vergangenheit ist Geschichte,
> Zukunft ist Geheimnis,
> aber jeder Augenblick ist ein Geschenk!

> *Every Moment*
> Past is history,
> Future is secret / mystery,
> but every moment is a gift
> (Falkenhagen 2012)

and this consideration, triggered by the class reunion thirty-five years after the end of high-school:

Mir bringt es Einhalt von dem immer vorwärtsstrebenden Alltag. Reflexion, was alles schon war. Genugtuung, dass das alles schon war und es kein muß gibt, keinen Zwang, dass ich alles immer weiter voran treibe. Ich werde zufriedener und sehe, wie die Zeit Veränderungen gebracht hat. Das Treffen ist zwar viel zu kurz, um ein bißchen tiefer von euerem heutigen Leben einen Eindruck zu bekommen. Aber ich sehe, dass es recht egal zu sein scheint, wo wir angekommen sind. Der eine etwas reicher, der andere alleinlebend, aber der Abend zu kurz, um es zu erfassen. Es sind kleine Eindrücke, die zusammen mit der Erinnerung sich wieder zu einem Bild formen, das Erinnern fördern und den Wunsch hegen mehr Zeit damit zu verbringen, den ein oder anderen im jetzt zu erleben. Doch dann ist der Abend (bzw. die Nacht - ich bin in der Nacht mit Wolfgang noch bis zur Furth spaziert -) auch schon wieder vorbei. Unser Alltag ruft, ob Arbeit, Familie oder ein sonstiger Weg mit oder ohne Ziel. Und unsere Wege trennen sich - aber ich freue mich aufs nächste mal. Es kam mir vor, als wäre unsere gemeinsame Schulzeit erst vor kurzem gewesen.

It brings me a break from daily life that is ever propelling forwards. It brings me reflexion of all the things that have been. Gratification that all that has happened already and that there is no "must", no pressure that I always propel everything further. I get more satisfied and see how the time has brought about changes. The class reunion was far too brief to get more of an impression of my former classmates' current lives. But I see that it seems not to matter where we have got to. One was a little more well-off, one was living alone, but the evening was too brief to grasp it all. These are small impressions that, together with memories of the past, re-form into an image that strengthens the memories and trigger the desire to spend more time to experience the one or the other of the former class-mates in the here-and-now. Then, however, the evening is over again. Our daily lives beckon. No matter whether work, family or other paths with or without goal. Our worlds move apart, but I am looking forward to the next time. I felt as if our mutual time at school together had been only recently. (Schwarz 2012)

Finally, this response:

Du hast mich gefragt, warum Nostalgie solche Bedeutung für unser Leben hat. Dazu kann ich sagen, dass sie erst dann Bedeutung bekommt, wenn man im Begriff ist zu altern. Vielleicht deshalb, weil man erst dann begreift, dass man keinen Schritt, den man jemals getan hat, verändern kann. Diese Erfahrung, nämlich einen Schritt zu gehen und ihn nicht rückwärts machen zu können, hat etwas Endgültiges, also schlussendlich auch irgendwie etwas mit "erwachsen werden" zu tun. Wenn man jung ist, dann ist man sich dessen unbewusst. Und wenn man älter ist, dann ist man traurig, weil man um die Endlichkeit dieser Schritte weiß. Und vielleicht noch ein paar Dinge gern geklärt hätte. Manchmal ist es auch so, dass man jemandem Unrecht getan hat, mit Worten oder auch Taten, und die Reue folgt erst nach Jahren. Sich entschuldigen zu wollen hat sicherlich nicht unmittelbar etwas mit Nostalgie zu tun, aber ist doch um die Ecke damit verknüpft. Denn wenn man keine nostalgischen Gefühle hätte, würde man vergangene Geschehnisse abstreifen, wegschieben, verdrängen oder auch ganz einfach vergessen.

You asked me why *nostalgia* has such meaning for our lives. I can say that it gets meaning only when we start ageing. Perhaps because only that is the time when we realise that we cannot change any step we have taken in the past. This experience, taking a step forward and not being able to back-track that step, has something finite, and ultimately this is part of growing up. When you are young, you are not aware of it. And when you get older, you get sad because you know about the finiteness of these steps, and because perhaps you would have liked to have settled some issues. Sometimes it is the case that one had done an injustice to someone, in words or deeds, and remorse follows only after years. Wanting to apologise is not directly related to *nostalgia*, but is linked to it indirectly: because if you did not have nostalgic feelings, you would simply strip off past events, push them aside, suppress them or simply forget them. (Hadamovsky 2012)

These are some examples of the statistic that most people think they know what *nostalgia* is and have encountered experiences of it on a regular basis. However, in an academic context, *nostalgia* is a concept that is neither well defined nor understood. General and consumer psychology, as well as cultural studies are the main academic disciplines that have subjected *nostalgia* to research, considering it a form of homesickness, a medical condition, a nervous condition, or an emotion. *Nostalgia* carries positive value and is therefore desirable, or it carries negative value and is therefore undesirable as an experience in daily life. *Nostalgia* is either of considerable value to the future of humankind, in so far as it may serve as a vehicle allowing humans to (re-) connect with their source and essence, which in turn will be beneficial to well-being and thus productivity in all contexts. If that is the case, *nostalgia* should be enhanced and supported. However, *nostalgia* may also turn out to have a considerable detrimental effect on humans, that of supporting escapism, and in the process wasting a huge amount of energy on futile delving into the past without much impact on the present and the future. The issue at stake in relation to *nostalgia* is thus whether it enhances the quality of human life, or reduces it; whether it supports well-being or weakens it; whether it enables humans to deal meaningfully with the problems that face them, or whether it depletes energy, thus preventing humans from that very important task.

Studying nostalgia in drama and theatre
In these broad academic and personal contexts, drama, theatre and performance (both in their historical and contemporary aspects and dimensions) may offer approaches to answer that question. The overall aim of the discussion, therefore, is to establish how plays depict *nostalgia*: as unambiguously positive, desirable and helpful to those engaging in it, or as negative, undesirable and not helpful, or whether *nostalgia* is depicted as multi-layered, complex and hence problematic.

The term and concept
The term *nostalgia* is derived from Greek: *nostos* means "return to one's native land", and *algos* means pain or suffering. Taken together, the original meaning of *nostalgia* is "suffering caused by longing to return home" (Hepper et al. 2011, 1). The phenomenon was described vividly by Homer in the *Odyssey*, as Odysseus nourishes memories of his home during his 10-year journey. The term *nostalgia* was coined by a Swiss physician, Johannes Hofer, in the 17th century specifically to describe the condition of homesickness suffered by Swiss soldiers serving away from home. In the 17th and 18th centuries, *nostalgia* was considered a neurological disorder, in the 19th century as a psychological disorder involving melancholy and depression, and in the majority of the 20th century it was considered as related to psychosis, mourning and depression (Wildschut et al. 2006, 975). Since the end of the 20th century, research into *nostalgia* has seen an unprecedented upsurge. The definition changed to "sentimental longing of wistful affection for the past" (*New Oxford Dictionary of English*, see Hepper et al. 2011, 2). *Nostalgia* now attracts a wide range of approaches, depending on the equally wide range of interpretations. According to Hepper et al., *nostalgia* has been described as an emotion (including a self-relevant and higher order emotion), but also as having cognitive and motivational underpinnings. The nature and function of *nostalgia* are equally contested. People develop *nostalgia* because they yearn for positive

memories when they encounter difficulties in life. Marketing psychologists argue that *nostalgia* allows predictions of consumer behaviour. Organisational psychologists have emphasised the role of *nostalgia* in developing "organizational coherence, management, and change". Hepper et al. also point to the range of research positions on the aetiology and valence of *nostalgia*. Those positions range from negative, such as "grief for the loss of an irretrievable past", via ambivalent to positive, with a predominance of either negative or positive impact. Related to this, some research considers *nostalgia* as healthy, possibly even useful as a therapeutic tool, other authors argue that it is maladaptive and thus unhealthy (2011, 2-3).

Nostalgia and Foucault's concept of power
It is perhaps useful to think about *nostalgia* not as something that is done to us or that is monolithic, but more along the lines of Foucault's concept of power, as something that circulates and is traded and exists even in places where you would not think it is there. In terms of power, it is implicit rather than explicit in drama in so far as characters rarely talk about their power explicitly. In Pinter's *Birthday Party* (1957), Goldberg trades in both power and *nostalgia*. *Nostalgia* is one of the tools he uses to take on a powerful position at the boarding house that he visits: he will sit down and reminisce about his childhood, but the stories that he tells are incompatible with each other, there are different names and different childhoods. He moves this *nostalgia* around and uses it as a way of dominating other people. As soon as they get into a particular discourse, when they think that he is pulling up something authentic from his past, he shifts it and they can no longer believe it.

Related concepts: melancholy, yearning, and déjà vu
In terms of yearning, *nostalgia* has more of a direction towards the past, and often the person engaging in *nostalgia* does so with quite specific time periods of the past, or contents of the past, in mind, such as specific people and specific circumstances. Yearning, in contrast, is likely to be less specific in so far as the person experiencing this feeling might find it more difficult to say precisely what they are yearning for. Yearning, moreover, is directed towards possibilities and potential of the future, rather than related to sadness about something that has been lost. It is captured well in a scene from Willy Russell's

Educating Rita (1981): the title character, a young hairdresser in Liverpool who decides she needs education and enrols in an Open University literature course, joins her family in the pub, where they are all singing a song from the juke box. She notices that her mother is crying and asks her why. The mother responds: "There must be better songs to sing" (1981). In the context of the play's plot, this incident supports Rita's determination to continue with her new and difficult path of education despite a series of setbacks, including alienation from her husband and her family that will shortly lead to her husband seeking divorce, and a phase where she does not (yet) belong to the group of educated people that she wants to be part of—in the scene before she sees her mother cry in the pub she could not bring herself to join a party that her OU tutor, Frank, had invited her to at his place. *Plenty* (1978) by David Hare (b.1947) moves backwards and forwards in time, and is thus able to alternate between *nostalgia* for what has happened, and then, when the plot goes back to the past, the characters can indulge in yearning for a possible future, which the audience or reader then know does not come to pass. This play thus has both sides of the melancholy equation. Déjà-vu is an inversion of the *nostalgic* sense of being separated, because it is an instant accessing of a moment that one feels has happened before. It shares with *nostalgia* the feeling of time travel, but déjà-vu comes unexpected and uninvited, rather than one that is yearned for as in *nostalgia*.

Nostalgia and ageing

This consideration brings the phenomenon and concept of ageing into the discussion of *nostalgia*. Ageing brings with it a consideration, possibly reassessment, and possibly *nostalgia*, for our youth. This applies to our perception and feeling of our body, where we notice difference between now and then, and the nature of memory, where imagination and truth may tend to become more distinctly separate. *Nostalgia* then becomes related to what we think we were, in terms of body and memory, in some past. This interaction of perceptions of the past shapes the present. Susan Traherne in *Plenty* becomes active in wanting to impose her own myth on others. Ageing allows us to recognise that the idea of who we were at some time in the past needs adjustment and change from the perspective of hindsight afforded by ageing. These in turn may shift again with time, leading to the insight that it is hardly ever possible to know fully what our identity is at any point in the present or what it may have been in the past.

Nostalgia for the future

There is also *nostalgia* for the future. A revival of a play by Alan Plater, *Close the Coalhouse Door*, is relevant; a Northern Stage / Live Theatre co-production directed by Samuel West, it toured the UK in 2012. The play was a hit in the late 1960s. It is a history of the miners in the North-East of England. The play started out in Newcastle and ran in the West End for a considerable amount of time. For the current revival the production team had to invent a framing device to allow the play, which takes the history to 1968, to take place in 2012. The frame is provided by an academic in a time machine. He acts as our guide to take us back to the past and explain the working class house we are going to visit, where they are having a 50th wedding anniversary where they are talking about the great mining victories and disasters and strikes of the past from the very early 19th century, re-enacting it with all the different voices. Arriving at the end of the context for the original play, they embarked on inventing a future, from 1968 onwards, that did not happen: for example, when Maggie Thatcher was not elected Prime Minister in 1979.

Constellations of nostalgia in drama

A close look at descriptions of plays on the large database of 146,000 plays, at www.doollee.com, that come up in response to the search term *nostalgia*, reveals a number of distinct categories. Further examination, in the context of the plays discussed in this chapter, confirms those categories. In the majority of plays, *nostalgia* is triggered by the device of having friends and family, in all possible constellations, meet (again), often after several years without having met, and exchanging memories or establishing where they are now in comparison to where they were when they met last. In some cases the play about a family unit may serve as representative of the nation. *An Inspector Calls* (1945) by J.B.Priestley (1894-1984) and *Chicken Soup with Barley* (1956) by Arnold Wesker (b. 1932) are examples. Although *Chicken Soup with Barley* is set against the backdrop of twentieth century history, it is more specifically about the loss of political faith of a Jewish, socialist family. Thus it is about how national and international affairs have an impact on a family's belief systems.

Personal relationships revisited are at the centre of a further sub-category of plays in which *nostalgia* plays an important role. Some plays focus on one individual character's psychology and some are set in the past that can trigger feelings of *nostalgia* in the audience. The plays of Tennessee Williams relate to these two categories of friends and family and personal relationships: they often look at failed family relationships; his memory plays dramatize characters looking back at their youth. His two semi-autobiographical plays are particularly interesting: *Vieux Carré* (started in 1938, premiered in 1977) set in New Orleans, and *The Notebook of Trigorin* (1980), an adaptation of Chekhov's play *The Seagull*.

One play on doollee.com is identified specifically as critical satire, several US-plays focus on *nostalgia* in the context of baseball, a revival of a controversial (fictional) production of *Twelfth Night* opens up *nostalgia* as a means of political opposition, several plays specifically deal with characters in exile and the role *nostalgia* has for them, and finally there are a number of plays that have celebrities of the past as main characters and celebrate their lives and successes. *Nostalgia* can be addressed and discussed explicitly in plays, or it is implicit. In sum, plays reflect the full range of attitudes towards and positions about *nostalgia* that we find in the academic debates.

Revivals

In a way every revival is a *nostalgic* engagement with the original staging conditions (note the recent production of *Death of a Salesman* in the USA which explicitly recreated at least the set of the original production). Certain plays must be set in period, because that's how they work best, or it may even be the only way they work. In the case of Oscar Wilde's plays, we perceive them in the light of an understanding that they are about a class and social system of which he fell foul in the end. We admire the world he creates and are aware of the sharpness of its teeth at the same time. Thus one form of quite simple *nostalgia*, of the "oh wasn't it wonderful in the elegant days of the 1890s when men and women were decorative" kind, is tempered and in the process a melancholy outsider *nostalgia* is created for the loss of the years we were robbed of Wilde's genius because prison broke his health and his artistic impetus. Plays about Oscar Wilde necessarily reflect on that historical moment and become nostalgic for a man we never knew, recreating situations which are historically documented, fleshing them out.

It would be possible for a seasoned theatregoer to see the revival of David Hare's *The Judas Kiss* in 2012 and become nostalgic, not for the imaginary 1890s, but for the 1990s when plays about Wilde were in vogue, with restagings of the trials, (*Gross Indecency: The Three Trials of Oscar Wilde* by Moisés Kaufman [1997]), and one-man shows (such as Simon Callow's revival of Micheál MacLiammóir's *The Importance of Being Oscar* [1997]). The play's use of male nudity, and its portrayal of taken-for-grantedness of promiscuous sexuality in Wilde's circle, might have been deemed controversial in the 1990s; in the 2010s, such attempts to show the 'real' 1890s underworld are probably less shocking. As with that other ephemeral art form, pop music, one theatrical generation's desire to shock is likely to be read as rather sweet and naive by the next, a kind of *nostalgia* for simpler times that is overlaid on the play's anti-*nostalgia* for the 1890s. The casting of Rupert Everett as Wilde in the 2012 production of *The Judas Kiss* adds a further layer of reminding the audience of the parts he played in productions of Wilde plays on film in the 1990s and early 2000s.

The Wooster Group's re-staging of Grotowski's "Acropolis" and their 2008-2012 staging of *The Wooster Group's Version of Tennessee Williams' VIEUX CARRÉ* are equally relevant in this context. The play itself is a memory play, it is partly autobiographical and marked by the author's *nostalgia* for the days of his youth; as a theatre show, one can say it is marked by the Wooster Group's own attitude to *nostalgia* and memory, since it is part of their ideology to carry past productions into the new performances.

Ibsen's plays, and those by Chekhov and Wilde, can take us back to the times before the great revolutions, the great wars and the period of stability. Through the productions we revive, we keep telling us (about) our theatrical heritage. The syllabus of drama studies at university will tell us that the plays of Ibsen set us free and made us think about drama in a modern way. In fact, at the time not Ibsen's plays filled the theatres in London's West End, but plays like Arthur Wing Pinero's *The Second Mrs Tanqueray*.

Re-enactment

Re-enactment of history is certainly an expression of *nostalgia*. In the UK, Prime Minister David Cameron recently announced plans to commemorate the outbreak of the First World War in terms of the need to create a legacy, just as the organising committee for the 2012 Olympic Games was preoccupied with creating a 'legacy' for the Games. Indeed, sports fans were encouraged to get nostalgic about the 2012 Olympics only one year on with the Anniversary Games, held in July 2013.

The way people talk about World War I now suggests a strange hybrid of second-and third-hand sets of memories, many of them filtered through the 1960s, a complex decade characterised by a reaction against the idea of war itself with the Vietnam War. Joan Littlewood's *O What a Lovely War* was equally influential in that. The ways in which we talk about and dramatize the First World War, from revivals of *Journey's End* to productions of the stage version of Michael Morpurgo's *War Horse* are saturated in that melancholy, as well as the way in which the war poets Owen and Sassoon are taught in British schools.

All these create a mental landscape which someone 80 years ago would not have recognised at all as how they recalled or commemorated the First World War. We convince ourselves that the rag bag of history is a direct line to the past, that it is in some way authentic. The audience of *War Horse* is interesting in this context, as there are many retired people with their grandchildren. They seem to be the most obvious targets for popular sentiment. This sentiment is the component of *nostalgia*. Attending such a performance includes an aspect of bearing witness, paying due respect to this aspect of history, no matter how problematic. Here the public act of going to the theatre is different from more private *nostalgia* of TV. Thus collective and personal *nostalgia* need to be differentiated.

Nostalgia in the context of popular culture

Popular culture is most easily identified with *nostalgia*, in terms of TV, film and musical. More towards theatre, there are historical re-enactments. Marketing for long-running musicals takes up *nostalgia*. It is by now for some productions a question of generations, and the way those musicals are produced internationally with the same sets and mise en scène, ensures they will be the same over the decades.

Simon Reynolds, *Retromania: Pop Culture's Addiction to its own Past* (2012) specifically draws on Derrida and Boym's ideas, as well as some sociological work from the 1970s on *nostalgia*. Amy Holdsworth's *Television, Memory and Nostalgia* (2011) allows drawing connections between what happens in theatre with developments in television. An example of this 'feedback loop' between the media is the popularity of stage adaptations, particularly of Austen, Brontë and Dickens novels, in the wake of the costume drama boom on British television since the mid-1990s. Indeed, a further example is the annual reinforcement as Christmas entertainment of Dickens's *A Christmas Carol* (and the musical *Scrooge*), Lewis Carroll's *Alice in Wonderland* and L. Frank Baum's *The Wizard of Oz*, which takes place on television in the screening of various versions, and also in the theatre, in revivals and fresh adaptations of the same texts. Despite the tenuous links of the latter two works to Christmas, their traditional appeal as family entertainment in television programmers' schedules—from back in the days of only three terrestrial TV channels in England—has been nostalgically translated to theatres, many of which have become financially dependent on the familiarity and cross-generational appeal of their Christmas shows to subsidise the theatre's work for the rest of the year.

The way the media package and shape collective history influences our own personal histories and personal *nostalgia*. As a result, we no longer remember only our personal histories, but what we have been told was happening, was vital or important about a period, as it is being historicised in front of our eyes by the media. Here is a major input to the psychological perspective on *nostalgia*: the act of remembering actually changes the memory itself. The more you revisit, the more this smooths things or changes the shape. In her work on postmemory, Marianne Hirsch deals with second generation survivors who do not have the direct memory of the Shoah, but are haunted by its horrors as powerfully and unavoidably as their parents. We can stretch the definition of this term and apply it to the distinction between real engagement and nostalgic engagement with the past. Hirsch describes postmemory as the imaginative investment, as a process of projection and creation, in which one is actively constructing memories to fill in gaps and to create a past that makes sense to you (1997, 1998, 2008). There are many plays in Canada and former Eastern bloc countries about 2nd or 3rd generation characters who deal with the guilt of war, the plays that can be read in in the context of Hirsch's postmemory. For example, the English Canadian *East of Berlin* (2007) by Hanna Moscowitch (b.1978) focuses on the experiences of the son of a Nazi war criminal (medical doctor) growing up in Paraguay.

Haunted by the past: critical positions towards *nostalgia*

In line with the injunction that Orpheus should not look back if he wants to retrieve his wife Eurydice from the Underworld, drama has been sceptical and critical of the human tendency to look back, to delve into the past and yearn for the assumed ideals of times gone by. The theatre is an ideal place for raising such doubts, because in the theatre, the narrator, for example, may well say that something did indeed happen, and it is authentic because I am describing it, and I know for certain this happened because it happened to me and I remember it as if it was yesterday. However, because it is an actor on stage delivering those lines, framed in the theatrical context, the assurance of authenticity and truth is rendered problematic and the actor in fact also dares the audience not to believe. *Nostalgia* or memory can have a distinctive role not only in a dramatic text, but is equally important as a feature of a theatrical performance in terms of the relationships to the theatrical venue itself in which the performance is presented.

In *The Haunted Stage*, Marvin Carlson develops an interesting take on this phenomenon. He discusses how every new performance created in a stable theatrical venue that has its own history and traditions carries in its aesthetics and inner artistic code the memory of past productions done in that space (2003). This is of course interesting in the context of theatre reception and the knowledge that different audiences bring to the auditorium. Thus *nostalgia* might mark our reception of the well-known works that carry a history of glorious productions or performers, such as Olivier's Hamlet. These traditions would be very much culture-specific and the degree of *nostalgia* the audience members could feel toward those productions would vary, depending on their own theatre experience and education.

A very interesting example of this phenomenon can be found in the 2012 MET (New York) staging of the opera *The Tempest*, composed by Thomas Adès and directed by Robert Lepage. The play on which the opera is based provides a very particular take on *nostalgia* in many aspects, including the story itself, the characters' psychology, and specifically Shakespeare's testimony on theatre art itself. Lepage heavily builds on this tradition: he situates his version in the 19th century and in the building of La Scala, in Milan. So the opera presents Lepage's meta-theatrical take on the action: everything is a theatre magic designed by Prospero, whose powers rest with the old theatre machinery, where everything is done by hand in the authenticity of the experience of the real, the imagery popular with the MET's audiences. This particular staging is very nostalgic for the magic of theatre illusion that would rest with the hands-on experience of the theatre makers themselves, something that can take us away from the power of technology and multimedia that has taken over theatre stages in the last decade. In this opera, Lepage does use theatre machinery, but only that which originates in theatre (acrobats, catwalks moving up and down, stage hands assisting Ariel in her flights and magic tricks and so on) with very minimal projections at the beginning of Act 1. This is an example of *nostalgia* as it can be experienced and manifested on stage in theatre, and perhaps something similar to the *Christmas Carol* phenomenon, discussed in the following paragraphs.

Christmas

Christmas is an interesting time and event in terms of *nostalgia*. Nowadays, Christmas seems to be predicated on the idea that Christmas is not what it was. This is evident, for example, in the lyrics of *White Christmas*, "Just like the ones I used to know". The "white Christmas" is lost in childhood, and it is something you are trying to regain. Even the song itself is a Bing Crosby classic (he first performed it on Christmas Day 1941).

A *Christmas Carol* is a good example of the English myth-making in relation to Christmas. Scrooge is returned to the past by the Ghosts of Christmas Past, and grieves for the opportunity of love with Fanny that he rejected. His grief also appears to be for the lost sense of community embodied by Fezziwig and his Christmas party; those days are gone, Fezziwig is gone, and that live-in-the-moment gaiety can never be retrieved (even though, paradoxically, in order to understand this, we as readers have to be shown, and encouraged to experience, Fezziwig's Christmas party anew). The starting point for

Scrooge's journey is to the Christmas that is past and gone, and these people can never be brought back. Our idea of a traditional Christmas has, in fact, already been borrowed from somewhere else. For many years in England there was the idea of the traditional German Christmas, which has its origin in Victorian times and Prince Albert, while in the last few years the idea of a traditional Scandinavian Christmas was promoted—other countries' Christmas traditions seem to be considered more authentic than English ones. To elaborate further: there is a substantial class dimension to Christmas in the UK, and over the past decade, celebrating a 'traditional' Christmas with Stollen and Lebkuchen, bought from Waitrose, has been a marker of middle-class Christmas consumption (where the default Christmas lower down the social scale has been Americanised). The 'Scandinavian Christmas' theme seems to be an extension of this middle-class trend, implying travel and cosmopolitanism, but also a displaced *nostalgia* for 'old-fashioned', simpler Christmases which in fact requires a further round of consumption. It's *nostalgia* by proxy, because the actual British Christmasses of the middle-aged and middle-class had always already been commercialised with bad-taste 'tat'!

The ultimate ingredient of *nostalgia* in the context of Christmas is snow. It features heavily in Dickens, because in the early 19th century there was uncharacteristically very much snow in England in the winters. With global warming we see that less and less, and thus it becomes fetishized, it becomes obsessed about. The measure for whether we have white Christmas is whether one snow flake falls on the BBC weather centre—if only one falls, it is a white Christmas and the betting organisations have to pay out. When we yearn for the white Christmas, we do not at the same time yearn for the things that went with that in the past, such as coal fires, hypothermia, frost bite and starvation.

Many Christmas productions in the theatre thrive on this context of *nostalgia*, such as many productions of *A Christmas Carol*, and the theatrical dimension of having all the spectators in the room witnessing Scrooge's transformation. *A Christmas Carol* was one of Dickens's favourite pieces to read on his reading tours, in a special adaptation lasting 90 minutes.

Christmas productions of the ballet *The Nutcracker* exist in a comparable context of *nostalgia*, and the other typically British seasonal phenomenon is the panto. A few recent developments add new dimensions to the *nostalgia* of "I am taking my children to the panto because I was taken to the panto when I was a child", and the *nostalgia* involved in statements from actors in interviews that their first experience of theatre, which triggered their desire to become actors themselves, was their experience of panto. The *New Wimbledon Theatre* has developed the trend of getting American TV and film stars, who have never done panto before, to join their annual Christmas pantomimes. In 2012 it was Priscilla Presley, before that it was Pamela Anderson, playing to *nostalgia* for 1970s American TV. The best example of this trend was their 2005-6 production of *Peter Pan* which starred Henry Winkler (The Fonz in *Happy Days*) as Captain Hook. The show thus combined *nostalgia* for childhood (Peter Pan itself; the pantomime experience) with childhood *nostalgia* among the fortysomething parent demographic for the TV show *Happy Days*, screened in the 1970s, which was itself a nostalgic recreation of the American 1950s.

On a different note, there has been the resurgence, over the past ten years, of adult panto, especially at the Barbican, with writers such as Mark Ravenhill involved, and some high-profile gay actors, such as Ian McKellen, as the dame. The idea is to revisit panto in a very knowingly out, post-queer-movement way that plays up all the double-entendres. They are selling something that is explicitly family entertainment, but the venue puts a warning on it that this is adult panto. Although it seems very garish and very family-orientated, because it happens at the Barbican it is in inverted commas, it is ironic, and it will have very racy contents. The result is a strange mixture of an irony relating to a past form, but at the same time almost an urge to step back into the closet, and to indulge in those double-entendres that were so popular in an age when it was not possible to be "out" about your sexuality on prime-time television. This genre plays with grown-up gays' memories of childhood, and memories of things being kept quiet and hushed up because they could not be said out loud.

The Victorians
In plays in which the Victorians haunt the present time in the sense that the present day is still dealing with the fall-out of the things the Victorians inflicted on each other and thus inflicted on the national

psyche, a strong sense of anti-*nostalgia* is discernible. The two examples that Poore has written on in detail (Poore 2012: 145-173) are *It's A Great Big Shame* by Mike Leigh (Theatre Royal, Stratford East, 1993) and *Abandonment* by Kate Atkinson (Traverse Theatre, Edinburgh, 2000), although there are numerous other examples: Emilia di Girolamo's *1000 Fine Lines* (1997), Judith Cook's *Ill at Ease* (1992) and Shirley Gee's *Ask for the Moon* (1986). In these anti-*nostalgic* plays, the past is not viewed as better, but instead history is cyclical, the same patterns of exploitation (particularly of women) being discernible in the modern-day and the Victorian plots that these plays stage concurrently.

Yearning for the 1960s

Other examples of anti-*nostalgia* in the context of plays set in the past are Mike Bartlett's *Love Love Love* (2010) about the legacy of the 1960s, Richard Bean's *Harvest* (2005), and *Clybourne Park* by Bruce Norris (2010). *The Last of the Haussmans* by Stephen Beresford premiered at the Royal National Theatre, London, in 2012. The question raised by the play's main character, Judy, a woman in her sixties who was a hippy in the 1960s, is whether it is possible to continue living in a 1960s hippy headspace? Her two children have been affected by her lifestyle: the daughter is very resentful and feels that she has to do all the organising and has to be the realistic one. Her son, Nick, is a drug addict who disappears for long periods, going off to "find himself". Judy lives in a big house which is falling to pieces, it is very much in need of repair. She had a cancer scare and both children come to look after her, but there is always the question in the air of who will inherit the house. Judy's behaviour, and how the other characters respond to her, raises questions about whether it is possible to continue a 1960s countercultural lifestyle into the 21st century, or indeed, into old age. The play's conversations interrogate the *nostalgia* that has accrued around the 1960s. The children are very critical of their mother's tendency to lapse into *nostalgia* and to lapse into this reassuringly universalist way of thinking, ignoring the political changes that really did take place over the last forty years that have left her in this house.

The one moment in life

In terms of drama, there is something Chekhovian about the way *nostalgia* is understood: people sit and cultivate their feelings, instead of actually doing something. Those nostalgic characters nursing their grievances about the past no longer being available can be found in *Plenty* by David Hare, with regard to a particular moment. What Hare manages to do is to create a quite unlikeable character in Susan Traherne. She fixates on one moment during the war, when she was fighting for the resistance, and she returns to that moment over and over again, as the moment when she was seventeen years old, she was in a foreign country, she did not know where she was going or what she was meant to be doing, she was nervous, she was meeting many unexpected people under very high pressure circumstances, and she has never lived as fully as that ever since. It is thus the opposite of the idea of home, of comfort that is at the centre of her *nostalgia*; rather, it was the very fact of being thrust into this chaotic World War situation at such a young age that has meant that nothing since has lived up. The pattern of the play allows us to see that the marriage that she has made is unsatisfactory to her on many levels, and disintegrates. It provides her with comfort but nothing like the excitement that she had as a teenager. She finds her way back to the soldier who parachuted in in the second scene, and in the penultimate scene they are shown sleeping together in a seedy hotel in Blackpool, as an attempt to recapture that moment—this is of course doomed to failure: he starts talking about his life and how dissatisfied he is with it. The play here carries a warning about trying to go back and trying to recapture what one perceives as a moment in the past mistaken as the essence of one's identity. The importance of Susan's war-time experience at the age of seventeen is emphasised by the fact that the play does not provide us with any information about her life before that age, and thus any information about her upbringing or education.

There is a clear connection between *Plenty* and *Hedda Gabler* in this context: in a couple of scenes, Susan waves a revolver around, as an attempt to solve an awkward situation. On one occasion it seems to do the job effectively, on others it seems to be quite disastrous in terms of her husband's diplomatic career. She has retained the firearm from her exciting past, and when she feels, in the present, that high drama is called for in the resolution of situations, she lets off the gun. This parallels Hedda Gabler's embitterment: she has had choices, and the choices she made clearly dissatisfy her. She feels she has been destined for something different from what she has got at the moment, and her idea of Lövborg with vine leaves in his hair seems to be one of the images of an alternative future that she envisaged for herself that has not come to pass.

All the above are examples of a trend of using time in order to formulate some idea about the state of the nation now. Guilt, on a personal or national level, is never far from the surface in this trend, because specifically in the UK we cannot "do" *nostalgia* without guilt. Self-pity comes in as an equal. This is probably not limited to the UK, and not to the present either: for example, J.B. Priestley's *Dangerous Corner* (1932), *Time and the Conways* (1937), *I Have Been Here Before* (1937) from the 1930s, and as a late addition to that *An Inspector Calls* (1945). The latter in particular is quite anti-*nostalgic*, taking us back from the perspective of the end of the Second World War to the Edwardian period (1901-1910) before the First World War (1914-1918), i.e., it is set in 1912, and tells us that we were never innocent: we were always hypocrites and we have not learnt lessons from history. Time-travel serves as a corrective or critical interrogation of *nostalgia*.

From critique to ambiguity

The majority of plays considered in the context of this chapter display a critical stance towards *nostalgia*, while at the end of *The Last of the Haussmans*, for example, there seems to be a twist towards a position that this intolerable woman, Judy, was not so bad after all and that there is something productive in her *nostalgia*.

A further example is *Jerusalem* by Jez Butterworth (2009). This play seems to have a dual-track attitude towards *nostalgia*. The folk songs intrude into the prose dialogue, and in parallel to that a contrasting between a fake, corporate *nostalgia* pedalled by the local brewery which makes the staff of the pub dress up as Morris dancers and perform these dances during the festival. This is imposed from above. In contrast, there is people's *nostalgia* that they refer to in conversation for what the fair used to be like twenty or thirty years ago—in living memory that is, before it became ruled by health and safety regulations and where you could do very dangerous things such as motorcycle jumps over a double-decker bus. However, it is never quite clear whether those memories are true or pieces of mythmaking desperately believed in by this group of outsiders. The pseudo-authentic Morris-dancing tradition, superimposed from above, was evidently false. Whether the actual tradition from below added up to anything was left much more ambivalent. However, it is perhaps difficult to pin down a play's stance towards *nostalgia* even if there are characters who say something anti-nostalgic, because characters can be interpreted against the grain and are open to critique from audiences.

Recent developments
It would appear that times have changed quite rapidly over the past twenty years or so in many respects, with euphoria after 1989 shifting to disillusionment by the mid-1990s and very conservative outlooks by 2000. In the context of the UK, there seems to be a high level of *nostalgia* for the certainties of the past, the black and white ideological divisions of the 1980s that were in place before the New Labour government came to power and muddied the waters by suggesting that the only way forward was to engage with capitalism and to use the profits of the City in order to finance social welfare projects. In many respects, *nostalgia* can be seen as a symptom of something that has broken down, that cannot go forward and therefore has to look back.

The tendency towards *nostalgia* as a tendency towards black and white, as examples of stable binaries, is everywhere, not limited to Britain. Elections over the last few years show a tendency towards conservative governments that give you the sense of stability, of right and wrong. It would be interesting to establish how theatre over the past ten to fifteen years has reacted to this development. In fact, *nostalgia* may have taken on a different tone over the past five years: in the boom years it was very easy to be comfortable with the ideas that history is this big junk yard which we can play around with at will, and that we are above and beyond all that now because we are all civilised and creatures of the media age. However, because the boom and the story related to it have come to a crashing end, we are now no longer comfortable with these ideas of progression towards a wired, networked, modern, global citizenry. This development must have had its impact on the way *nostalgia* developed during those years. For example, the timeliness of the revival 2012 of *Close the Coalhouse Door* (discussed above) has much to do with a sense that a Marxist view of history's repetitions and capitalism's internal contradictions is reasserting itself in the wake of the banking crisis. Plays dealing directly with financial mismanagement, such as David Hare's *The Power of Yes* (2009) and Lucy Prebble's *Enron* (2009) also suggest that our recent history is not something to be played with but which must be interrogated and understood urgently.

Red Ladder Theatre's *Big Society!* (2012), a musical play set in a music hall in 1910, draws attention to the lack of progress—indeed, the regression—on matters like economics, policing, privilege, education and social mobility, and democratic accountability, since the era before the World Wars. In 'unmasking' the UK's current coalition government as Edwardian 'toffs', the play staged an angry interrogation of Prime Minister David Cameron's collectivist rhetoric of voluntarism, Victorian values and Blitz spirit.

This critical position towards *nostalgia* is also the mainstream position within British academia. This position implies an appeal to people to wake up, and an image of *nostalgia* as a sleepy state, a stupor that coaxes people into a dream that is not reality. It is easy to connect this position with the Marxist notion of 'false consciousness', and with it, the assumption of an external reality that *nostalgia* seeks to hide from us or distract us from. Andrew Higson's recent article, "*Nostalgia* is not what it used to be" (in *Consumption, Markets and Culture*, 2013) extends this debate about how academics think around *nostalgia*.

Nostalgia, exile and choice

From explicit critique of—via ambiguity towards—*nostalgia*, at the core of Poore's thinking about *nostalgia*, we now move on to the broad topic of *nostalgia* in the context of exile, which in turn has been at the centre of much of Meerzon's research to date (Meerzon 2005, 2009, 2010a, 2010b, 2011, 2012, 2013, and Meerzon and Jestrovic 2009). The main characters in *Educating Rita, Plenty* and *Hedda Gabler*, Rita (Susan), Susan and Hedda, face a number of crucial and defining moments in their lives in which they have to make choices that will have significant impact on their future lives and on their looking back at those choices, in the cases of Susan Traherne and Hedda Gabler, in terms of *nostalgia*. In exile literature and drama, the question of choice is at the forefront of writing in so far as the exile of a novelist or dramatist, or the exile of a character in a novel or play, is a matter of choice or not. In cases of a character's banishment, in classical or Shakespearean plays, there is no choice. If a political regime gives a person, real or fictional, the choice of leaving the country or going to prison indefinitely, there is a sense of choice, although in real terms probably quite limited. A person or character may find the circumstances of life in their home country unbearable and decide to leave, even if that means giving up a lifestyle in relative comfort for a much less comfortable one. In all those cases, exile means a rupture.

The crucial moment for an existence in exile is not the moment of leaving home, but the moment of arriving in the country or place of exile. This is the moment when reconstruction of self must begin, and that brings with it the issues of whether this is possible, in each individual case, at all, how it is possible, to what extent it is possible, and what strategies that person or character employs in the process.

In the aftermath of the 1917 revolution, for example, many Russian writers, theatre artists, officers, philosophers and their families, all refugees from the Soviet regime, left their homes. In the 1920-30s, they collectively and individually engaged in resisting history and *nostalgia*, living in expectations to return home in the foreseeable future. These artists often had difficulties adapting to their new homes. Unwilling to master the language of their chosen exile fully, they frequently had to seek menial jobs (such as taxi drivers, domestic servants, or waiters in pubs and restaurants), often surviving by cultivating their memories of the past, their native language and culture. Their exile centred in the European cultural centres of Paris and Berlin, as well as Harbin in China (well documented in the work of Olga Bakich 2000, 2002); their literature, theatre, and visual arts have been marked by deep personal *nostalgia*. Vladimir Nabokov's novels and plays of the period (among many), specifically the 1926 drama *The Man from the USSR*, look at the life of Russian émigrés in the Russian diaspora in 1920s Berlin and convey the feelings of displacement, estrangement and individual loss.

Another example of *nostalgia* in exile is also found in the works of Mikhail Bulgakov, an exile within his own country and culture. Bulgakov's personal experience of displacement was marked by his forced escape from his native Kiev (Ukraine) to Moscow, in Soviet Russia. His famous novel *The White Guard* (written in 1924-1925 but published only in 1966), as well as his plays *Flight* (1926-28) and

Days of the Turbins (premiered on October 5, 1926 in the Moscow Art Theatre) present his semi-autobiographical account of the atrocities that awaited Russian aristocracy during the times of the Russian Socialist Revolution and Civil War. The novel and the plays depict the desperation with which the remnants of the White Army had been resisting the Red Army in Ukraine and Southern Russia, their fall and subsequent exile. The play *Flight* is particularly interesting in this context: set in four acts or eight dreams, it looks at the lives of Russian refugees seeking protection first with the White Army officers in Southern Russia and then in exile, in Constantinople. The play features the university professor Sergei Golubkov, the White generals Charnota and Khludov, and Serafima Korzukhina, the abandoned wife of the Deputy Minister of Commons/Trade of the Russian government in Crimea, Korzukhin. The Moscow Art Theatre took this play on but never had a chance to present it for the public. The play was banned by the Soviet authorities (till 1957) for sympathising with their enemies, the Whites, suffering from pain, humiliation and *nostalgia* in exile.

Hence, exile heightens the duality of past and present. There are many stories from real life and from fiction in novels and plays about people, often artists, who did not succeed in exile, with the reasons for failure ranging from a personal unwillingness to adapt, to people not fitting in with their new environment despite their diligent to desperate attempts.

However, when it comes to the exilic experience, at the opposite end of the spectrum, there is one's conscious decision to make the most of being in the country of exile; to continue one's life abroad as if there has been no rupture; to seek the continuity of before and after, and to make one's creative work in a new language a medium of that continuity.

Taking as her point of departure a view of *nostalgia* as more of a negative than a positive force, Meerzon looked at scenarios of exilic existence from an intercultural perspective, not limited to Russia. She proposed a new scenario of exilic being where *nostalgia* is not the major driving force. The premise of her work on exile was to create a study that would resist a traditional view of exile as banishment and suffering. The idea was to introduce a slightly different view on exile as a creative possibility, as a second life chance that sometimes people openly embrace and explore. Specifically, she looked at six cases of "success", discussing how the personal stories of escape by each one of the chosen artists dictate and are also reflected in their artistic work "after exile". Her inspiration for this approach came from the artists' themselves, who each to a different degree would articulate their position on *nostalgia*[2]. Each of them would acknowledge that *nostalgia* is a given condition of the exile flight and experience, but that one must develop his/her own attitude to this emotion.

The life and work of Joseph Brodsky, the Russian poet exiled to the USA, serve as an example of such paradigm. In the summer of 1972, Brodsky landed in the West, forced into exile by the Soviet authorities. However, Brodsky regarded his exodus, in the words of Brooke-Rose, as a "force for liberation, for extra distance, for developing new structures in one's head, not just syntactic and lexical but social and psychological" (Meerzon 2007: 196). Exile became his pursuit in creativity, a spiritual and aesthetic journey, and a condition that generated new energy and ideas. Instead of turning into a state of constant suffering, disorientation and displacement, Brodsky's expulsion became a creative paradigm. It caused an expansion of his artistic interests, when the Russian poet not only willingly embraced his forced bilingualism but also found it stimulating to think, write, and teach in English. Moreover, it is the exilic condition that instigated Brodsky's exploration of the forms of writing which he regarded as "foreign" when living at home: in America he not only composed poetry in a new language but also probed the artistic challenges of writing scholarly essays, prose and drama.

One can argue in other words, that Brodsky's response to the exilic stigma—*nostalgia* for the past, for one's home and culture— was his conscious acceptance of this new condition, his willingness to explore its linguistic, social and artistic challenges. The feeling of *nostalgia*—*nostalgia* for the landscapes of his native city St. Petersburg, for his elderly parents left behind, for his young son, with who he never had a chance to properly communicate—penetrates his poetry and prose. But it also generates new energy, rhythms, images, and values, now conditioned by the poet's new life, in the language and culture new to him.

---

[2] The artists are Joseph Brodsky, Wajdi Mouawad, Eugenio Barba, Josef Nadj, Atom Egoyan and Derek Walcott.

One of Joseph Brodsky's few dramatic texts, *Marbles* (1982), was first written in Russian and later translated into English by the author, with the help of Alan Meyers. The text is a projection of Brodsky's philosophical stance. It depicts two prisoners, Tullius and Publius, serving life sentences in the city's tower. Set as a Platonic dialogue, the play unfolds within the three classic unities of place, time, and action. The time, "the second century after our era" (Brodsky 3), has traces of Ovid's Rome. The place is a penitentiary, similar, at the same time, to Bentham's panopticon as analyzed by Foucault in *Discipline and Punish,* to the jail in Brendan Behan's *The Quare Fellow* and Harold Pinter's *The Dumb Waiter* (Meerzon 2007: 186).

Janusz Glowacki's play *Hunting Cockroaches* (1986) depicts a figure of an intellectual in exile and looks at the major inner conflicts a displaced artist faces. They include the loss of his/her social status and economic security; culture shock, sudden artistic insignificance; and a sense of personal humility new to the artist. The play presents a Polish émigré couple—a writer and an actress—who spend one sleepless night after another in their cockroach-infested New York apartment in the lower side of Manhattan, the area known for its poverty and democratic life style, with many of New York's artists and other eccentric personalities living there. In order to bear their new reality, in which Anka impersonates generic East European "babushkas" in the museum of anthropology and Jan volunteers in the local college with lectures on world literature, the characters engage in the series of games or role-playing, re-enacting for each other the events from the past and their new encounters in America. The play begins with Anka reciting Lady Macbeth's monologue, the role she used to play at home, while Jan is pretending to sleep. The action takes on an increasingly surrealist tone, when in the middle of the night the Polish policemen and the homeless person from the Central Park appear in Anka and Jan's bedroom from under their bed.

Although originally written in Polish, the play was translated into English and had its world premiere in New York. In 1986, it was selected by the American Theatre Critics Association as an Outstanding New Play; and in 1987 it received the Joseph Kesselring Award and the Hollywood Drama League Critics Award. The play received wide recognition in America: it was originally produced at the River Arts Repertory Company in Woodstock N.Y., then at the

Manhattan Theatre Club, (starring Dianne Wiest and Ron Silver, directed by Arthur Penn), and the Mark Taper Forum, (with Swoosie Kurtz and Malcolm McDowell), among many. It continued Becket and Mrozek's tradition of surrealist one act plays providing social and existential satire on the life on the margins. Glowacki's irony is more directly targeted: first at his new audiences, when both of his characters tell us that the ability to sleep through the night makes one an American and a person of success; and then at the characters themselves.

As with Chekhovian dramaturgy, *Hunting Cockroaches* engages with *nostalgia*, the *nostalgia* of exilic experience that the intellectuals prefer to deal with using irony and laughter as the devices of self-distancing and defence. It inevitably finishes with a very sad sight, Anka going over her old phone-book trying to locate someone from the past who might be able to pick up a receiver on the other side of the globe. The wretched truth is that no number is going to bring hope or happiness to the characters. Nobody from the old world is available: death, emigration, and betrayal emptied Anka's book and hence, they have nothing else to do than to return to their games of love and self-deception in order to make it through one more sleepless night in the city of New York, the capital of the Western wealth, prosperity and entertainment.

Glowacki's next play, *Antigone in New York* (1992), is relevant in the context of exile drama and *nostalgia*. The play also has an émigré character; Sasha is surrounded by other outcasts who share with him the living quarters of the Central Park in New York. The play is a take on Antigone's story, with the Prostitute Anita taking the place of Antigone, and the Policeman character taking the place of Kreon. Sasha, Anita and other homeless people live in the Central Park; they represent the "people" or the "population" of the polis—the park is the polis—with whom the Police fights. It is interesting that in this play Glowacki does not distinguish between the Russian émigré and American homeless people living in the park.

Among other plays written by the East European writers, the former dissidents and the prominent figures of the American exile, Slavomir Mrozek's *Emigrants* (1974) deserves a special mentioning. This play

> reflects both the philosophical and the mundane dilemmas of émigrés from Eastern Bloc states living in the West. Commenting on his own

immigrant experience in a letter, Mrozek wrote, "I never experience such a sharpening of [my] senses and thoughts as in an unfamiliar country, an unfamiliar city, among unfamiliar people, whose language preferably I do not know. [This offers] such intensification of life, of my whole existence." (Listerud 2010)

Goran Stefanovski's plays *Sarajevo* (1993) and *Hotel Europa* (2005) present a continuation of the same trend in exilic dramaturgy. Silvija Jestrovic's *Not my Story* (2000-2008) engages with hope, *nostalgia*, friendship and personal trust as they've been experienced by the Yugoslav-expatriates in 1990s Canada:

> Sonya, Lela and Nena are childhood friends now living in Toronto. A mutual friend, Sasha, visits from New York to make a documentary about them. A comedy of errors ensues as Sonya (a former Belgrade actress now a dental receptionist), Nena (a former photographer now a waitress) and Lela (a former art historian now working in a peep show) relate false tales of success and happiness to avoid public embarrassment. They try to re-invent themselves, running from their true story, only to find themselves face to face with it. Alluding to Chekhov's *Three Sisters*, *Not My Story* toys with cultural stereotypes and role-playing, while revealing the fragility of one's identity and how we are all implicit in making and unmaking each other's sense of self. (Jestrovic 2004)

On the other side of the exilic theatre spectrum are the plays written by the playwrights expressing the voice of the community and writing on behalf of and for it.

The conflicts between generations feature prominently in many plays focusing on diaspora families, where members of the parent generation are often portrayed as ignorant of the ways of the "new" cultural contexts, while the younger generation are in between that level of ignorance and full acculturation. Those plays tend to be formulaic, and in turn relate to a *nostalgia* for the important plays of this kind of the past, such as Lorraine Hansberry's *A Raisin in the Sun* (1959, film 1961), or, more recently, *Fences* by August Wilson (1983). It is a classic formula for naturalism, which has been co-opted by the diasporic family play tradition. There must be conflict, and in a family context that is most frequently between older and younger generations.

In both cases of diasporic exilic experience and individual exile, the tending to one's sense of connection to the homeland, and keeping it going, is an imaginative project both on individual and collective levels. Only a projected return would reveal the extent to which the imagination of the homeland is accurate in relation to the real circumstances in the homeland at any point in time during the period of exile.

Here one could add the "intergenerational" plays that dramatize the conflict of generations as found in the émigré families. These plays often feature the first generation émigrés (parents) struggling to find their way in the new country, without proper knowledge of the adopted language and culture. In the centre of such plays would be the second generation émigrés (these parents' children) who are trying to find their ways in the new country and feel limited by their parents' inability to deal with the new circumstances. Some dramatic examples include *Mom, Dad, I'm Living with a White Girl* (2001) by Chinese-Canadian playwright Marty Chan, and *Trying to Find Chinatown* (1996) by American writer David Henry Hwang. There are a number of collections of plays, such as *Playwrights of Exile: An International Anthology* (which features Wajdi Mouwad's *Wedding Day at the Cro–Magnons*; Eduardo Manet's *Ladystrass;* Anca Visdei's *Class Photo*; Leila Sebbar's *My Mother's Eyes* and Noureddina Aba's *Such Great Hope*), *The Exile Book of Native Canadian Fiction and Drama* (2010), and *Testifyin': Contemporary African Canadian Drama* (2000), *Je me souviens* by Lorena Gale (2000), *Paradise by the River* and *The Carpenter* by Vittorio Rossi, *Paradise Garden* by Lucia Frangione, *The Refugee Hotel* by Carmen Aguirre, *who knew grannie: a dub aria* by ahdri zhina mandiela, *You Fancy Yourself* by Marja Ardal and *RETURN (The Sarajevo Project)*, which is a unique international co-creation developed by an ensemble of Canadian and Bosnian theatre artists.

Finally, the existence in exile can be characterised by a feeling of survivor's guilt. That sense of guilt is often not founded on real omission of any action that would have been possible. However, the sense of guilt projects back into the time before exile and shapes that time into one of innocence in terms of *nostalgia*. *Tales from Hollywood* by Christopher Hampton (1983) is about major literary figures from Germany as exiles in Hollywood after escaping from the Nazi regime, such as Thomas Mann, Heinrich Mann and Bertolt Brecht. Some of the characters are nostalgic about their past lives, and as individuals and as a group they feel guilty because they are not very efficient in their discussions as to how to contribute to the resistance against the Nazis.

Nostalgia and new historical narratives

Svetlana Boym distinguishes between *two types of collective nostalgia* that characterize the post-communist *zeitgeist* in the Russia of the 1990s. The concepts can be applied to other situations as well. *Nostalgia* marks "one's relationships to the past, to the imagined community, to home, to one's own perception: restorative and reflective" (Boym 2001: 41). *Restorative nostalgia* "puts emphasis on *nostos* and proposes to rebuild the lost home and patch up the memory gaps. *Reflective nostalgia* dwells on *algia,* in longing and loss, the imperfect process of remembrance" (Boym 2001: 41).

The first type, *restorative nostalgia*, leads to the resurrection of a nationalist mythology. The examples include a large number of the post-Soviet Russian TV series and films that dramatize historical facts (specifically World War II) and figures (from the Soviet hero-aviator Valery Chkalov to the war hero, General Zhukov). These events and people are often looked at through the *nostalgia* lenses that add glitter to the Soviet past.

The second type, *reflective nostalgia*, "suggests a new flexibility, not the reestablishment of stasis" (Boym 2001: 49). This type of *nostalgia* takes into account the experience of an individual who is inevitably drawn into the macro-machine of the monumental history (Foucault). More importantly, "restorative *nostalgia* takes itself dead seriously. Reflective *nostalgia* [...] can be ironic and humorous" (Boym 2001: 41). Brecht's philosophical play-dialogue "Conversations in Exile" (1940-1941, Finland) can be considered an example of how the lenses of reflective *nostalgia* can be used in the exilic experience of re-thinking one's past and his/her individual position within the movements of the national and world histories. The book reveals creative possibilities that *nostalgia* might enable. Hence, there is an important differentiation between *reflective nostalgia* and *restorative nostalgia* in Boym. Derrida's *Spectres of Marx: The State of the Debt, the Work of Mourning and the New International* (2006) feeds into the Boym book, dealing with the fallout of the fall of the Berlin Wall, and the *nostalgia* for a future that did not happen.

The historical narratives of pre-Soviet times and Soviet times have been reintroduced to the public in a different way. Russia is notoriously known for re-writing its history. Every time it does so in order to espouse a new ideology. In the last decade there was a wave of reuniting the population with the Church, bringing back the mechanisms of manipulation and control through religious discourse. Classical icons have been rethought, remodelled and recontextualised for other consumption.

Recovery, return and creation
We have mapped how we understand *nostalgia* to function, in terms of grand historical narratives and irony, which need to be part of a definition of *nostalgia*. Equally important are images and analogies in relation to *nostalgia*. It is always history re-remembered: it has been packaged and processed already and is encountered only then. It is thus not a fresh encounter with history. This brings in the notion of return, the dangers and adventures and pleasures one might encounter in this process of return, and the role of *nostalgia* as a safety net to avoid having to re-engage, to return in a real way. I can look at photos of the house in which I grew up and I can think about my memories of it, but if I actually went there and found that it had been knocked down, or turned into a supermarket, that would jolt me out of *nostalgia*, or might place me in a more anxious frame of mind compared with the comfortable, secure knowledge of "this was the house where I grew up". An example is the novel *Everything is Illuminated* by Jonathan Safran Foer (2002), in which an American boy returns to the Ukraine. It was made into a film in 2006.

Paul Basu's *Highland Homecomings: Genealogy and Heritage Tourism in the Scottish Diaspora* (2006) is about the role of the Scottish Highlands in the imagination of the descendants of emigrants who investigate their family history and their genealogy, and are particularly drawn to the Scottish Highlands, even if they have family branches that were Swedish or English. The Scottish Highlands are a particular draw and have specific associations for these descendants. They go through a process of imagination, use relics, engage in creative writing, and make an imaginative investment that is about creation rather than recovery.

Recent developments

In Russia in the 1990s, *nostalgia* was part of a cultural renewal process from within. More recently, however, the much more powerful government uses nostalgic attitudes in order to make the population conform and to manipulate ideology. As discussed earlier in reference to academic modes of thinking, the critical position towards *nostalgia* would regard it as a false consciousness, a way in which the powers that be cloak their activities with the intention of manipulating popular sentiment with regard to the past, and creating a version of the past that serves their purposes. This is probably closest to a popular understanding of *nostalgia*. It is a political position that steps outside of this circle and proposes not to allow ourselves to be manipulated.

In general, Russian drama of the post-1991 era has been marked by what we call *chernukha* style, something close to the British *in-yer-face* theatre. Beumers and Lipovetsky discuss this in their book *Performing Violence*:

> New Russian Drama is (...) one of a few artistic and cultural phenomena shaped entirely in the post-Soviet period and this book investigates the violent portrayal of identity crisis of the generation as represented by theatre. Reflecting the disappointment in Yeltsin's democratic reforms and Putin's neo-conservative politics, the focus is on political and social representations of violence, its performances and justifications. *Performing Violence* seeks a vantage point for the analysis of brutality in post-Soviet culture. (2009)

Going back to the older, stable, canonical works is a sign of people looking for continuity in history and looking for new narratives, in response to years of fragmentation in post-structuralism and postmodernism, in a popular and accessible form. You can use that tendency for propaganda and control, but it is also a sign for a return to a desire for clarity and for the reinforcement of moral values that had been rejected over the past thirty years. Adaptations of modernist novels or texts for performance can be considered also in terms of *nostalgia*, in this case for certainty of form and narrative, in view of developments of postdramatic theatre that abandons narrative. Linked to this is the *nostalgia* for the grand narratives of the past, which in turn brings us to the genre of historical drama, in which the combination of satire and irony as reflective devices, may not allow *nostalgia* much of a chance.

Relevant plays on doollee.com

The following plays, details about productions and plot summaries, are from *doollee.com*, edited for grammar and spelling.

Al-Bassam, Sulayman. *The Speaker's Progress*. Performed at MaM Harvey Theatre, New York, 2011. Not published. A condemned 1960s staging of Shakespeare's *Twelfth Night* has become the focal point for political resistance blogs and underground social network movements. The state, eager to suppress this dangerous mixture of *nostalgia* and dissent, commissions The Speaker, a once-radical theatre producer now turned regime apologist, to mount a forensic reconstruction and public denunciation of the work. As The Speaker and his group of non-acting volunteers delve deeper into the "reconstruction" they find themselves increasingly engaged with the material they are supposed to be condemning. They soon discover in the act of performance and the growing participation of their audience a solidarity that transforms the gathering itself into an unequivocal act of defiance of the state.

Alam, Pervaiz. *Safar (The Journey)*. Performed at Waterman's Arts Centre, Brentford, London, 2002. Not published. The play *Safar* in Hindi/Urdu was staged in London, Leicester and Birmingham. It was invited to the Fringe Festival of Edinburgh 2003. *Safar* (The Journey) is a tale of exodus from imaginary homelands and of perpetual, irrepressible longing for such paradises lost. It's the journey of an immigrant into the unknown who discovers his past in London. The plot is woven through the personality of the protagonist Vishal—descendent of a Hindu family that migrates from the Pakistani Punjab to India in 1947 under forced conditions. The same Vishal comes to London as a migrant worker. What happens when we migrate from one country to the other? What happens when we are forced to live in exile? How does the trauma of migration affect our relationships? Vishal's journey into the unknown world of *nostalgia* has just begun.

Ayckbourn, Alan. *Life of Riley*. Performed at the Stephen Joseph Theatre, Scarborough, UK, 2010. London: Faber and Faber, 2011. With a few months of his life remaining, George Riley's closest friends remember with love, *nostalgia* or occasional bursts of fury, how deeply he has affected all their past lives. George, though, is plotting one last final farewell which threatens to upset all their future lives. What exactly is the eccentric maverick Riley playing at?

Bennett, Alan. *The Old Country*. Performed in Oxford, UK, 1977. London: Faber and Faber, 1977.

Brittney, Lynn. *Wine and Wisdom3: Nostalgia*. Axminster: Playstage, 2009. It is New Year's Eve at Roy and Jean's house. Celebrating with them are Roy's close friends, Maurice and Eve, and Eve's wayward brother, David. Jean has decided that they will all play a board game, called "*Nostalgia*", and the questions are all about the 1960s. Roy, Maurice and Eve, being some ten years older than Jean and David, have mixed feelings about the period in question. While playing the game, some very interesting memories come to light. Simmering resentments surface from the older age group about the fecklessness of those who were teenagers during the 60s, which only draws Jean and David closer together as they share their experiences of the "swinging scene". The moral of the story is: beware of marrying a younger woman, especially one who yearns to recapture her youth!

Byrne, Colm. *Nostalgeria*. Performed at Vienna English Theatre, 2001. Not published. Two couples meet after years apart and discover very different memories of their past, threatening the relationship of each.

Calvert, Robert. *Cattle at Twilight*. Performed at Pentameters, London, UK, 2008. Not published. Imagines a purgatory peopled by Hendrix and Noel Coward, in epigrammatic despair at the rampant march of *nostalgia* across the land of the living.

Canino, Frank. *All Dressed up and Nowhere to Go*. 2002. Not published. In a funeral parlour two middle-aged brothers and their wives keep watch over the body of their dead brother. Memories, accusations, *nostalgia* and embarrassing revelations spill out under the pressure of grief—or maybe relief! Was the dead brother a hero or a thief? Who should get his jewellery? and what happened to those bonds?

Casiano, Karina. *Rootless: La No Nostalgia*. Performed at P.S. 122, New York, 11 May 2010. Not published. This is part of the 7th annual soloNOVA Arts Festival. Here's the official festival blurb: "Sexy. Bold. Bilingual. Take a journey through the emotional life of migrants with songs ranging from tango to rock. Unravelling the psychological toll of displacement, Karina Casiano ferociously and personally criticizes the role of newcomers and probes their responsibility toward their own countries."

Chatterjee, Sourabh. *Thakuris Nostalgia*. Performed at Lark Theatre, New York, 2002. Not published. A father and his daughter struggle against shifting cultural, religious and generational values in modern-day Goa, India.

Creedon, Conal. *Glory be to the Father*. Performed at The Forum Waterford, Ireland. 2001. Not published. Mossie Buckley and his mother had only one thing in common: neither of them knew their father. Now faced with the imminent prospect of fatherhood, Mossie struggles to discover a personal sense of family through the recollections of his youth, his *nostalgia* conjured up through a blend of magic realism and the surreal.

Drabek, David. *Akvabely / Aquabelles*. Rehearsed reading at Nottingham Playhouse, 2011. Not published. A view of the contemporary generation of thirty-somethings. Three university friends conceive a secret hobby: they meet at a hidden reservoir and "dance" in the water. After school their paths had diverged. Kajetan had taken the post of TV moderator and became a true celebrity. Petr stayed at the university as a lecturer and continued his stubborn struggle against consumerism. However, the two friends are caught off guard by Filip. He decides to stay in the reservoir for ever, returning to an existence as a prehistoric water element. Things take off : Petr leaves his wife, Kajetan, influenced by the loss of his friend, causes a brawl in the TV studio. Over a few seconds their certainty has crumbled to dust. In spite of all its gags and humorous situations, the play is permeated with the *nostalgia* of a generation and in places even a frosty surreal quality.

Evans, Lisa. *Keep Smiling Through*. Performed at the Keswick Theatre by the Lake, UK, 2011. London: Oberon, 2011. Keswick, 1940—Britain is at war with Germany. Maggie's life is under invasion too: Gran knitting for England, evacuee lodgers, helping with the war effort and now a fund-raising concert party! Husband Rob is due home on RAF leave and best friend Peg has just learnt that she's pregnant but no such luck for Maggie and Rob. *Nostalgia*, romance, laughter and tears all feature full of live music, songs and dance from the war years.

Farrell, Bernard. *Kevin's Bed*. Performed at the Abbey Theatre, Dublin, 1998. Cork: Mercier Press, 1998. *Kevin's Bed* is a play of *nostalgia*, expectations and broken dreams. The setting is the celebration of the golden wedding anniversary of Dan and Doris a time for them to return to their old house, join in their celebrations, contemplate a life in disarray and remember the joy of their silver anniversary, the Sonny and Cher days, the optimism and the expectations they had of their sons, John and Kevin.

Findlay, Jim. *Accidental Nostalgia*. Performed at St Ann's Warehouse, Brooklyn, 2004. DVD: New York: Accinosco, 2005. Operetta. *Accidental Nostalgia* is an operetta about the pros and cons of amnesia. The main character is one Cameron Seymour, a neurologist specializing in the memory function of the brain, who is delivering a lecture about an autobiographical book she has just published called *How to Change Your Mind: A Self-Help Manual for Psychogenic Amnesiacs*. She begins to tell the audience the story of the research she did to write the book, which was an investigation of her own psychogenic (emotionally driven) amnesia. The audience then follows her journey back to the house she grew up in—located in her home town of Carlson, Georgia—where she hopes to trigger missing memories of her childhood, and to find her father, from whom she has been estranged for many years. It turns out that her father is missing and that she is wanted for his murder, though it is unknown whether he was murdered, committed suicide, or simply disappeared. And from that point on, the show becomes a bit of a thriller. The narrative of *Accidental Nostalgia* is punctuated by songs, dance numbers, and interactions with peripheral characters who appear on a large film projection screen. The screen also serves to shift the atmosphere via projections of text and images, manipulated live by designers/ performers Findlay and Sugg. It is a hybrid form containing hybrid content, from the outlandish to the philosophical to the deeply personal. It is a mixture of truth and fiction, song and text, movement and stillness.

Gibbons, Frank. *Baby Sparklers*. Performed at Ucheldre Centre, Holyhead, Anglesey, November 2010, by the Ucheldre Repertory Company. Published by Lazy Bee Scripts 2010. "Nostalgic one act comedy". This is the one-act version of "Sparklers", an evocation of children growing up in an industrial town in the 1970s. The characters are aged 7 to 9, but are intended to be played by adults or teenagers. Run time is approximately 50 minutes. November 4th 1970—a time for learning to swear, a time for discovering friendship, and a time for earning respect. Armed with dustbin lids and iron railings, Rachel, Susan and Tommy are prepared to guard their modest bonfire pile against an expected raid by the dreaded Dawson twins. But an even greater danger threatens to engulf them when a member of the group is lured away by the Firework Man.

Gordon, Eric. *Nostalgia Brand Chewing Gum*. Performed at Pentameters, London, 1999. Not published.

Gotanda, Philip Kan. *The Wash*. Performed in Los Angeles, 1985. Portsmouth, N.H.: Heinemann, 1992. Nobu Matsumoto has separated from his wife Masi at her request, though both of them are in their sixties. Nobu's newfound bachelor life is regularly interrupted by Masi who comes by to pick up and drop off Nobu's weekly laundry as part of the duties she still feels a Japanese wife owes to her husband. Their two daughters have opposing feelings about the breakup; Marsha, the more traditional of the daughters, wants to reunite her parents, but not even Nobu and Masi's *nostalgia* for their courtship in a World War II Japanese-American internment camp can bring them back together again. The other daughter, Judy, who's been estranged from her father since marrying a black American, has been supportive of her mother's attempt at freedom. It is not until Masi tentatively begins a relationship with Sadao, a widower, that the severity of Nobu's traditional values reveals itself; he is inconsolable, obstinate and reclusive, leaving Kiyoko, a widowed restaurant owner who has fallen in love with him, unable to break down.

Gregory, Sean. *Reeling*. Performed at the New Century House, Manchester as part of the 24:7 Theatre Festival 2010. Not published. They say, all that remains in an empty house is memories. Jude and Alice didn't expect to find theirs next door. A forty-five minute play about *nostalgia*, family, mistakes. . . and ninety minute cassette tapes. To understand the past, you have to relive it.

Gurney, A. R. *Ancestral Voices*. Performed at Lincoln Center NY, 1999. New York: Broadway Play Pub., 2000. If the family is the key theme of American drama, A R Gurney's play is a beautiful chamber work in that great tradition. The short play is staged as a concert work, with five performers sitting on chairs in front of music stands, where they've laid their scripts. The five are playing members: grandfather, grandmother, father, mother, son of a rich wasp family in Buffalo NY between 1935 and 1942, with a brief coda from the 1960s. The son, Eddie, who goes from age eight to twelve, is our narrator, guide and point of view. This lovely play unites the microcosm of family to the macrocosm of America at war. On Eddie's first date he brings his girl a paper `war-sage'. It's also about something in between a city. It's an elegy for Buffalo, a once-glorious place whose fortunes are declining. The texture of life in Buffalo is heartbreakingly evoked in ways reminiscent of *The Magnificent Ambersons*. This is a magical play, not a mere exercise in uncritical *nostalgia*, but a nuanced reminiscence full of time and change and loss and suffering—as well as joy. (Donald Lyons, New York Post)

Hampton, Brian. *Checking in.* Performed at June Havoc Theatre, New York, 2009. Not published. Six mis-matched friends from Virginia now struggling to make their way in the world reunite for a weekend in Atlantic City. They rehash the past and catch up on the present. But, when they discover one of them has been hiding a shocking reality, her reasons send them into a tailspin—questioning whether there's more to their bond than a case of beer, a carton of cigarettes, and a room full of high school *nostalgia*.

Ingleton, Sue. *Aunts with Hot Flushes.* Performed at Darlinghurst Theatre, Sydney, Australia, 2006. Not published. Music, *nostalgia*, secrets and lies… sometimes sharing can be the most liberating experience of them all. It's New Year's Eve 1959. Three female friends, (and a ring-in), gather to celebrate the dawn of the 1960's, a time filled with the promise of emancipation and change—whether desired or not. The women share a common bond, in that they're all childless, somewhat set in their ways, and approaching, or in the sweaty throes of menopause. What begins as a light-hearted gathering of female friends swapping familiar tales and singing familiar songs, soon veers into uncharted waters. As many martinis are consumed, defences slip and reminiscence becomes disclosure. Secrets are shared and lies revealed which will change these women's lives and relationships forever. Suzanne Ingleton's funny and touching play explores the lives of four women at a time when being childless was synonymous with being frigid, barren, or unattractive. Through humour, song (including "Where The Boys Are", "Que Sera Sera", "White Cliffs Of Dover" and "Three Coins In The Fountain") and the bonds of friendships shared and forged, they cope with loss of opportunity and the 50's social expectations of women on the eve of feminism.

Kelly, Alexander. *The Lad Lit Project*. Performed at the Oval House, London, UK, 2005. Not published. About stories of mates, girls, sex, love and loss. It's about going to pubs, meeting other blokes: it's about *nostalgia*, times past rewritten in the present.

Knight, Cheryl. *Turn Back the Clock*. Performed at the Edinburgh Fringe, 2011. Not published. In honour of Joyce Grenfell's centenary year, hidden in this comedy revue can be found some of her more delicate and poignant pieces. This gem of *nostalgia* from the golden age of revue is suitable for all ages, all will delight in the truthful, funny and moving characters. Older audiences will enjoy the evocation of one of the greatest female entertainers of the twentieth century while fresh faces will tune into the current trend for vintage revival.

Kramer, Seth. *Name*. Performed by Gallery Players, New York, 2001. Not published. Four friends from high school gather on Zack's 27th birthday. From pop cultural *nostalgia* to anxiety over Susannah's first pregnancy, they look at where their lives have taken them and where they might be going next.

Landsman, Aaron. *Even the Nostalgia was Better Back Then*. Performed in 2005. Not published. Three men confront how normal they are not.

Lucas, Kristen Renee. *A Heart Given is never Lost*. Performed at the Manhattan Repertory Theatre, 2010. Not published. Thick-headed, ruggedly handsome, charming and married, Seth lives in two worlds. Madly obsessed with his past he begins to see that marriage is often more work than warm passionate feelings. He decides to escape his mundane marriage and take up with his past love, Kate. When he encounters Kate, he sees that she is everything he remembers and more. Somehow reuniting with Kate has made all the bad things in their past relationship disappear. The problem is there is really nothing wrong with his current wife, Katherine. She is beautiful, kind and helpful to the point of exhaustion. Kate, however, can't seem to get over the ugly truth of her and Seth's not so perfect past and won't let him ruin his marriage for something that is not, and has not ever been perfect. In the end Seth, Kate and Katherine all have to face *nostalgia* for what "was" or reality of what "is." Which do they want to live in?

Martinez, Rogelio. *Asphalt Green*. Performed at the Mile Square Theatre, Hoboken, NJ, 2005. Published in the collection *The Baseball Plays: 7th Inning Stretch*. New York: Playscripts, 2010. Divine intervention and *nostalgia* combine to defend a hallowed urban baseball lot from becoming an apartment complex. Father Joseph, a staunch defender of the lot, confronts contractor Dennis in an effort to show him what the lot means to the neighbourhood children. Will Father Joseph's stand be enough to keep this sacred space from being destroyed forever?.

McPherson, Nancy. *Mamie McCall's French Fancy*. Performed in Stewarton, Ayreshire, 2011. Not published. Two retired ladies meet up in a Coffee Bar. They discover that they share *nostalgia* for a more genteel type of afternoon tea experience. Gentle humour arises from the fact that they are obviously out of place in this environment. However, underneath this humour, it is poignant to observe that what they share most is their loneliness. They are each unable to break out of the barriers which prevent them from savouring a more eventful life. In the end, they settle for a less exciting, but acceptable substitute for the real thing.

Moroney, Molly, *Kithless in Paradise*. Performed at the Lion Theatre, New York, 2011. Not published. The McCalls and Barretts share a life in the lap of luxury and decades of friendship. A rollicking, lavish dinner party that promises to be full of laughter, wine and *nostalgia* takes a foul turn when a guest pushes the boundaries of friendship too far. Secrets spill forth, leaving all to question the tenuous binds that hold marriage, kith and kin, and lifelong friendships together.

Parker, Stewart. *Spokesong*. Performed at the King's Head, London, UK, 1975. Published in *Plays and Players* 1976. The story of a bicycle-shop owner, Frank, who is passionately convinced that bicycles will be the salvation of the modern city. Frank is a romantic with great *nostalgia* for the past. His brother Julian, who had been in London, where he became an anarchist, has now returned home determined to destroy what he sees as a hopelessly corrupt society. The conflict between these two brothers lies in Parker's exploration of the roots of the present-day conflict between Protestants and Catholics in Northern Ireland. The story really concerns Frank's painful education into the realities of Belfast life. The play includes a conventional love story and a chorus figure called the Trick Cyclist who sings most of the songs and embodies the spirit of Belfast. Jimmy Kennedy, who wrote "Red Sails in the Sunset," "Isle of Capri," and "South of the Border," did the music for the songs. There are seven songs, ranging from an 1890s music hall song to a 1930s Noel Coward type of song.

Poliakoff, Stephen. *My City*. Performed at the Almeida Theatre, London, UK, 2011. London: Methuen, 2011. Beautifully atmospheric and infused with a sense of yearning *nostalgia*, the play presents a series of strange, seemingly coincidental encounters with others which evoke momentous trends in the city they live in and the shifts of society throughout history. Two former school friends are reunited with their erstwhile teacher, the glamorous, gracious Miss Lambert who is now engaged in nightly pilgrimages on foot across London as an antidote to her chronic insomnia. In the course of these nocturnal journeys, she witnesses a paradigmatic range of incidents reflecting today's society: the kindness and the violence, the glut of discarded rubbish and the sanctity of that which is carefully preserved, as well as the ghostly vestiges of the past.

Potter, Gareth. *Gadael yr Ugeinfed Ganrif.* Performed at the National Eisteddfod of Wales, Blaenau Gwen, in August 2010. Not published. During the dark days of the 79 referendum, Wales had lost its nerve and the Welsh rock scene was wallowing in *nostalgia*. But the raucous visit of the Sex Pistols to Caerphilly had stirred one schoolboy's imagination. He had to be in a band—and from then on things were never quite the same. Weaving images, music and a true life story, this is the autobiographical adventure of one man, spanning the last two decades of the Twentieth Century that brought us Cool Cymru and finally a Senedd in Cardiff Bay. An energetic and heartfelt portrayal of a time in our history when a restless generation insisted that the world came to Wales and that took Wales to the world.

Rebeck, Theresa. *Off Base*. Performed at the Mill Quare Theatre, Hoboken NJ, 2005. Published in the collection *The Baseball Plays: 7th Inning Stretch*. New York: Playscripts, 2010. The line between *nostalgia* and reality is compromised as a couple argues over the morality of modern day baseball. While Amanda insists that steroids have tainted America's favourite pastime, Jimmy clings to the glory that the sport once was. Though they both love the game, each must choose between the fantasy of what baseball represents and the politics of what it has become.

Scanlon, Rosalind. *Dance Hall Days*. Performed at the Riverside Studios, London, UK, 2006. Not published. There are folk songs and farmhands and comedy Catholics; milkmaid simplicities and mellifluous wit. Boozing and gambling and bittersweet romance—we can only be in Ballyanywhere, the global village of Irish *nostalgia*. It's now the permanent home of comfort-zone comedy; so much so that it's easy to forget that this familiar small world was made up from the memories of the lads and lasses who left it. 'Dance Hall Days' rolls the recollections of Hammersmith's ex-pat Irish community into one musical night in 1955 at the Ballybannion village dance. (Caroline McGinn, Time Out London)

Sherwood, Normandy Raven. *The Golden Veil*. Performed at The Kitchen, New York, 2012. Not published. Conjuring the intimacy of a séance and the wild abandon of a hootenanny, *The Golden Veil* is equal parts pastoral ballet, backwoods jamboree, Punch-and-Judy show and forlorn testimony, an exposé of the lives of the rural poor and a celebration of their lovely handicrafts. In the inimitable style of the National Theater of the United States of America (NTUSA), *The Golden Veil* is a violent and lusty revenge fantasy, unfolding via the traditional domestic arts of reading aloud, singing along, making faces, charades and parlour tricks. Through the telling and retelling of the story, the play explores the ways that we use narrative to render the painful picturesque while it prods the perverse underbelly of our *nostalgia* for simpler times. Like much of the NTUSAs work, *The Golden Veil* is a concatenation of the past. It uses multiple narrators and multiple modes of narrative play to tell the same simple story, revealing through its incon- sistencies a nonetheless consistent other and otherly world.

Spitz, Marc. *P.S., It's Poison.* Performed at The Red Room, New York, 2011. Not Published. Four old college friends reunite in Manhattan and what starts as a stiff and awkward game of catch up devolves into a drug and rancor soaked mess when old rivalries and affections boil to the surface; abetted by drugs, professional jealousies, a new cultural divide and the arrival of their favorite college professor; a famous and deeply troubled novelist with a pretty, young girlfriend and a mysterious box in tow. Twenty years on, class is back in session and if they can get out of this cocktail party alive, they just might learn something of value once again. A dark look at the peril of the aging hipster and what it means to be an artist, a parent and a "perennial favorite" and how challenging it is to remain intimate and engaged in your surroundings in middle age. You don't have to remember 1993 to relate but it doesn't hurt.

Spratt, Claire. *Blitz Bride.* Performed at the Buxton Festival Fringe, 2011. Not published. It's wartime Britain and ATS girl Ruby is set to wed Henry, although sooner than planned (if Henry and her Dad, Arthur, have anything to do with it) for Ruby to avoid a posting abroad! Stationed away from home it is left for her mother, Peggy, and her heavily pregnant best friend, Nancy, to organise the lot. Based on true anecdotes and full of *nostalgia* and laughs. This is a semiautobiographical one act play lasting approximately 1 hour 04 minutes, followed with an 11 minute war-time sing-song at the curtain call.

Sunde, Sarah Cameron. *A Summer Day*. Performed at the Cherry Lane Theatre, New York, 2012. Not published. A visit to an old friend sparks the memory of a visit years earlier and the mysterious disappearance of a loved one. Set in two time periods in the same idyllic house, *A Summer Day* evokes the *nostalgia* of the end of an affair, capturing love both in the moment and as a distant memory.

Taylor, Richard. *The Go-Between*. Performed at the West Yorkshire Playhouse, Leeds, UK, 2011. Not published. The past is a foreign country: they do things differently there. In the heat and humidity of the rural Norfolk summer in 1900, a young boy comes of age as he is unwittingly enlisted as a messenger in an adult affair of deceit and desire. This is the world premiere of a moving new musical adaptation of LP Hartleys beautifully wistful novel of naivety, *nostalgia* and the end of innocence, perhaps best known as a film of the same name starring Julie Christie and Alan Bates.

Thompson, Helena. *Open House*. Performed at the Croydon Warehouse, London, UK, 2004. Not published. A full length play, it revolves around eccentric Charlie, a cheery old man who is so open minded he lets his daughter's friends share his house. But when the house favourite dies and his unknown brother knocks on the door, the house is thrown into jeopardy. In this city tale of *nostalgia* for what never was the housemates learn that their beloved betrayed them all; it takes deluded Charlie's death to let them finally mourn and move on. This is a play about corrupt ideals and the bitter sweetness of facing the truth.

Traiger, Larry. *The Gay Barber's Apartment*. Performed at the Sanford Meisner Theatre, New York, 2008. Not published. Larry Traiger's *The Gay Barber's Apartment* is a provocative dark comedy centering around the lives of soon-to-graduate prep school students in late '90s New York City. Henry and Jonas spend their time getting acquainted with cocaine in the apartment of Venice, a 50-year-old gay barber with a troubled past. Henry and Jonas are haunted by the presence of their prep school Dean, Richard Hunt. After they introduce their love interests Mary and Bunny to the apartment, worlds collide, accentuated by the appearance of a long-lost friend, Rob. Each character is faced with *nostalgia* and the unravelling of relationships.

Woolland, Brian. *Getting Over You.* Performed at the Etcetera Theatre, London, UK, 1995. Not published. Set in 1995 and 1968. In 1968, Mick, a 17 year old rock star meets Dee, a young black student, trying to take control of her own life. They have a passionate love affair, but are trapped by Mick's failure to perceive Dee on her own terms; and by Dee's inability to accept Mick's vulnerability. When Dee flies out to San Francisco, where Mick's band are in the middle of an American tour, the relationship finally collapses into recriminations. In 1995, Mick is married to Rachel (twelve years older than him). They are living comfortably by the Thames. 'Dee' (who now goes under her real name as Lahadi) is producing a television series about the sixties and seventies, in which she wants Mick to appear. Although delighted to see Lahadi (Dee), he is reluctant to dig into his past. The collision of past and present reveals a series of shifting relationships with their past—dependency, *nostalgia* and sentimentality; rejection, anger and guilt.

Chapter Two

Daniel Meyer-Dinkgräfe, Gayathri Ganapathy, Shrikant Subramaniam

Towards *intuitive collaboration* as a concept for discussing intercultural performance

Introduction

Despite extensive academic debate, intercultural collaboration in the context of performance is still problematic with regard to fairness and equality of exchange and levels of power and authorship among collaborative partners. Positions in this debate range from, in general terms, the view that intercultural performance collaboration cannot and should not develop in terms of fairness, equality and democracy, as such attempts restrict artistic freedom to the view that intercultural performance must seek to address these issues and to achieve appropriate balance between artistic freedom and professionalism and fairness. Analysis of the literature reveals that the debate has been conducted almost exclusively in terms of concepts assuming that at the basis of intercultural theatre practice is a rational, strategic approach to that practice, where every aspect, stage and step can be explained in terms of logic (Meyer-Dinkgräfe 2002).

This basis is in line with the conventional, object-oriented paradigm that seeks to exclude the subjective (such as intuition) in principle. It is the predominant paradigm of science. However, the majority of artistic work does not result from intellectual thought processes and strategies, but evolves in terms of tacit intuition, which may be hard to express in words. It stands to reason that any discussion of a tacit, intuitive process in terms of ratio, strategies and logic may not yield reliable insights. To enhance insights about intercultural performance, the chapter develops the concept of *intuitive collaboration* with reference to an intercultural performance project at the University of Lincoln, UK, from February to April 2012.

Who we are
In this article, we introduce our work to date on the rehearsals and performance of a dance-drama entitled *Hiranyala: An Unforgettable Journey*. We are Daniel Meyer-Dinkgräfe, Professor of Drama at the University of Lincoln, UK, Gayathri Ganapathy, PhD Student in the School of Psychology at the University of Lincoln, UK, and professional Bharata Natyam dancer, and Shrikant Subramaniam, professional Bharata Natyam dancer and story-teller, and at the time Dance and Education Officer with Manasamitra, a South Asian cultural organisation in West Yorkshire. As co-authors of this chapter, we will refer to "us" and use the pronoun "we" where appropriate, and write in the third person, using our first names (Daniel, Gayathri and Shrikant) to indicate the level of familiarity that has developed between us across the duration of the project, against the background that we had not worked with each other before, at least to the extent we did for this project.

The outward frame of the project
On 2 February 2012, Daniel had the idea of approaching Bharata Natyam dancer Gayathri by email about her interest in working with him on the adaptation of a fairy tale. On 3 February they met in person to discuss the feasibility of the project, and agreed the rough time frame. From 10 February to the end of March they met for seven rehearsals of one to two hours each, and were joined on 1 April by Shrikant. Four day-long rehearsals with Gayathri, Shrikant and Daniel followed in Lincoln on April 1, 7, 21 and 22. The performance of a showcase of four of eight scenes of the script took place on 27 April 2012 in the Dance Studio of the Lincoln Performing Arts Centre.

Motivations
The material at the basis of the project was a fairy tale written in 1987 in German by Daniel's mother. The story had the title *Hiranyala*, the name of the story's heroine. Daniel's mother had retired a few months before writing the story after a forty-year career as a stage actress, and had written the story over Christmas after getting the idea on the way

back home from the local supermarket. Here is the full text of the story, as translated by Daniel:

> Once upon a time there was a young woman called Hiranyala. God liked her very much and was always with her. One day they went to a beautiful lake. The clear water was covered with blossoming lotus in all colours. Elves were sitting on them and waved and laughed, and sea maidens looked out of the water. One of them -- she had beautiful dark eyes and eyebrows -- talked to Hiranyala. She handed her a golden bowl and said that Hiranyala should pour water all over herself. She did this, again and again, until she had had enough. Then God and Hiranyala set out on a long journey.
>
> They came to a dark pine forest, which was really very dark and musty and uncannily quiet. They walked for a long time until they finally arrived at a small wooden house, covered with moss. Having knocked on the door they went in and greeted respectfully an old woman with a round, clear face and kind eyes, who lived in the house. The woman gave Hiranyala a little bone, a golden spindle with golden thread and a golden apple. Hiranyala would have to make use of her gifts, she said.
>
> The journey went on. The pine forest came to an end, and in front of them lay the valley of the snakes. It was teeming with big and small, poisonous and non-poisonous snakes. No living creature could cross. But there was Hiranyala's small, invisible girlfriend, Shipala, the little Naga-girl, who was around her all the day, although invisible, to protect her. Shipala was a daughter of the King of the Nagas. She led God and Hiranyala through this valley, and the snakes allowed them to pass by quietly and without touching them.
>
> At the edge of the valley of the snakes started a region in which a wild, crackling fire was raging. No living creature was in there any more. But there stood a tall, black horse. It was looking at them. They mounted it and were able to ride through the fire without any harm. The black horse disappeared.
>
> They found themselves faced by a desolate, barren area in which no tiny blade of grass could grow. They went ahead. Suddenly they saw in front of them the appearance of Death, who blocked their way. Hiranyala, however, gave him that small bone which the old woman in the forest had given her. From this small bone many, many skeletons emerged, about which Death was so happy that he no longer took any notice of Hiranyala.
>
> The landscape changed again. Mountains towered one over the other, bare rocks, covered with snow. They had to climb them. It was very cold. On top of the highest rock a woman sat spinning. She was spinning rough, grey thread, she felt cold and she was not happy. Hiranyala handed her the golden spindle with the golden thread. The woman's face began to shine, she removed the old spindle with the old thread from the spinning wheel, and put in the new ones. Now

everything changed. The snow disappeared, a warm wind came up and grasses and flowers grew everywhere. The sun was shining. 'Now the threads of enlightenment can become visible to everyone, all over the world', said the woman, and she bowed her head to God.

God and Hiranyala rose up towards the sky. They went higher and higher until they stopped at a large, hard gate, which was made of solid gold. In front of it stood an equally large, hard lion of solid gold that guarded the gate. Nobody was allowed to enter. Now Hiranyala took the golden apple, which the woman in the forest had given her, and threw it towards the lion. He caught the apple in his hard muzzle of solid gold and devoured it greedily. The lion changed: he became a quite normal, lively, and nice lion. The gate was opened from inside, and a large host of cheerful, garlanded children crowded towards Hiranyala. 'We have a mother again', they shouted, 'We have a mother again'. And they surrounded Hiranyala: 'Will you cook something for us to eat, then?', they asked.

'What would you like?' asked Hiranyala.

After a little while they shouted: 'Sweet snowmilksoup!'

Hiranyala cooked a huge pot full of sweet snowmilksoup and all the children ate from it until they had full stomachs. Suddenly all the children grew pretty, snow-white wings and they all were small angels.

They went with God and Hiranyala towards God's palace in heaven. All bowed their heads to the two tall angels who stood at each side of the gate. A golden path led towards the many shining white steps of the palace with its pillars and turrets, which rose equally white and shining into the sky. They went to the big round hall of the palace, which was filled with golden light radiating from the dome. The floor consisted of transparent golden topaz. On a seat opposite the entrance, God and Hiranyala sat down. By now all the angels had the most beautiful instruments and played heavenly music. Hiranyala's heart was fulfilled with warm joy, and thus fulfilled, it found its home in God's heart.

In late January 2012, considering possibilities for a special event to celebrate his mother's eighty-fifth birthday on 27 April 2012, Daniel came up with the idea of a performance of *Hiranyala*, and approached Gayathri with a copy of the text. At that point in time they had met on three occasions: soon after Daniel had been introduced to Gayathri by email as a PhD Student in the University of Lincoln's School of Psychology by the Head of School in autumn 2010, as audience members of a dance performance in the Lincoln Performing Arts centre in 2011, and on the occasion of Gayathri's attendance at a meeting of the research working group *Consciousness, Theatre,*

Literature and the Arts on 24 January 2012, which Daniel had founded within the Lincoln School of Performing Arts.

Gayathri was interested in the project initially because it would bring her a much longed-for opportunity to have a dance studio available to her to practice Bharata Natyam. She was first and foremost a PhD student in Psychology, busy with her literature review and subsequently her data collection (in the form of developing and carrying out dance work with school children aged seven to ten and doing empirical tests with the children before and after her dance practice with them to establish what the impact of her work with the children had been). Her time to practice was limited, and, at least equally important, she did not have much access to suitable spaces, in which a sprung floor is essential for the dance so as to avoid injury— the dance studio in the sports centre was available only against a hire fee, and the dance studio or the stage in the Lincoln Performing Arts Centre were reserved for students and staff affiliated to that School, or incoming productions. In addition, Gayathri found the text of *Hiranyala*, as included above, very conducive for her particular art form, the South Indian dance form of Bharata Natyam, as the text was very descriptive in a way that made the vocabulary of movements, gestures, facial expressions and means of rendering emotions available to her from her more than eighteen years of training in Bharata Natyam particularly apt for the performance of those textual details.

In the week commencing 27 February, Gayathri worked with children in Grimsby, as part of a project organised by Shrikant in his role as Dance and Education officer of Manasamitra, a South Asian arts organisation based in Dewsbury, West Yorkshire. Shrikant was part of that project. Throughout the first few weeks of rehearsals, at the back of Gayathri's mind had been a worry as to how just one artist would be able to attract an audience to an art form they may have never seen or just heard of in the past. Against this background Gayathri showed Shrikant the script of *Hiranyala*. Shrikant was attracted to the project because the script seemed to him very imaginative and profoundly emotional. The idea immediately sprang up in him that this was performable using the paradigms of Bharata Natyam, a remarkable art form that can meander with imagination with its perfect interplay between song, gesture and movement. Shrikant felt that he could express the thoughts and the varied spectrum of emotions in the script through the technique and vocabulary of Bharata Natyam. He found this script had a lot of scope to have two bodies creating different shapes and layers to the meaning of the words. For example, the description of a *pine forest* can be portrayed beautifully with eloquent hand gestures but again working with four arms rather than two arms enhanced the whole effect of the forest.

Phase one: Gayathri and Daniel
The project work thus developed in two distinct phases, each characterised by a specific kind of collaboration: the first phase saw the collaboration between Gayathri and Daniel, the second phase that between Gayathri and Daniel, Gayathri and Shrikant, and Shrikant and Daniel. In the first phase, the choreography of the first four scenes was prepared with only one artist in mind, Gayathri. The starting point for Gayathri and Daniel's work was the text of the story, *Hiranyala*. On the basis of that text, they independently considered, and brought to the rehearsals, music they found suitable for each scene, listened to each suggestion repeatedly, and then decided.

Once the music had been decided, Gayathri would listen to the music quietly at first, eyes lively at work with the imagination of possible movements. This was followed by an exploration of *mudras* and movements of hands, wrists, and arms from the elbow down. She played the music repeatedly during this process, shifting from performance mode of exploring movements to more personal mode of artist in rehearsal—still different from daily life. When new ideas worked in performance mode, Gayathri's face reflected her satisfaction (in artist mode); at other times a slight frown, in artist mode, indicated that more work was needed to achieve a better result in performance. Such a frown usually preceded a stride from the end of the performance position to the computer to replay a section that was more energetic than her artist mode walk after a sequence she was more obviously pleased with.

Gayathri then combined the exploration of hand and arm movements for each section with full body movements and steps in line with the rhythm of the music. At certain intervals, after a phase of intense work on a small section of the scene, she started the sequence of movements as from the beginning of the scene, to get a sense of the place and position of the newly developed sequence within the piece as a whole.

This creative process came across to Daniel as fragile and vulnerable, and Gayathri experienced it as "nascent". On occasion Daniel would raise explicit questions of detail. At other times, Gayathri would briefly explain a decision in favour of one movement, or sequence of movements, over others, or an element of the artistic process of creation. Most of the time, however, communication was tacit, pre-verbal, and genuinely pre-expressive in Barba's sense of the concept.

As very close observer, Daniel went beyond rational association of observed input with concepts and theories, allowing him to make intellectual sense of what he observed: processes, patterns, mechanisms—essentially fragments. A holistic perspective developed for, and through, his observation, in which he eventually not only visually perceived Gayathri's moving, dancing body, but became her body, in a mode of true embodied cognition combined with empathy, defined as an individual's ability to "partially and temporarily suspend the functions that maintain one's separateness from others (usually called ego-boundaries)" (Stern 1980: 81). He felt the creative process within her body in and as his—a new experience as he does not have a history of either training or performance in Bharata Natyam or any other dance form. While that high level of bodily empathy allowed Daniel to experience Gayathri's creative development of the project as and in his own body, it would never have allowed him to emulate, copy and carry out her movements himself. The extent of that empathy varied from rehearsal to rehearsal, dependent on aspects of both Gayathri and Daniel's daily condition, such as distraction by other events of demands in their lives. In phases of the highest degree of empathy, Daniel experienced instances of a non-ordinary mode of exchange of information between Gayathri and him that he had already encountered in a workshop with Sandra Reeve at a conference in 2006:

> One of the exercises consisted of workshop participants teaming up in pairs of their choice. Partner A would sit at the side of the space observing partner B move in the space. As instructed by Reeve, A would then engage in movements him or herself, which B was expected to pick up and use as inspiration for the development of their own movements. After the exercise was over, A and B would discuss

their experiences, and swap places for a second run of the exercise, with A moving and B at the side, again followed by discussion. When I was moving, I occasionally glanced at my partner and intuitively integrated the inspiration from her movements into mine. When I sat on the side, I first engaged in movement, as instructed, and observed how my partner in turn integrated my suggestions into her movement. In the course of the exercise, however, I found myself no longer moving but, in a state of very high concentration and alertness, which felt, at the same time, very relaxed, suggesting just in thought. Seeing her lying on the floor, for example, I thought: "She could now start movements like a mermaid". Later, my thoughts became less fully expressed, turning from sentences to phrases (up, left, right, more gentle, etc.). To my surprise, my partner followed my mental suggestions one by one. We realized, in our post-exercise discussion, that she had different images from the ones I had; thus, what I envisaged as a mermaid movement was for her the swinging of a clock pendulum, but still, she had made the movements I had wanted her to make. I would rule out, with hindsight, the possibility that I "merely" observed some latent component of her position, which then triggered me to think "mermaid", for example, and then her latent component indeed developed into what I confirmed as "mermaid" (and which was "pendulum" for herself). What happened was that my thought (the cause) resulted in her movement (the effect). (2006: 3)

A challenge to Gayathri was the work on the third scene, for which the music of the third movement of Mendelssohn's violin concerto was chosen, played, characteristically fast, by Jascha Heifetz. The challenge, for Gayathri, came from the implicit expectation to use ballet movements. She quickly, however, detected the rhythm underlying the piece, and found ways of shaping her movements around that.

Phase two: Gayathri, Shrikant and Daniel
Shrikant joining the project in April was most welcome, and led to a very attractive development of the choreography. Initially the choreography was just music and movement. With Shrikant and his rich background of experiences in storytelling and his unique way of presenting artistic material, the script was given a new dimension. Creative process, or any form of creative problem solving is said to go through four stages: preparation (research: collection of information or data); incubation (milling over collected information); illumination (light bulb idea—aha moment) and implementation (actual making, creating: verification). This phase of the *Hiranyala* rehearsals was

indeed in every sense an 'illumination' according to Gayathri. The verification of the first four scenes was achieved in such a way that there was an equal balance between the storytelling and movement-based choreography to music.

The first two scenes were mainly designed within the storytelling framework to help capture the interest of the audience to the art form as well as to provide them with ample time to register the characters. The third and fourth scenes concentrated on pure choreography where Bharata Natyam was presented in a contemporary format. In addition to Shrikant and Gayathri as the performers, Daniel joined the performance in the active role of narrator, reading passages from a large fairy tale book. There was continuity between the narrator (Daniel), the storyteller (Shrikant) and the protagonist (Gayathri as Hiranyala). According to Gayathri, though each of us performed our individual roles, we still remained connected. Similarly, the points at which we finished in the first three scenes were poignant. They gave enough time for the artists to experience the emotion and let it sink in and feel the moment. Daniel observed after the first joint rehearsal that Gayathri and Shrikant worked very well together, each bringing their own strengths to the collaboration, and recognising, appreciating and fully integrating the strengths of the other. It was interesting to note the common starting point in the story, followed by music (or rhythm without music) and then movement.

Specifically with regard to the text of the first three scenes, Shrikant was pleased that scenes one and two had a smooth transition and a very interesting connection. The 'bodily freezes' at the ending of the two scenes were poignant yet unique in their positioning on the stage. For example, the first scene ended with the three characters in three different spotlights like the shape of a triangle. The three spots are like three subject positions—the protagonist (Hiranyala, performed by Gayathri), the text (embodied by Daniel) and the inscribed dancing body of words (Shrikant). There was a common thread passing through all the three subjects, from the text of the narrative to an inscribed body which expressed the text to the main character of that narrative. The second scene and the third scene had a unique inter-connectedness of text, breath and motion. The description of the pine forest (scene two) and the valley of the snakes (scene three), in both cases conveyed through eloquent hand gestures, bodily stances and sharing of two voices, two forms of energy, one volatile and the other more graceful on the stage (from two genders—one masculine and one feminine) also added a new dimension to the concept of physical energy on the stage.

The showcase
On 27 April 2012, around forty spectators, who had responded to an announcement sent by email to all staff and students within the University of Lincoln, attended the showcase performance. The date coincided with an extremely busy schedule in LPAC due to technical rehearsals for assessed student performances. As a result, the allocated technical team had altogether forty-five minutes to set up the venue for the performance, from arranging chairs to rigging, setting up light cues, and arranging projection and sound systems. It was thus in the performance that all light and sound came together fully for the first time. We used the width of the space, with grey curtains as a natural backdrop. For the scene at the lake, a blue gel was mixed in with normal light, a green gel for the forest, an amber gel for the valley of the snakes, and a red gel for the fire.

Images were projected on to the stage right wall, using a projector placed on the outskirts of the stage space stage left. For the opening moments, the image was that of Hindu god Vishnu, to represent the God mentioned in the text. For the narration describing Hiranyala's beauty (an addition to the text of *Hiranyala*, suggested by Shrikant and composed by Daniel), an image of Gayathri in an environment of nature was used, which faded into an image of Vishnu and his consort Lakshmi, to indicate God and Hiranyala travelling together. An image of a small lake with lotus blossoms accompanied the later moments of the first scene when Shrikant described the lake. For the scene set in the forest, two images, of a forest increasing in density, were followed by the image of a hut in a forest to accompany the narration of God and Hiranyala reaching a hut in the forest. The items they receive from the old woman who lives in the hut were also shown as projections, a bone, a spindle with thread, and a golden apple. The image for the valley of the snakes was that of a barren canyon, and for the fire scene fire was projected.

The positioning of the projector on one side of the stage rather than on the rig above led to an additional effect of the performers casting clear shadows on to the projections. In the context of those circumstances the performance went ahead without major problems and as well as could be expected.

At the beginning of the performance, Gayathri had to get used to the presence of the audience. Although the performance took place in the same space where all of the rehearsals had taken place, in conditions of performance, with a live audience present, the space is transformed. Gayathri was not merely dancing for herself, but had to carry an audience along with her. Getting herself acquainted with the audience thus took up the duration of the first scene, and confidence grew with every step and intensity of expression increased equally slowly, together with opening up. At the beginning of scene two, when all three performers stood in a row facing the audience, with Daniel at the front, Gayathri behind him, and Shrikant behind Gayathri, the positioning of the projector light caused their shadows to be projected on to the stage right wall, over the image of the dense wood. Gayathri noticed this and the appropriateness of the combination of image and shadows struck her as very impressive. This impression served as a trigger for Gayathri to settle into the performance and relish the detailed depictions of objects Hiranyala is given by the old woman (the bone, the spindle and thread, and the apple). In the third scene she enjoyed the challenge of dancing with Bharata Natyam based movements to a Western music that might raise expectations of ballet movements to accompany it. The first three scenes build up well towards the climax of the fourth scene, which turned out to have become everyone's favourite, for both performers and members of the audience.

For Shrikant, the transformation of the venue from a bare rehearsal area to a performance space brought with it a surge of energy. When the spectators entered the space, it was obvious from observing their faces that they came with a considerable level of joyous expectation, which shaped the energy in the space to make it warm and welcoming to the artists. He sensed a difference in energy between himself and Gayathri, in particular towards the end of the performance, which he explained with regard to Gayathri not having had the opportunity to practice her dance regularly since she had moved to the UK for her PhD studies, whereas he had practiced on a daily basis. He brought more of his own energy to the performance when he noticed the imbalance, to restore balance.

The intercultural dimension and the concept of *intuitive collaboration*

The project worked with a text written by a person of German nationality, translated into English by a German working in the UK, and performed by him and two dancers from India in the UK. This is the outer framework of the intercultural nature of the project. The German context came into the project because the author of the text at the basis of the project, Daniel's mother, happens to be of German nationality. Her work, however, was already intercultural because it was strongly influenced by her exposure to Indian thought mediated through her then involvement with the Transcendental Meditation movement, Sri Sri Ravi Shankar's Art of Living movement, both based in India, and earlier exposure to Indian Hatha Yoga courses held in Switzerland. On first reading of the text, both Gayathri and Shrikant intuitively realised that they were able to relate to the text, independent of the cultural origins.

The linking factor for the intercultural nature of the project was that all three performers were working in the UK, not their country of birth (India and Germany). Each one of us uses material from our own cultures, seeking to fit material from our own cultures into a different cultural context, with the help of a text from a different culture, and performing it to yet a different culture. This brought many different perspectives to the project: even though Shrikant and Gayathri are from the same country, they brought their different training backgrounds with them, apart from the gender factor. Shrikant's background in this respect is the Kalakshetra style, while Gayathri has trained in a range of styles—Kalakshetra, Vazhuvoor, and Tanjore. The different energies conditioned in these different ways were allowed to come together freely and naturally, and thus to create a performance that was interesting for the performers, for the members of the audience with an academic theatre studies or dance studies background, and members of the audience without specialist knowledge of the performing arts.

Confronted with frequent claims in the debate around intercultural theatre concerning issues of inappropriate hegemony, neo-colonialism, cultural exploitation and cultural theft, Shrikant emphasised that the original idea for *Hiranyala* was that of Daniel's mother, but all performers brought their own ideas to the rehearsals and the production, and thus claimed their own ownership in relation to the material. In this way, ownership did not become problematic. In the same context, Gayathri pointed out that if you are secure about your own culture, your own roots, if you know where you come from and what you have to offer, and if you know your limitations, such problems do not arise. In the *Hiranyala* project we all knew our strengths and limitations, and worked together on the basis of being honest about both, not boasting with the former nor feeling downhearted about the latter. On that basis we were able to be open-hearted, interested and curious to accommodate new learning from other cultures. For clashes to occur, there is no need for the clashing parties or positions to be from different cultures. Personal attitudes are more important in determining whether clashes will arise. In working on *Hiranyala*, all three performers did not merely work for themselves, on their own contribution to the performance, but together, for each other in the sense that, for example, we were able to portray the vision that Daniel had, that his mother had with the original story.

In the process of translation Daniel was not influenced by the fact that it was his mother's text. In rehearsal, Daniel was able to answer specific questions from Gayathri and Shrikant about the details of the text on the basis of his knowledge of what his mother intended, and on some occasions was able to ask her and provide them with first hand response. For the performance, Daniel added a few lines of text describing Hiranyala's beauty:

> God as sculptor had created the beauty of Hiranyala's face, because no human sculptor could have created such an infinitely finely chiselled countenance, with so many, infinitely delicate yet robust, infinitely nuanced features and shapes, gentle, flowing, sweet, but not too, all in just the perfect proportions on their own and to each other, and each individual feature with its own infinity of further layers just as perfectly proportioned and relating to each other.

Daniel arrived at this version of the description in discussion with his mother, thus ensuring the text agreed with her impression of the overall fit.

In the rehearsal process, the team made the fairy tale, *Hiranyala*, accessible to the audience through the combination of distinct components or elements, such as narration, story-telling and dance, and achieved an appropriate balance of those elements. Rather than studying the text of *Hiranyala* in an intellectual, analytical manner Gayathri worked intuitively, on the basis of the experience that her artistic creativity works best when she allows it to flow in the moment. Prior analysis leads to compartmentalisation and fragmentation, whereas creation in the moment allows integrated wholeness to develop. Once an initial sequence of movements had been created by Gayathri in this way, further development took place through thinking about the created material, and discussing it with Shrikant. Then they would find a point in the discussion where it was best not to talk any further, so as to allow the material to settle within their own minds. At the next rehearsal, Gayathri would then seek to incorporate all aspects of the discussion, and their further tacit development within her intuition, in her performance. The broad shape of the production emerged predominantly through intuitive processes; the same applies to the detail, in particular the specific use of Bharata Natyam as the chosen dance form. The relationship of the narrative and the means of expression in this dance form, such as footwork and mudras, is not an issue of discussion or consideration for a dancer trained in Bharata Natyam: there are set ways in which any object or action or person will be depicted.

In the context of Indian dance, including Bharata Natyam, there is the *tandava*, the dance of Lord Shiva, the male dancer, who dances when he is angry. When he dances the three worlds tremble. To calm him down, his wife, representing the feminine principle, dances as well, *lasya*. Thus it is part of the dance form that male and female energies are definitely different, with more exuberance, more footwork and jumping for the men and more graceful, soft movements from the women. Thus Bharata Natyam does not deny, but acknowledges and works with gender difference.

Overall, the team was thus aware of differences in levels of input into the creative process, but this was not perceived by any team member as an infringement of their own of any other team member's space, or authority. Here, a new concept emerges as a solid and valid response to issues of intercultural performance: *intuitive collaboration*. The impact of this concept is based on two related insights: first, most of the debate about intercultural theatre has been conducted in the domain of reason, well within the conventional definitions of the objective, scientific paradigm, assuming that creative work, including performance, functions in terms of rational processes, of strategies, and logical decisions. Second, much performance work, as creative work, is actually predominantly, and at least at its origin, intuitive. It stands to reason that academic discussion of a predominantly intuitive phenomenon in terms that seek to exclude the intuitive will not lead to many useful insights. Thus an approach that allows rigorous investigation of intuitive processes promises to yield long-overdue insights into intercultural performance.

Chapter Three

Daniel Meyer-Dinkgräfe, Per Brask, Harry Youtt

Appropriate forms of praise of acting in theatre criticism

Hierarchy: the performer comes last

In the past, some notable theatre critics have published collections of what they considered the most important examples of their reviews. The majority of theatre criticism, however, is relatively inaccessible in newspaper archives. The internet age, and, for the UK, Ian Herbert's launch of the *Theatre Record* (as *London Theatre Record*) in 1981, which collates all available reviews on productions in London, and to some extent beyond, in bi-weekly editions, have changed this to ensure wider accessibility. Such enhanced access allows the general observation, statistically speaking, that the larger part of each review of theatre is likely to be spent on the play (the dramatist's text) and the production (the director's ways of interpreting the text in his or her process of putting the text on stage), and the scenography (some or all of set, costume, lighting and sound design). The people whom the audience see on stage for the entire duration of the performance, the actors, usually and typically receive the least of all the words available to the reviewer.

This arguably deplorable and unfair practice is mirrored in many books about theatre that carry photos from productions. In most cases the image captions provide information about the director, the year of the production, the name of the dramatist, the title of the play, the name of the scenographer, and the name of the photographer (see, for example, Rubin, 1994). The names of the actors in those images are only provided in very exceptional cases.

The conclusion is obvious: theatre critics do not do justice to the work of actors. "Critic" is the worst insult in the exchange of verbal abuse between Vladimir and Estragon in the English version of Beckett's *Waiting for Godot*. Estragon throws it at Vladimir "*with finality*", and with exaggerated pronunciation: "Crritic!", to which Vladimir responds with "Oh". The stage direction immediately afterwards implies how genuinely and deeply hurt Vladimir is: "*He wilts, vanquished, and turns away*". In the German version, the insult comes without the "*with finality*" stage direction and the English "Crritic!" is replaced by the "Ober...forstinspektor", with the three dots suggesting hesitation; the chosen insult is ridiculous, and Vladimir's response, an exaggerated "Ohh!", does not suggest at all that he is adversely affected by this insult. The French version leaves the insults to the production. (1971: 186-7). Many autobiographies of, and interviews with actors suggest that they have an often tense relationship with theatre critics.

Against the background of this observation, in this article we want to discuss some of the reasons of why the actors receive short shrift, and the limited range of vocabulary that critics employ to express their appreciation of an actor's work. We analyse the status quo, position it in a wider context of the philosophy of praise, and discuss the way forward with reference to relatively exceptional examples of past good practice that may serve as a pointer to future developments.

The time frame we cover in the article is restricted to the contemporary situation, from the 1970s to the present. We are not covering the comparisons of theatre and opera criticism, or theatre and film or television criticism, comparisons of the contemporary with previous time periods, cross-cultural comparisons beyond the countries we cover, i.e., the United Kingdom and the USA, or the comparison of newspaper versus academic criticism. Research can emerge in those fields, possibly informed or inspired by our work, or is happening elsewhere already, such as the material covered in the 7 June 2012 University of Kent conference on *Cultural Criticism in the Digital Age: Media, Purposes and the Status of the Critic*.

There are at least two possible reasons for the hierarchy of text, director, scenography and finally actor. First, there is the tendency among academics and academically oriented journalists to feel it necessary to appear text-biased in order to preserve their reputations as respected critics. In this context, it is problematic to write too enthusiastically about a performer: because it could be perceived as an indirect demeaning of the text, and an acknowledgment that perhaps emotion has overcome the critic's intellectual-rational assessment of the work itself and its underlying text. The second reason is that at least in consumer criticism, there lurks in many drama critics the frustration of a thwarted Thespian dream. This could account for an unconscious begrudging of a performer's significance in a particular drama's successful rendering.

Vocabulary in theatre criticism
So much for initial arguments relating to reasons why the work of actors gets fewer words in theatre reviews than the play, the director and scenography. When we look at the words that theatre critics do allocate to actors, the disappointment continues. Critics are rarely at a loss to find suitable, often ironic, witty, or sarcastic words of describing in detail what precisely they did not like about a particular actor's performance. Billington in *The Guardian* tends to be most gentle in the descriptions of what he finds problematic, as in these comments on the actors playing Professor Higgins and Eliza Doolittle in a production of Shaw's *Pygmalion*:

> Rupert Everett's saturnine Higgins strikes a note of rasping anger from which he scarcely shifts. There is little suggestion of either the scholarly obsessive or the sadness of a man who awakes too late to Eliza's vibrancy. While nothing can douse the comedy of Eliza's trial outing at Mrs Higgins's tea party, Honeysuckle Weeks also lacks the chiselled articulation that can endow the scene with ecstasy. (2010)

The *Times* is not as gentle: the actor playing film star Bette Davis in Anton Burge's *Whatever Happened to the Cotton Dress Girl*, received this sentence in the *Times* review: "And Wilcox? A good actor. But, sorry, she's no Bette Davis" (Maxwell, 2008). The tone in the *Daily Mail* is even blunter: commenting on a production of *The Prince of Homburg*, Quentin Letts wrote: "Mr McDiarmid, despite his amazingly deep voice, is miscast. He hams and camps and rolls his eyes. For God's sake, man, you're playing a Prussian autocrat, not some goose-stepper from *The Producers*" (2010).

When it comes to praise, the direct vocabulary is limited to words such as "good, very good, stunning, extraordinary, moving, beautiful, admirable" for stage actors. Billington considers "acute interpretive intelligence" as a characteristic of great acting, and thus a description of how a character comes across in a specific actor's performance represents praise for him (1993: 8). For example, he describes (and thus praises) Alec McCowen's performance as psychiatrist Dysart and Peter Firth as Alan Strang in Shaffer's *Equus* as

> a brilliant study of a man of reason, soured by the need to bottle up and contain his instincts; and as always, he articulates arguments beautifully. And Peter Firth matches him admirably as the haunted, hapless, soft-featured boy who has given reign to his fearful passion. (1993: 35)

Billington describes the impact of the acting and adds the key words of "beautiful" and "admirable".

Good critics, like *The New Yorker*'s John Lahr, will often include exceptionally evocative descriptions as part of their evaluations such as in Lahr's review of Sam Mendes's production of *Richard III*. Here is his opening impression of Kevin Spacey as Richard,

> We first encounter the flamboyantly shameless would-be king in his cups, scrunched into a leather chair, with a wine bottle at his feet and a purple paper party crown askew on his head, while a TV screen behind him broadcasts footage of the King's son Edward, Duke of York, and his victorious army returning home – a narrative of success that Richard clicks off with a fillip of disgust. As he draws his twisted body out of the chair and skitters buglike down stage to us, propelled by the weight of his humped back and his ungainly left leg, whose foot turns in at a ninety-degree angle. (Lahr 2012a).

This is both beautifully written and keenly observed and more importantly it gives the reader confidence in the critic and his general assessment of how the actor's performance fits into the tenor of the drive of the show as a whole. The actor can also get a sense of whether what he and the director intended actually came across. This is valuable for all involved.

Even as fine a critic as Lahr, however, can have an off day and descend to unfairness against an actor as he does in the subsequent issue of *The New Yorker* where he reviews Cynthia Nixon's performance in the New York revival of Margaret Edson's *Wit*:

> Nixon can paint likable stage pictures with an effective emotional palette, but intellectual sinew and humor are not among her primary colors. Vivian [the character's name] trades in the paradoxical gaiety and wisdom of sarcasm; Nixon trades in charming sincerity. She doesn't savor the pitch and roll of Vivian's swagger; she can't see the wink in the words. Too often, she shouts Edson's lines. (Lahr 2012b)

This statement comes uncomfortably close to a personal attack on the actor and not a description of what she is actually doing. Lahr frames his evaluation of Nixon within an appreciation of Edson's play and the virtues he finds in the main character as written, the previous and by him highly regarded performances of this character by Kathleen Chalfant on stage and by Emma Thompson on film, and by the mention that Cynthia Nixon is "known to one and all as Miranda Hobbes in 'Sex and the City.'" This review then does not describe what Cynthia Nixon actually did (apart from her too often shouting the lines) and how what she did (including the shouting) contributed (or did not) new insights into the issues and interactions addressed in the play. What the review does assess is the magnitude of Lahr's disappointment. More importantly it makes (or ought to make) a reader distrustful of the critic's evaluation of the performance. It is also unhelpful for the actor who, after all, cannot change the fact that she was once on a TV show and is "known to one and all" as the character she played in it. Nor is she likely to be able to change her primary colours, whatever that means.

Some critics are aware of their problems with appropriate language to do justice to the impressions they have encountered on the stage: thus, Alison Croggon, an Australian journalist, poet and playwright, comments:

> It's very, very difficult to write well about performance, for a start. I don't think I've yet quite found a way. And when you're confronted with artists like Romeo Castelluci, say, the stakes go up further, because he just gets rid of language altogether, or puts it in such a questionable place that language seems particularly inappropriate in response. I'm sure there's a way to write adequately, but I haven't found it yet, there's always a sense of ashes about it, the traces of fire. (2007)

Daniel Bye notes that

> even the sainted Kenneth Tynan consistently reviews the play until the
> very final paragraph, when he finally deigns to pass judgment on the
> acting. This despite a few pieces on actors (e.g., Olivier) or directors
> (the two Peters) showing he had an extraordinary ability to write
> perceptively and well on areas beyond the purely literary. (2007)

Alex F has this to add to the debate:

> Everyone—on the subject of writing about theatre specifically—could
> it be that part of the problem is that we do not yet have the tools or the
> shared language to articulate what we may wish to say about it?
> Whereas a literary critic has a long tradition of highly engaged
> criticism to draw from, if you want to write about performance rather
> than the play, you are to a large extent going to be seeking out a new
> way to do so. . . . I say all this, and yet I normally find it very easy to
> talk about performance in the bar after the show—perhaps there's
> something about the social nature of theatre that lends itself to
> conversation in a way that it doesn't to the solitary act of writing. Then
> again, perhaps not - I'm speculating wildly off the cuff now and I
> should probably control myself. (2007)

Perhaps the issue is not so much how we describe what we experience
but how we render our response to that experience. If we look at it this
way, we are no longer searching for the appropriate comparison, but
for an articulation of something that is at once more personal and truer
to the nature of the theatrical event itself—an event which needs not
just the empty space and the actor to walk across it but also the
audience: not to observe because that is too passive, but to audiencify
the event into theatre.

Virtues of critics and of good acting

The problem that confronts a discussion of the philosophy and
vocabulary of praise in relationship to acting is (at least) twofold. On
the one hand are the virtues of the critic and on the other, the virtues
manifested in good acting. Both sets of virtues are context-sensitive
but in different ways. The critic must be aware that the achievement
aimed for by an actor operating within the Stanislavski tradition in a
play by Chekov is not the same as the achievement aimed for by an
actor operating within a Brechtian aesthetic. Indeed, neither is aiming
for the physical body and vocal constructions an actor working within
a Grotowski-Barba tradition would be striving for. Thus one of the

intellectual virtues a critic must possess concerns her ability to discern the kind of theatre she is evaluating. Within that she also needs to know what genre or category the performance is part of before her assessment can begin to be trustworthy. In other words, the assessment cannot simply depend on whether the critic likes or enjoys this kind of theatre, which means that in addition to discernment, she must also exhibit the intellectual virtues of open-mindedness and aesthetic judgment.

The actor, of course, must also be sensitive to the kind of play or event she is part of. The kind of training she has undergone will often set the limits of her creative capabilities. It is difficult for an actor who has spent years of rigorous training in a Stanislavski-based school to begin operating with Barba's required physical expressiveness until she has also undergone a significant amount of relevant training in this form. The actor in the Chekov play will traditionally want to seem to disappear into the role, to limit the perceived distance between herself and her role—and to make any effort seem to be the character's and not her own. The Brechtian actor will want to make this distance part of the stage narrative, in order to emphasize the constructed aspect of the performance and point towards the social and political circumstances of the role being portrayed—and he may make strenuous and exaggerated effort when playing, for instance, Arturo Ui. The Barba trained actor will attempt to find an extra-daily expressiveness (with body and voice) based on a given assignment—an assignment only the director and the actor may ever know.

The performance to be adjudicated as good in these examples naturally depends on what was achieved in each case. The assessment that such and such an actor was "every inch an Arturo Ui" would be beside the point, whereas the assessment that the actor persuasively revealed the circumstances that someone like Arturo could exploit for his own benefit, would be high praise. That the actor in the Chekov play seemed hard at work would be an insult. But, in a Barba-like event, it could be praiseworthy if the actor had found a strenuous vocal resonator. In other words, praise must relate to the intended achievement (as of course must blame).

In the aesthetic of verisimilitude in which the actor enters a fictional situation and behaves as though it were real (i.e. the prevailing aesthetic of major theatres in the West, and especially in

North America) the task of the actor is not first and foremost interpretation in the literary sense. At least not the kind of interpretation that asks: what is the meaning of all this? The actor first and foremost looks for what it is she is supposed to do in the situation of her character. Most often actors will determine what the character wants in a particular situation, (most often) from another character. She then tries to execute an action instantiating that want/drive while adjusting to the other character and what that other character is in pursuit of. Hopefully the two pursuits are at odds and a dramatic moment becomes possible. The praiseworthy actor is the one who is able to define the minutest goals of her character in such a way that her actions (including voice and movement) will keep the audience's attention. Her achievement in the execution of these actions is what must be evaluated. In rehearsals, this praise may be called out from a director as, "you've nailed it." That is, the actor managed to make her actions (even the smallest ones, like the turn of the head at a certain time, the modulation of a line) so specific and so nuanced that people in the rehearsal hall were utterly convinced of the reality of the moment (though of course everyone knew that it was played). In actual performances on different nights what all audiences will get is a sense of the somewhat larger goals laid down in rehearsal, the tiniest goals can rarely be laid down firmly, as they risk then becoming mannered. There must be room for some improvisation – more or less, depending on the kind of show—and some room to respond to a specific audience, for example through minor changes in pacing.

Sensitivity on the part of the critic to the kinds of goals the actor is pursuing is necessary for the assessment of a performance, as is the way these goals through their behavioural manifestations succeed in suggesting the life of a character. The appropriate categories of praise for a successful achievement in this context relate to terms such as clarity, specificity, precision, aliveness, focus, persuasiveness, sensitivity to the goals of fellow actors, intelligent or imaginative or inventive choices, attention-holding, flexible vocal delivery and subtly revealing movement patterns, etc.

Many critics may have difficulty assessing (and hence adequately describing) their own responses to a performance, which may be related to their shyness, or unwillingness, to show vulnerability, in other words their ability to express what the performance makes them feel, imagine or want to do. This argument is related to the position discussed earlier, that actors get short shrift by critics in general either because of the perceived or implied superiority of the text, or due to the critic's possibly unconscious desire to avoid the impression of stage struck awe, fearing to say too much, lest their own performance insecurities be exposed. The second reason for the critics' apparent lack of suitable vocabulary of praise is that they might not know what actors do, to an extent sufficient to allow them to assess it and put that assessment into words that make sense to their readerships: we live in a culture where the main aesthetic we are exposed to focuses on believability, which means that the performer as much as possible must hide what she does and since critics don't investigate the techniques of making that happen (after all everybody knows how to pretend, right?), they are unable to evaluate what the actor has done.

The result of such criticism is that it is of not much practical use to actors, beyond evoking feelings of being pleased or hurt, as the case may be—a conclusion well supported by many actors' comments in autobiographies or interviews.

So far, we have noted the dominant position, in theatre criticism, of the dramatic text over the achievement of the actors, and have discussed some possible reasons for it. We have also noted that in the few lines critics tend to reserve for their comments about actors, they are better equipped to find suitably precise words for negative criticism, but tend to be vague when it comes to praise. We discussed this observation in terms of critics' problems with assessing their own responses and in daring to stand by them, and critics' problems with understanding what acting is all about. Those contexts represent the issues inherent in the institutions of the theatre and consumer criticism themselves. The causes for those problems with praise of an actor's achievement are, however, not restricted to those intrinsic to the art and its institutions.

The wider philosophical context of praise

In philosophy, praise is almost exclusively dealt with concomitantly with blame, as a major binary opposite in moral philosophy: the *Oxford Dictionary of Philosophy*, for example, defines praise and blame thus:

> Praise is the public expression of approval and admiration; it acts as a reinforcement of the qualities or actions that are praised, perhaps

> encouraging their repetition, or their display as a model for others to follow. The opposite of praise may be simply disappointment or regret. Blame implies that the agent could have done better or ought to feel guilt or shame. It therefore raises issues of free will and responsibility. (2005, 287).

Implicit in most philosophy that deals with praise and blame, in the context of moral philosophy and discussions of free will and responsibility is a preference for engaging with blame rather than praise—a choice explicitly made and justified by Williams in his entry on "Praise and Blame" in the *Internet Encyclopedia of Philosophy*:

> In fact, blame will get the greatest attention here. This is partly because praise seems less problematic: misplaced blame is felt as deeply unfair, not least because being exposed to blame is unpleasant and costly in a way that being praised is not. But it is principally because blame has a closer connection than praise to matters of intense philosophical interest, including freedom, responsibility and desert. We often *praise* inanimate objects (such as art works or buildings) and animals (a loyal pet, for example), although we could not *blame* such entities, however deeply dissatisfied we felt with them. The focus of this article, however, will be upon entities that are clearly open to blame as well as praise: human beings.

In a religious context, in Christianity, praise is due to God for having created the world and all that comes with it and Him. Humankind is marred by the primordial sin and thus not very praiseworthy, unless it is to do with their worship and praise of God.

The fields in which praise is being written explicitly have been at the fringes of the academic and societal norms and thus approval: *positive psychology* and the self-help section of popular science. Praise has been a key characteristic and research topic in *positive psychology*, defined as "the study of the conditions and processes that contribute to the flourishing or optimal functioning of people, groups, and institutions" (Gable and Haidt, 2005: 103). This movement has been a relatively recent addition to the discipline of psychology, introduced as such in the late 1990s, and although it has its origins in humanistic psychology (Abraham Maslow, for example) of the 1950s, it still suffers some of the criticism reserved by the establishment for newcomers.

This criticism is probably not helped by sound scientific research seeping into the field of popular science and the self-help dimension of the book market and the internet. In popular psychology, represented in the printed and internet formats of magazines such as *Psychology Today*, praise is a popular topic in main features and blogs. For example, University of Cambridge academic Terri Apter argues that "Praise is an important learning tool, but it is a difficult tool to use correctly", and proceeds to differentiate the kinds of situations where praise is, and has been, successful, and provides striking examples of praise gone wrong (2009). Praise and its pitfalls are equally central to the research by Carol S. Dweck, Professor of Psychology at Stanford University, culminating in the publication, on its basis, of *Mindset: The New Psychology of Success* (2006), a book that has been successful in the self-help bracket of the popular market.

Despite the growing interest in positive psychology, its underpinnings and techniques, popular culture is permeated by a desire of seeing someone voted off some island. We do not wish to imply that one of the functions of the critical journalist is to encourage an actor to become a better actor through the use of praise. We are not suggesting the effective critic has to assume the role of acting coach or motivator. A critic is not a therapist. Our real aim is to counter the negative-bias-as-a-positive-value of popular culture or at least to establish and reinforce that a critic's ethical obligation is to overcome popular culture's tendency toward negativity for its shock and retail values, and strive towards an ethic of dispassionate honesty in reviewing performance—although it could be argued that "being honest" is not as philosophically or psychologically simple a state as it might appear. How can we ever truly know we're being honest?   .

We thus note that philosophy mentions praise in passing, also preferring to deal with its opposite, blame, instead; religion does not find much about humans praiseworthy, hence the development of a vocabulary of praise could not expect much support from that quarter either, and psychology, which so far has tended to focus predominantly on "negative" manifestations and phenomena of human life, is only gradually carrying out and accepting research into positive action such as praise.

Against the intrinsic and extrinsic backgrounds revealed in this chapter, theatre critics cannot be blamed either for not having been able to break the pattern of spending more printed space on blame than on praise, or for finding better words for such blame than they are able to muster for what praise they are prepared to offer. It might be worth considering whether this applies to the Western (European and American) contexts only, and whether the situation is different in other cultures.

The way ahead

In the context of theatre criticism, it is equally possible to discuss existing "best practices" for critical review of a performance, and to develop those ideas further.

A read-through of Frank Rich's reviews as Chief Drama Critic for *The New York Times*, 1980-1994 (republished in book form as *Hot Seat* in 1998), reveals him as the highly intelligent, discerning and knowledgeable writer a demanding editor like Arthur Gelb would have required for the person succeeding Walter Kerr. Rich became known as "The Butcher of Broadway," but from the perspective of the present time he doesn't seem to have been especially vicious in his reviews. Rather, his reviews tend to be well-written and argued, often filled with detailed description. The quality of his writing could lead one to suspect that readers of his reviews came to trust his judgments and hence his influence grew—to the detriment of shows he didn't assess very highly. He did not become influential because he was unreasonable, outrageous or grandstanding.

Rich, during his career as drama critic, was a sharp observer of acting performances and many of his reviews contain evaluations of actors' achievements grounded in examples. In a few cases, his evaluation of an actor would form the primary focus of a review. A particularly apt example is his review from February 24, 1981, of Nicol Williamson's "marathon performance" as Bill Maitland in John Osborne's *Inadmissible Evidence*. Here Rich states,

> As delivered by Mr. Williamson, Bill's lengthy diatribe is not the teary wallow in self-pity or self-hatred that one might expect: It's a lawyer's objective tallying of the facts of his own bankrupt life. By thinking through every specific gesture of his character, the actor gives a performance that is beyond pity and is far too complex to devolve into a sentimental archetype. He shows us Bill clearly for what he is: the case is presented without prejudice. Mr. Williamson is something to see. Standing tall in a pin-striped three-piece suit, he enters the stage in darkness, then stands weaving in a blinding spotlight (…). His voice sputters and whinnies as words tumble out in babbling incoherence. He searches his vest pockets for his pills and then sends his long hands flying up to his temples – as if he were trying to push his spilling brains back into his skull. (…) Mr.

> Williamson sits behind his desk and hurls verbal darts at all comers
> (…) Mr. Williamson explodes with a withering insult—only to turn
> ashen a second later and beg like a child for forgiveness." (1998: 57)

This kind of review is evidence of keen observation. Rich pays close
attention to what the actor does. It stands as a beacon of good
reviewing of an acting achievement.

Taking a closer look at his first three seasons as drama critic for
The New York Times, one finds phrases for praise of acting, such as
the following sample (all page numbers refer to Rich, 1998):

> the magic of infectious charm (5); spirited contributions (6); a
> Vesuvius of rebel yells and outlandish homespun wisdom (8); The
> actors are in character (11); the first Nick ever to capture the
> character's ambition, boorishness, and casual ruthlessness without
> falling into clichéd Sammy Glick mannerisms or sacrificing the role
> humor (12); she manages to straddle all the play's moods at once (12);
> her whole body seems to shriek (12); four thinking actors shed
> startling new light (13); sensitively played (18); a whirlwind of
> graceful energy (18); doesn't disappoint (28); one of the comic
> treasures of the literate theater (28); a deft pratfall artist (28-29); the
> perfect note of farcically youthful ardor (29); he delivers his knock-
> 'em-dead speeches with raucous relish (34); dominates the evening
> (38); every bit the magnetic, inspirational leader (39); the performers
> are good (41); touchingly straddles that boundary between hysterical
> laughter and tears (43); boundless imagination and a split-second
> precision that is breathtaking (45); towering performance (47); a
> remarkable transformation (47); he's the frisky Ellington spirit
> incarnate (59); by making life and art look as easy and elegant as a
> perfect song, Ms. Bacall embodies the very spirit of the carefree
> American musical (64); precisely conveys his character's mixture of
> princely arrogance and unspoken despair (68); with commanding
> assurance and wit (72) in the hands of people who know how to milk
> it for every last gasp, thrill, and laugh that it's worth (74); she has the
> killer instinct—and the skill to project it from a stage (74); he shows
> us the serene, almost senile face of a man who's taking a private final
> tally of an entire lifetime (75); delivers a beautiful closing speech
> (81); an uncommon knack for revealing the inner workings of a
> slippery lowlife's restless mind (86); giving fresh, clean performances
> (87); the whole cast is strong (89); outstanding (95); elevates a comic
> type with rending poetry (100); we see a man unravel to the terrifying
> point where the audience's loathing must give way to a compassionate
> embrace (100); brilliant (105); the actress walks a tremulous line
> between hilarity and hysteria (107); priceless (107); never less than a
> brilliant actor, has outdone himself (109); a charming, Woody Allen-
> esque fellow who brings fire to the shows angriest song (112); Ms.

Hepburn, to say the least, is still yare (114); the passion, the stubbornness, the vulnerability (114); does keep you guessing about which part of her personality she'll reveal next (115); his strong voice, as well as his characteristic sweetness (118); brings full honesty (118); a fascinating performance, full of contradictions that always leave the audience on edge (118); one of the most powerful theatrical coups (123); a sensational actor in peak form (128); wittily accomplishes the crucial task of making Iago a double-edged blade. We never doubt that his victims would mistake his poisonous deceptions for the devotion and counsel of an honest friend (129); impressive (130); effective (132); a towering presence (139); her force of personality is mesmerizing (144); this actress makes us believe in the warped logic (149); shading her portrayal with carefully considered nuances (150).

A number of these summary abstractions might be considered offhanded [e.g. "brilliant," "priceless," "outstanding," "impressive," "in peak form,"].

Though this list exhibits a wide ranging vocabulary in assessing good acting it does not really do justice to Rich's accomplishment as a critic, namely that he rarely tosses off an adjective and lets it stand. His usual method is to exemplify what he means and what he saw, and he usually assesses a performance in context. Often acting is described along with the storyline. Of course, the most telling statement of what he looks for as the basic elements of good acting is his explicit, "the bread-and-butter qualities of good acting: feeling, stage presence, physical, vocal, and facial expressiveness" (52). The focus here is what can actually be seen. Yes, an actor must interpret, and Rich evaluates highly surprising and insightful acting choices, but it is the expressiveness, what actually comes out, so to speak, and allows the audience to interpret, that he takes as his purview for assessment.

Art as the expression of emotion, a view Rich is at least close to endorsing in the above quote, has had a distinguished career in aesthetic philosophy, explicated variously by thinkers like Croce, Dewey, Collingwood and Oakeshott. It is currently (by some) considered to be a conservative (in the old sense of the term), even an old-fashioned (a historically and culturally limited) view of art. Expressiveness is, of course, a somewhat slippery term hard to define with any kind of philosophical precision, but in regular non-philosophical conversation it is usually meant to convey that the work of the artist is evoking or communicating some feeling or emotion, possibly having been felt by the artist (or having evolved in the creation of the work), but certainly by an audience. And what Rich does in his best reviews is to give an account of how a performance made him feel and of skills and techniques employed by an actor to make him feel this way.

Rich's approach can be generalised to imply that the challenge to all critics is to identify what aspects of the performance are evoking or communicating some feeling or emotion to give an account of how a performance made the critic and the audience feel, and to identify the skills and techniques employed by an actor that make him feel this way. However, many contemporary practitioners, especially academic practitioners, would probably disagree because they would shiver at having to endorse its underlying aesthetic assumptions. To elaborate: post-modern critics, in particular, would find it difficult to endorse "art as the expression of emotion" and to take their interpretive stance from that claim. They would probably want to look at performance as a kind of gestural language or see it as part of a cultural context of codes that are repeated in order to "ground" (there is no ground for them) or occasionally challenge cultural assumptions (a performance that caused such a challenge would be valued highly by them)— whether they are felt or not would be beside the point for them. In contrast to such post-modern critics, Rich values meaning-seeking art that operates on and challenges the emotions as a means of (hopefully) eventual shared insight by artists and audience, and many readers of the better papers and magazines would probably agree that this is precisely what they find interesting reading.

A further example of exemplary reviewing does not refer to an individual critic, but provides a case study of reviews of a specific production: the 2012 revival of Arthur Miller's *Death of a Salesman*, directed by Mike Nichols in the Ethel Barrymore Theater, New York, with Philip Seymour Hoffman (Willy Loman), Linda Emond (Linda Loman), Andrew Garfield (Biff Loman), and Finn Wittrock (Happy Loman) in the main roles.

Perhaps because this play is a well-worn text about which much has been written, and because Mike Nichols is the iconic eighty-year-old director who might be perceived as a semi-untouchable sacred cow, there is ample discussion of the performances in the reviews. This is no doubt also attributable in part to the fact that there are at least a couple of celebrity star turns that increase the focus upon performances. It is also noteworthy that Nichols' principal contribution seems to be that he has adhered to the traditions of the play's staging, sets, lighting, and musical background. Perhaps there is not a tremendous amount to be said about his contribution. The review of the production in the *New York Times* indicates very clearly that the production triggered many responses and thoughts in the critic, Ben Brantley. He is impressed by the profiles of the actors, and refers to their achievements on screen and stage. At the same time he is not in awe of them to the extent that he merely flatters them; rather, his detailed assessment in particular of Hoffman demonstrates his ability to identify and express both his achievements and shortcomings in terms that are neither condescending and dismissive nor sycophantic, and never general but always very specific: Hoffman brings "exacting intelligence and intensity" to his performance, making "thought visible", but it is the thought of an actor "making choices" rather than of a character "living in the moment". His "reading of certain lines makes you hear classic dialogue anew but with intellectual annotations." As a

> complete flesh-and-blood being, this Willy seems to emerge only fitfully. His voice pitched sonorous and low, his face a moonlike mask of unhappiness, he registers in the opening scenes as an abstract (as well as abstracted) Willy, a ghost who roams through his own life. (And yes, at 44, Mr. Hoffman never seems a credible 62.) Mind you, there are instances of piercing emotional conviction throughout, moments you want to file and rerun in memory. Mr. Hoffman does terminal uncertainty better than practically anyone, and he's terrific in showing the doubt that crumples Willy just when he's trying to sell his own brand of all-American optimism. (His memory scenes with his self-made brother, played by John Glover, are superb.) What he doesn't give us is the illusion of the younger Willy's certainty, of the belief in false gods. For "Salesman" to work as tragedy (for which it does qualify), there has to be a touch of the titan in Willy, of the hope-inflated man that his sons once worshiped, so we feel an ache of loss when all the air goes out of him. That was what Brian Dennehy offered (some felt to excess) in Robert Falls's marvellous 1999 production. Mr. Hoffman's Willy is preshrunk. (Brantley 2012)

In contrast to Hoffmann (and a similar view on the performances of Linda Emond and Andrew Garfield, Brantley considers two performances as outstanding because of their uninterrupted authenticity:

> As Happy, the younger son forever in pursuit of Dad's affection, Finn Wittrock provides a funny, poignant and ripely detailed study in virile

vanity as a defense system. Bill Camp, as Charley, Willy's wisecracking next-door neighbor, wears on his face an entire lifetime of philosophical compromises, small victories and protective cynicism. And he speaks so deeply from character that he makes even a line like "Nobody dast blame this man" sound as natural. (2012)

Thus, Brantley's overall verdict is mixed:

At the end of this "Salesman" I felt that I understood Willy and Linda and Biff, and was grateful for the insights that the actors playing them had offered. But I felt I knew Happy and Charley, that I might run into them on the street after the show. I also felt *for* them. The gap between those two sets of reactions explains why "Salesman," now and forever a great play, never quite achieves greatness on the stage this time around. (2012)

Here is a further good example of a review finding appropriate, specific words for the range of performances:

Cripes, what a cast. Emond gives a disciplined, deceptively conventional performance that builds to a startling climax. The Broadway newcomer Finn Wittrock, as Biff's neglected younger brother, Happy, infuses a character often played as a boorish dullard with a subversive sexual ambiguity—never enough to be distracting or cartoonishly revisionist, but enough to fix our attention (and ensure his invisibility to his father). Fran Kranz makes a lasting impression as the Loman boys' nerdy foil, Bernard, and Bill Camp, as Bernard's father, Charley, radiates disgust and empathy in perfect balance. The card-game scene, where Willy splits his attention between compulsively insulting Charley and conversing with the mental apparition of his late adventurer brother Ben (John Glover, spectral and diabolical), is a perfectly conducted trio: a dead dream, a defiant dreamer, a rejected reality. And Molly Price, with little more than a shrill giggle and a poignantly hapless shimmy, makes The Woman more than just a woman. But the play belongs to Garfield and Hoffman, as it must. Both know how to weaponize language. (Garfield, especially, has used his Brit's ear for High Brooklynese to great declamatory advantage: He treats Miller like Shakespeare, finding the rhythms, then secreting them inside a natural reading.) And both are performers of demon strength who are always on the razor's edge of succumbing to their own "technique," but, miraculously, don't. Hoffman's habits as an actor are, of course, better known, and may register occasionally as habits; sometimes too good a fit can be as distracting as a bad one. This is, of course, the great challenge of Willy: to play a small man larger than life. Hoffman meets that challenge fiercely, dressed to perfect disadvantage. Isn't that remarkable? (Brown 2012)

The exception to this tendency of focus on the actors was John Lahr's review, which was almost entirely text-focused, as he analysed primarily the play's character motivations. This appears to have been written "for the ages," as some kind of testament to Miller that Lahr might envision will live on and become part of the critical canon. Here is the exception in that article:

> And Hoffman, an eloquent package of virulence and vulnerability, finds all the crazy music in Willy's disappointment. Gravity seems to hang on his lumpy body like a rumpled suit, tethering him to the shaky ground he stands on. (2012c)

In her book *To Watch Theatre* Rachel Fensham, among other moves, applies and elaborates insights gained from Elizabeth Grosz and comes to the enlightening proposal that,

> The Actor's body [...] deploys a thin psychic flesh to concentrate an emotional justification. Phenomenologically, these performing bodies produce simultaneously the maximum interiority and maximum exteriority that is needed to signify on the surface. These intensities need to be apparent and active on the skin if actors are to differ. (2009: 18)

Fensham thus operationalizes (and obtains a highly evocative understanding of performance) Grosz's metaphor of the helix or the Möbius strip to indicate the interconnectedness of inside and outside. With this move Fensham has made the reading of performance at once concrete, the actor's interiority must be "active on the skin," and suggestive, we, the spectators, attempt to understand that interiority, imaginatively (as we cannot, of course, ever really *know*). How apparent and active these intensities are "on the skin" is significant to our engagement (emotionally and/or imaginatively; i.e. interpretatively) as well as to the evaluation of the performance. The actor who in this way keeps us engaged is a superlative performer, is one who by setting our imagination into flight keeps us anchored in the now of the performance.

The praiseworthy qualities of an actor's choices and achievements may, as appropriate, include such words and notions (and their various (other) synonyms and riffs) as clear, bold, boisterous, sharp, unpretentious, intelligent, fluid, flowing, (or halting, jagged, crooked), daring, imaginative, innovative, surprising, specific, keenly rendered, balanced, gritty, poised, tightly executed, precise, detailed, reverent (irreverent), taunting, captivating, affecting, effective, dynamic, rhythmic, inspired, responsive, playful, textured, graceful, nimble, deft, lively, spry, sustained, intense, fearless, explosive, subtle, supple, focused, flexible, provocative, elegant, persuasive, etc., etc. All suggesting that a level of aliveness, presence, has been achieved.

Summary

We observed that in many theatre reviews, less space is used to write about the actor's achievements than about other aspects of the performance under review. Related to this, critics tend to have problems with expressing their praise in as much precise detail as they are able to express negative criticism. In this chapter we have discussed the reasons for this state of affairs. The historical context, in terms of philosophy and religion, demonstrates why it might be difficult for critics to get out of a blame/negative mode, because blame is so deeply rooted in our culture. Our position and argument here is to raise a concern about the danger of blame becoming a popular fetish; we are not suggesting that praise might somehow be, or become, a moral imperative. Instead, we have made clear what kind of positive vocabulary is available to the critic, and pointed out what the critic might "search" for, pay attention to, and evaluate, such as the performer's aliveness and presence. Thus we do not expect critics to praise at all costs, which might involve losing some desirable distance between themselves and the performance under review, but to have at their disposal a set of criteria to be alert to, and a set of related, suitable words to make use of in expressing what they have observed and experienced, so as to share it with their readers.

The two sample reviews that follow represent an aspiration, and a model of what reviewing might be when freed of constrictions of word limits and therefore of having to choose between, say, describing the day and the venue, or telling the readers what happens in the play.

Sample review: *Medea / Macbeth / Cinderella*
At the Oregon Shakespeare Festival, Ashland, OR
(April 18-November 3, 2012)

It's a sunny and hot August day in Ashland, OR. My wife and I go for a walk in Lithia Park right next to the theatre, on a walkway alongside Ashland Creek. The park is a mixture of nature and culture in the sense that as well as indigenous trees and bushes many species have been planted from other habitats. It's almost too beautiful a day to consider entering a dark theatre, though the idea of air conditioning grows increasingly attractive as we walk.

On a sunny... Once in the theatre we don't know what to expect. We know the title and the fact that Bill Rauch has worked since he was an undergraduate on the idea of mixing the three most popular theatre forms in the western canon, Greek tragedy, Elizabethan drama and the American musical. We have also seen plays directed by Bill Rauch such as *Hamlet* and *Measure for Measure*, and *Servant of Two Masters* and *The Imaginary Invalid* directed by the co-creator and co-director of this show, Tracy Young, so we know that in those terms we are in good hands, but still...?

On stage is a huge black set at the top of which was a platform whence a ramp angles from stage right across the back wall to meet up with a staircase that angles in the opposite direction down to the floor. A work lamp stands stage right.

The show begins when an usher enters. He's wearing a backpack like he's ready to go home, possibly on a bike. He moves the work lamp to centre stage and as he does he whispers lines from plays. He may be imagining seeing/hearing characters and interacting with them. Then shadows begin to creep out from the dark. Among them I notice the three witches from *Macbeth*. There's a flash and then we're thrown into a different world, perhaps a world generated and powered into being by the usher's imagination.

Though the stage picture starts in black it quickly becomes colourful, the colour provided by the lighting and the costumes. The set designed by Rachel Hauck, the costumes by Deborah M. Dryden, and the lights by Christopher Akerlind together create an immensely useful and effective playing space and striking colour combinations. What makes this visual feast so effective is that it never overpowers, everything supports the actors' performances.

Hope, ambition, despair are central to *Cinderella, Macbeth,* and *Medea,* respectively, and transformation is a theme in all three. The three plays are kept separate, though some props move about and stage spaces serve many purposes. The different acting styles are tightly delineated and one could have expected jarring effects, this is actually what makes the production work as a whole. The strands each have their own world and overlaps of words provide sudden ripples across the plays.

The only character who operates in all three plays is the usher, played by Mark Bedard, who sets the whole thing going.

Jeffery King as Macbeth illustrates clearly how idea becomes embodied action when he "consults" the witches. After having been beset by fear, his body opens up and out, his head lifts and his voice becomes brighter. By the end he carries his body lower, burdened, bewildered. Sitting on the stairs King delivers The Tomorrow soliloquy in a state of near collapse, willing the words out against massive resistance – his experience far exceeds the wisdom of the words. It is as though Macbeth is saying, "I know this, and this is what we are. But, still, what just happened?" This moment is a uniquely forceful acting achievement. Never has that speech been so meaningful for either of us.

Medea's love for her children becomes physical counterpoint in Miriam Laube's performance, moving between not being able to kiss or embrace them enough and her desperate need to punish Jason for his betrayal. Laube, who shifts from sensuous temptress to loving mother, to entranced sorceress sitting on her knees bidding occult forces come to her aid, depicts Medea's despair with her expansive vocal range and beseeching hand gestures, outstretched as though what she wants, her family with Jason, could be just inches away, if only, if only…. This is an actor whose body can slink, creep, slide, push, twist and coil in aid of her objectives.

Lisa Wolpe is particularly chilling in utter coldness towards Medea when Medea pleads with Jason to come back to her. He has simply got a better deal and surely Medea should understand that she should have behaved better with Kreon. As Jason Lisa Wolpe and Christopher Liam Moore, playing Lady Macbeth, accomplish persuasive gendered movements, gait and vocal delivery.

Lady Macbeth, now out of female dress, descends the stairs rubbing imaginary blood from her/his hands presents an image of haunted contrition that disallows any sense of blaming the woman behind the man. This is a moment of great theatricality leading to a deeply affecting realization. Her actions were not merely those of a pushy woman, desperate for social position. A man could as easily have committed them. S/he is not so much unsexed as double-sexed.

Lara Griffith captures Cinderella's change from deferring drudge to princess. When she enters the ball she towers over everyone and not only because she stands at the top of a long staircase but because the sweet, acquiescing girl has become a confident woman who is not shy under the gaze of others. She stands straight, is viewed, as she herself takes in the view of the prince, who is looking up from the bottom of the stairs.

When interwoven in this production the stories comment on each other and one cannot help but wonder whether Cinderella's good fortune could turn into a fate like Medea's or if she could become driven like Lady Macbeth, were her story extended.

The three-hour show is over so fast. Time's taken on a magical quality and has run away with itself. How could have seen all three plays in this short time? Much was cut but nothing was missed. How was this possible? Blending plays by Rodgers & Hammerstein, Shakespeare and Euripides could have been a train wreck, a mash-up, but the risk Rauch and Young took was worth it because the resulting show is simply genius –a testament to artistic daring, in this case replanting old ideas in new contexts.

We're both quite overcome after the show; uplifted by the power of the theatre to transport you into an imaginary world, to make you look at relationships afresh, and we're shaken by how easily those ur-emotions of ambition, desire and revenge can destroy hope and the bonds of love.

We need another little walk in Lithia Park to catch our bearings, to return to the world we came from, a world we now understand differently, enhanced and not a little enchanted, larger in scope than we knew before.

Sample review: *Tristan und Isolde*, Stadttheater Minden.
In September 2012, the Richard Wagner Association of Minden, a town in North-Rhine Westphalia, an hour's train journey from Hannover, mounted a full production of Richard Wagner's *Tristan und Isolde* in the municipal theatre of Minden. The theatre, built in

1908, whose auditorium seats around 500, does not have its own company: it is a receiving house, bringing a rich variety of touring productions to an audience of more than 70,000 per year. The orchestra pit is too small for a Wagner orchestra. As a result, the pit was covered and provided the acting space, bringing the singers literally within reach of spectators in the front row. The orchestra was placed behind the acting space, separated from it by a gauze curtain, and thus in full view of the audience throughout the performance. At the back of the stage was a screen shaped to represent the bow of a boat, with light projected on to the screen changing in relation to different moods expressed in the music and libretto. The auditorium became the boat's stern, with the audience's breath serving as the wind propelling the boat. The acting area, as the deck of the ship, was constructed with planks of wood painted in a lilac colour and sloping upwards towards the back; by way of props there were two small wooden boats on the deck of the ship, and a trunk in Act I, the boats shifted for Act II, leaving more open space, and for Act III several wrecked boats littered the acting space, making movement around it more difficult. Some intact boats were floating from the ceiling over the orchestra in Act II, and a boat wreck floated there in Act III.

The production had been publicised, in the local newspaper, with special reference to Matthias von Stegmann as the director as a guarantor of the approach to directing best captured by the term *Werktreue*, truthfulness to the work of art, as opposed to *Regietheater*, director's theatre, in which the director superimposes a concept over the libretto that may feel will not match the libretto and particularly the spirit of the music. Von Stegmann worked for many years as an assistant director at the Bayreuth Festival, including with Wolfgang Wagner on numerous productions. He assisted Wagner also for the 1997 production of *Lohengrin* at the New National Theatre in Tokyo, where he returned to direct his own productions of *Der Fliegende Holländer* (2009) and *Lohengrin* (2012). Von Stegmann has been known, in Germany, as an actor in dubbing; he has written German dubbing scripts, and directed dubbing; in particular, he has been in charge of the German dubbing of *The Simpsons* (translation and direction) for a number of years now.

The stage is open when we entered the auditorium, lit by the lights in the auditorium, and the orchestra musicians were at their desks behind the gauze which was lit blue. When the house lights went down, the lights on stage came on, Isolde took her place in one of the boats, Brangäne sat near another boat, Kurwenal was in the background. The conductor arrived, the overture started. Isolde was reading in a book, not quite able to concentrate, a number of books were piled on the floor next to the boat she was in, she flipped the pages, read here and there, nervous, agitated, possibly bored. Real life took place in front of our eyes: music, set, changing light, singers, singing, libretto, facial expressions, gestures, glances, all became one, illustrating in surprising detail what is likely the genuine meaning of *Gesamtkunstwerk*, total work of art.

Repeated viewing could possibly allow spectators to pick up on, and remember, all of the minute detail of what happened on stage. Most striking moments included the way Tristan and Isolde behave when they have drunk the love potion instead of the death drink. Both became love-struck teenagers, in very different, but clearly masculine and feminine ways, respectively, very moving and only slightly comical, so as not to distract from the serious nature of the situation as highly problematic within the opera's overall plot. Neither can help the power of the potion, neither is able to "think straight" any more, all they know is the attraction to each other, which is love in both a spiritual sense, as eros, and a physical sense as sexuality. The production manages to make this holistic level of their experience clear for example when Tristan and Isolde move closer to each other as if to kiss, only for Isolde to break away from the kiss when their lips are almost touching to place her face on Tristan's chest in a loving embrace.

Kurwenal is very surprised at what he observes, helpless, confused, and the realisation of what she has caused hits Brangäne quite visibly. Both have to use the maximum physical strength they have available to literally tear Tristan and Isolde apart so as to keep up appearances when King Marke arrives. When Marke has discovered Tristan and Isolde at the end of Act II, colour of Isolde's dress matches that of Marke's coat and suit. While Marke laments Tristan's betrayal, sitting on the sea trunk, Isolde comes over to him and sits next to him, sad at his suffering, sad that it was caused by her, but at the same time not showing any signs of feeling guilty: she is under the influence of the love potion, and is thus responsible for Marke's misery, and neither is Tristan. There is no conflict here for her, or for Tristan.

At the beginning of Act III, we see Tristan resting in a derelict boat; Kurwenal is busy washing out bloodied bandages from Tristan's wounds. There are many of them, and they are quote bloody, and Kurwenal tries his best with them, without achieving much. It is an image for the moving care that Kurwenal takes of Tristan, but it shows also the helplessness of the rather rough man in carrying out this work that he probably never thought he would be doing: he is awkward with the movements, clumsy, quite inefficient, without any idea of hygiene, as one would expect from a man like him, but the fact that he still tries, and tries so obviously hard to do something almost against his very nature is genuinely moving.

Chapter Four

Daniel Meyer-Dinkgräfe

New dimensions of consciousness studies

The Vedanta model of consciousness

At the centre of the Vedanta model of consciousness are distinct states of consciousness, each with its own range of experiential and physiological characteristics. Humans share the experience of three conventional states of consciousness, waking, dreaming and sleeping. The sleep state is devoid of immediate experience: we know, on waking up, that we must have been asleep, and we can gauge whether we feel rested after sleep or not, and depending on this, with hindsight we consider our sleep to have been "good, restful, deep etc.", or "heavy, restless, superficial etc.". The dream state occurs during sleep, and the range of potential experiences we encounter in the dream state of consciousness is much wider; all sensory perceptions can be aroused in dreams: we can dream in a wide panoply of colours or in black and white, and shifts can occur between them back and forth within seconds. We can hear, touch, taste and smell in our dreams. When we wake up after sleeping we may remember that we have had dreams, and we may have more or less vivid recollections of the contents of dreams; often, memory of dream contents seems to melt away almost tangibly as we attempt recollection. The waking state of consciousness is distinctly separate from sleep and dream, as in it we actively live our lives (while typically we cannot control the nature of sleep and the contents of dreams actively, or at least fully,).

Pure consciousness is a fourth state of consciousness, and serves as the basis for the six expressed levels of consciousness characteristic of the waking state of consciousness. Pure consciousness is also at the basis of the states of sleep and dream. It can be experienced either on its own, or together with waking, dream or sleep. Experienced on its own, it is a state of consciousness that is devoid of any contents otherwise associated with the senses, desire, mind, intellect, ego, or intuition, feeling or emotion. A person experiencing pure consciousness on its own is not aware of anything other than consciousness itself. The experience of pure consciousness together with waking or dreaming or sleep is characteristic of higher states of consciousness as defined in the Vedanta model of consciousness.

A fifth state of consciousness is characterised by the co-existence of waking, or dreaming, or sleeping, and pure consciousness. In this state of consciousness, the level of pure consciousness, which is never overshadowed in daily experience by the activities and experiences of the individual psyche, becomes a "stable internal frame of reference from which changing phases of sleep, dreaming, and waking life are silently *witnessed* or observed" (Alexander and Boyer 1989: 342).

In the fifth state of consciousness, the field of pure consciousness is experienced permanently together with waking, or dreaming, or sleeping. This level of functioning is maintained in the sixth state of consciousness and "combined with the maximum value of perception of the environment. Perception and feeling reach their most sublime levels" (Alexander and Boyer 1989: 355).

The final level of human development is called *unity consciousness*. In this state of consciousness, "the highest value of self-referral is experienced" (Alexander and Boyer 1989: 359). The field of pure consciousness is directly perceived as located at every point in creation, and thus 'every point in creation is raised to the (...) status' of pure consciousness. "The gap between the relative and absolute aspects of life (...) is fully eliminated" (Alexander and Boyer 1989: 360). The experiencer experiences himself and his entire environment in terms of his own nature, which he experiences to be pure consciousness. For further discussion and examples of experiences of higher states of consciousness, see (Meyer-Dinkgräfe 2005: 24-29).

Hans Binder—biography and approaches to knowledge and consciousness

Binder explains his background and the development of his abilities in the following way. Even as a child, he had a special relationship with nature because, when he was one with nature, he was able to perceive the aura of many trees and plants as well as being allowed to hear the fundamental oscillation of the universe, the OM sound of nature. This should, however, gain greater significance only in the second half of his life. He learned the crafts of reinforced concrete construction and horticulture, and was very successful in these areas for decades. In horticulture, he had a major business, which he gave up when his skills to investigate fault zones in houses, and to provide analyses of persons were in such demand that he was able to dedicate himself to them alone. In earlier times he used to dig deep into the gardens of the people, today he can do that in their subconscious minds to help them with the design of their lives. Until all was ready, he was able to learn a lot through training and studies. To this day, he continues researching and experimenting on his own in the field of consciousness studies.

He has supplemented his natural talents with the study of the Veda, of Vastu, dowsing, and geomancy, and has acquired knowledge of all the materials and radiations, as well as the anatomy of all human body parts, organs and all their features. This bundled set of skills and all the knowledge he acquired is invested into all the holistic analyses and in development and manufacture of products.

The entire universe, according to Binder, can be understood as an energy field that integrates smaller units also as energy fields and interacts with the parent field, and other fields, since they are in turn connected to each other via the "everything that is" principle. Each planet has therefore its own energy field and is connected via the "unified field of natural law" again with the great whole. On Earth, there are then earth energy fields at each level of manifestation, for all plants and each plant, and for all animals and for each animal, and for all people and every individual. The deepest and most important energy field of each person is that of their very own life plan. Since this plan of life for every human being is different and individual, according to their own primordial tasks of learning and *karma* from previous incarnations, each individual has the opportunity to change the past by living in the present and by addressing the tasks resulting from her life plan in daily life.

The intensity of this energy field is dependent on the extent to which every human being is able, at every moment of her life, to live life in accordance with his plan of life, or to what extent a person is engaging in a (necessary) detour that seems, for the time being, to represent a departure from the life plan. Everything affects everything and is connected to everything. If an individual engages in detours, a corresponding energy field is again produced, which in turn affects the overall energy field. The "free will of the individual" comes into this equation as well, as to how long and in what intensity they have to engage in this "detour / learning process", until she is back on the path determined by her life plan.

Everything that people have ever created and create, have manufactured and manufacture, in what form and with what material whatsoever, and what people have ever thought and think at this very moment, also represents energy fields within the unified field of natural law, brought into being by the respective activities of manufacturing, creating and thinking. All levels of complex energy fields now interact with each other and react to each other, in the sense that like attracts like in turn.

On the basis of this underlying set of thoughts, in Chapter Five, Binder will introduce further principles of his philosophy, and I will relate those to experiences of the theatre.

Chapter Five

Principles of consciousness and theatre contexts

Spiritual development
Principles (Hans Binder)
In the beginning was unity, which became, as the origin of holistic playfulness of nature, duality, and evolved from there to the infinite complexity we see around us today. From this time there was evolution. A person develops from unity into duality, evolving further with the ultimate aim of returning to unity. At the level of unity time does not exist. But at every level, for every form of expression of unity in complexity, the aim of time is to come back to the state of unity—this is a natural law governing the entire universe. For humans this means that every person will automatically, whether she likes it or not, develops in the direction of becoming one again with herself, and that means to enliven both his divine reference point within herself as well as becoming one with her dual soul, eventually dissolve in the whole of the universe as a unified, high-quality energy field.

On this journey back to the unity, the human being first dissolves accumulated karma and then he turns to the relevant tasks she has also brought from past lives. To the extent that she resolves her karma and completes her tasks, she becomes a human helper of God and helps to change the powerful energy field of mass consciousness and their entrenched beliefs and to bring them to a higher level.

Mass consciousness is a multi-layered complex of fields of oscillation that occur on Earth and throughout the universe by many people, creatures that live in the universe and their actions / karma (karma means action) that. Every living being contributes to the mass consciousness and influenced by it in turn. The energy or oscillation fields of mass consciousness cannot be grasped intellectually in their complexity and their multiple overlaps

When humans grow in their evolutionary development, when they have completed their individual tasks, they will be deployed, to the extent that they can handle it, as "divine helper" within a "divine plan" in working on mass consciousness. They will be used just for the transformation of those areas of life in which they were previously involved themselves and in which they have attained mastery. Here it is important that the helpers of God have developed an appropriate level of trust that allows them to play this role successfully. Their lives as helpers function in the way that they are guided by their divine plan into situations that do not feel different, in daily life, from the situations that served to remove karma or to tackle tasks. However, the situations with which the helpers are confronted, are in fact no longer their own situations, but reflect or even mirror situations that are important in the mass consciousness at a given point in time and are just suitable for being addressed by the helpers encountering those issues.

The energy field the helpers generate in their actions is very strong, and if the helpers are acting accurately in those situations that mass consciousness mirrors to them at any one time, then the energy that the helpers bring to the situation, and thus to the corresponding energy field of mass consciousness, colours the respective energy field of mass consciousness and thus brings about a positive change.

Theatre context (Daniel Meyer-Dinkgräfe)

If helpers create art (paintings, plays, productions) that correspond to their high evolutionary development, or if they interpret art as actors, singers or musicians, this will affect such forms of art that exist in mass consciousness and related oscillatory fields that still correspond to a lower stage of development. An example might be that in a national television competition it is no longer the obvious, gross act that wins, as in previous years, but the more subtle, which is evolutionarily more highly developed and which corresponds, therefore, to a finer level of oscillation and therefore to the "higher divine plan". The mass of the people who watch such programmes and cast their votes, becomes able to perceive these subtle impressions as more valuable. The helpers may contribute to this development.

To take this further and to make it more concrete, let us take as an example a helper who has completed her own life plan, which was equipped with *karma*, or who is a human being that was already born as a helper. This person's divine plan earmarks the helper as a dramatist. The playwright is characterized by a very specific primordial energy field that is dominated by the divine plan for this individual. In addition, the helper's energy field is moulded by the energy fields of home, education, lineage, environment, etc. All these individual energy fields are in turn influenced by the primal energy field and attracted to it. From this web of energy fields a play is created, into which enter the energy fields of the elements that make up the playwright. Also, the development of consciousness of the playwright flows into the energy field of the play, such as the degree to which the playwright experiences pure consciousness and therefore can bring this energy field of pure consciousness into the play.

Over time, the energy field of the play extends to include many additional impressions that arise from the many performances of the play and the way that readers and audiences react to the play and its performances. Therefore, the longer past the emergence of the play, the more complex, from today's perspective, the energy field, which accounts for this play or what surrounds it. Added to this is that people create actions through their "free will" (wrong action, which leads to the "negative *karma*"). This also takes its place in the form of an energy field and colours in the overall energy field of the play. Thus every action, whether positive or negative in the context of evolution, characterizes the overall energy field.

To sum up, creation consists of multiple energy fields that work together in shaping every aspect of life. This applies equally to the people and what they do. Theatre is no exception—the dramatist, the play, the performance, the spectators, and their interactions, all can be understood as energy fields that come together from many sources and interact in complex ways. A central principle of the interaction of energy fields, and thus also for the spiritual development of humans, is resonance.

Resonance
Principles (Hans Binder)
The entire life consists of sending and receiving. We can take up only something within us if the intellectual breeding ground for this has been created in us and if there is a match for it in us. We all have certain beliefs / ingrained attitudes structured in us and these beliefs write the script of our lives. It is mostly because of these beliefs that

we are not able to change our lives, because they are deeply embedded in our consciousness.

Recent findings in quantum physics or quantum biology make increasingly clear that it is always the power of human belief patterns that turns us into what we believe to be. True limits exist only in our heads. Otherwise the realm of unlimited possibilities is ahead of us.

In the meantime, there are even studies that show that beliefs affect not only our own lives but that of our entire environment. We can change our DNA through our beliefs but also stimulate our self-healing powers, our happiness and joy—or the opposite. Impossible is only what we consider to be impossible!

Our emotionally substantiated and stored beliefs generate a tremendous resonance field and everything that oscillates within this resonance field is taken up by this resonance field and cannot help but resonate, just as all the strings on a guitar resonate when a string is plucked. The law of resonance teaches us how everything in the universe communicates with one another via resonance. All things and beings in the universe have a natural oscillation and communicate with each other, as well as all the cells and organs of our body and of matter vibrate with each other, usually in different frequencies. Other people, beings, things or events cannot escape the resonance field that we generate, when they resonate with our generated frequency, for like always attracts like.

Resonance fields have a very strong force. Therefore, it is critical for us in which resonance fields we reside. Everything starts with thought. Thoughts are the building blocks of our lives. Thoughts come and go. The decisive factor is always, what thoughts we give access to our consciousness and which ones we allow to pass. It is possible to control our thoughts. If we cultivate the purity and clarity of mind, and therefore thoughts in us, we can avoid in the first place for unwanted resonance fields to form within us at all. We should add here that we owe a considerable responsibility to ourselves, especially with what we think, and how we put our thoughts into action.

When negative resonance fields have been created already, we will be confronted by divine nature with situations characterised by interactions with resonance fields that are both different and the same. Here is an example: we have a good day. Everything goes according to our desires and to our satisfaction and in harmony. Suddenly, a person appears and involves us, within seconds, in an incredible argument. It has broken out like a blazing bush fire. We get carried away and suddenly we say things we would never have said under normal circumstances. Or we make decisions that we later regret and that we would never have taken after prudent consideration. How could this happen? It is simple: we had the resonator or transmitter (aggression, emotions, or tasks) in us. This was only reason why it was possible to infect us within seconds, otherwise a quarrelsome person would not have been able to activate her negative vibration potential in us. She would have been able to reach us with his negative, aggressive behaviour, because we would not have been on his frequency. If we consider this from the opposite end, when, for example, we read an uplifting book, listen to good music or move in the energy field of pleasant people, we make use of their existing positive resonance fields. Thus we strengthen the desired positive energy, which in turn enhances the positive resonance field. Therefore it is good advice to surround oneself with people, music, entertainment and literature that exert a motivational and uplifting resonance force on us. If we see that someone is doing us no good, no one is forcing us to stay with them, or at least to tolerate his negative attitude and to continue, thus, to subject ourselves to this destructive energy. Otherwise, a certain sadness of the soul is created in us in the long run, forcing us into depression. If we surround ourselves with people who mostly convey to us just a feeling of inferiority, who devalue us and do not believe in our inner strength, we are discouraged in time and our talents, our creativity and our motivational forces in us are superimposed upon by these degrading resonance fields. That is why it is best to be, if possible, only with people who believe in us, who believe in our strength and our talents and recognize our potential.

Theatre context: coping with demanding roles (Nicola Tiggeler, Daniel Meyer-Dinkgräfe)
Most actors will, across their careers have to represent people they perceive as very different from how they see themselves. The actors do not share their characters' views and do not approve of their behaviour. From an ethical perspective, the question arises how far actors will go to further their careers (those who turn down too many roles, or even one, might never get another offer), which tensions between person and role they are able to cope with, and how they deal

with tensions that may arise out of this dilemma. In this section we outline research on this topic briefly, and by means of a current case study we develop new approaches that allow us to understand better the issue of coping with a demanding role.

In the context of theatre acting, there is consensus that actors may be affected emotionally by the roles they play" (Geer 1993: 151). Burgoyne found two major types of potentially emotionally distressing affect, which she termed *boundary blurring*.

> In the first type, the actor's personal life may take over in performance, leading to the actor's loss of control onstage...conversely, the actor's character may take over offstage, with the actor carrying over character personality traits into daily life (1991: 161).

Bloch conceptualises the same emotional affect of performance as emotional hangover (1987: 10), while Seton coined the phrase "postdramatic stress" (2006).

German actress Nicola Tiggeler (b. 1960) played the part of Barbara von Heidenberg in the German soap opera (called Tele-Novela) *Sturm der Liebe* (Storm of Love) from 2006-7, 2008-9 and 2010-11 in 548 episodes. Tiggeler describes Barbara von Heidenberg as a woman who is deeply driven by ambition and strategic thinking. She needs devotion, she needs love and attention, and all in extreme dimensions: with her, everything is above average. She puts to use all available means, such as outward allure, femininity, a cold, clear intellect and strategic thinking. She is certainly someone who had much to live through in the past and maybe she was even humiliated—at least she has felt this way, and against the background of such hurt she has always derived the right to take her fate into her own hands. If it serves her purpose, she will kill. This is beyond conventional moral judgment, because she creates her own laws: she sees herself not subject to any standard, neither religious nor moral. Rather, she constructs her own systems of justice and legality. Her needs must be implemented. When she has been injured, or if her trust has been abused, which she may have felt towards those other characters to whom she opened up, then these characters have to be destroyed.

During the years in which Tiggeler played the role of Barbara von Heidenberg, the role was a priority in life: the series was shot covering five 45-minute episodes in five days, not one episode per day, but five episodes over five days in such a way that allowed the most economical process in terms of content, actors and locations. All actors, therefore, had to prepare five episodes in advance and jumped back and forth between episodes. There was one team for filming in the studio, and another team for filming in the outdoors and a couple more locations on the premises of the Bavaria Film Studios. The day of shooting in the studio was from 9am to 8pm, the external shooting also began at 9 o'clock and ended a little earlier, with consideration for longer distances for travel. Sometimes, the actors were not scheduled to shoot all day, resulting in later starts to the schedule, or earlier ends, or waiting times in between.

The filming was therefore very intense, and the role of Barbara von Heidenberg was, as described above, such that Nicola Tiggeler personally had nothing in common with her. Tiggeler describes herself as loyal, and the character's planning for her own benefit is foreign to her. She could understand from her own experience Barbara's straightforwardness, but hers is on a completely different level. Much of what Barbara did was contrary and foreign to Tiggeler as a person, but when she played it, she had, as an actress, to be fully committed to the role and was. During filming, Barbara was natural and consistent for Tiggeler, but she found it straining to be that way.

She tried to keep her distance, and approached many aspects of the filming not by getting too involved, but by relying on her skills and craft as an actor. She defined the emotions of the role as primordial emotions such as sadness, anger, fear, and hope: all those things that drive and motivate people in general, but which are exaggerated and taken to their limits in Barbara's case. This made the character so extreme and polarizing. However, there were a few other moments that Tiggeler gave to the role, or that the authors endowed the role with: Tiggeler tried to make the role holistic and wrest from her soft, tender, erotic, seductive, maternal, and thus human aspects. Any one-sided emphasis on the character's ugly aspects would have turned her into monster, and thus more boring, and the viewers would have turned away from the character with horror, especially in the long run. That is why Tiggeler felt and played the affection that Barbara von Heidenberg developed towards some of the other characters. The fact that the screenwriters had written a son for Barbara allowed Tiggeler to bring in maternal feelings and genuine sensibility to the role. The feelings about Barbara's pregnancy and miscarriage go in the same direction. Every woman will be able to empathize with these moments and those when you fall in love, open up and then get disappointed and feel betrayed, in one's own perception of things. This is normal. What follows when Barbara experienced such situations was exaggerated, with a tendency to kill.

Tiggeler also tried to bring a certain humour to the role, irony, not necessarily in the sense of self-irony, but more in terms of black, snappy and quick-witted humour. Tiggeler achieved distance also by not engaging with the role too much in her spare time during the weeks of filming. The locations in the Bavaria Film Studios in Munich for the interior shots, and in a private castle in Bavaria for outdoor scenes gave Tiggeler the chance to continue living at her home in Munich, and not to have to stay at a hotel. When she was driven home after a day's work, she went through the workload of the next day's shooting, then had to continue learning her lines in the evening, because up to ten scenes worth of filming would translate into thirty pages of text. For difficult scenes she went through the emotions once, otherwise she tried to limit herself to relying on her craftsmanship, her intuition and experience. After the shooting she came home to her large household, with her husband and two school-age children, and different duties were awaiting her there. Over time Tiggeler developed a feel for the role, to the extent that she knew how the character speaks; she was able to make use of this knowledge to establish and maintain uniformity even when different scriptwriters were at work.

Tiggeler appreciated the communication with the fans of the series, the role and herself because she is aware that these contributed to the status she has reached in the TV world. She receives many letters and tries diligently to answer them. Most are fine, she says, with exceptions from writers who confuse reality and fiction, and believe they should insult the actress because she has accepted the role of Barbara in the first place—which supposedly reflects her own life. There was a lot of this at the beginning of the series, and while there is much less of it now, it still happens from time to time.

The terms "positive" and "negative" have been used in their generally understood, rather colloquial meanings. In order to contextualise the perhaps rather rare way that Nicola Tiggeler developed to deal with the negative side of her role as Barbara von Heidenberg, it is necessary to examine the hidden concepts behind the terms in more detail.

To sum up, the role an actor plays will influence the actor's life, and will in turn be influenced by the actor's life. In the case of Nicola Tiggeler, we have seen that she employs a range of approaches to be able to cope with the challenges of portraying, over a long period of time, a character with predominantly "negative" features. She seeks to provide a rounded portrayal of the character, actively looking for and actively foregrounding "positive" characteristics; at the same time, her enjoyment of playing the villain allows her to remain in command and not to be overtaken by the character's negative emotions. She balances craft and skills in engaging with the character's emotions, and actively seeks to keep her distance from the character in her spare time during the intensive weeks of filming, not neglecting her duties to her family. Finally, she keeps herself fit mentally and physically to withstand the strain of the work. In addition, Binder would suggest seeking to achieve the observer position so as to be able to be distanced from, and not overshadowed by, the "negative" aspect of the "positive – negative" polarity.

Resonance and time
Principles (Hans Binder)

Another important aspect within the context of laws of resonance is time. Again and again, you can hear various things about time: time does not exist as we imagine it; everything happens at the same time; in time there are different parallel planes of reality; time is running faster; the time does not pass; time flies; time exists only in our three-dimensional world, etc. Modern quantum physics has found that so-called quantum waves, such as our thoughts and beliefs, do not spread only geographically, but also in time, in the form of "time waves". Scientists found that there are so-called "quantum waves" that run from the past to the future. There are also energy waves that spread from the future into the past. The waves that travel into the future are called waves of offer and the waves that go back to the past are called echo waves.

If both waves meet each other—that is, if an echo wave of the future hits an offer wave emitted by us, the one wave modulates the other and as the product of those two waves a so-called event probability is created. Thus, past and future communicate when appropriate signals meet each other halfway—that is the present. It is at this interface, in this presence, which we also call the *here and now*, that we have the opportunity to employ the power of our thoughts to change the polarisation of real events that are actually already a fact, and that will take place around us in the very near future. If we are directed towards spirituality and evolution, we will be able to transform our negatively polarized thoughts that have formed already, in the unified field of natural law, into huge positive energy fields. This means nothing else than that the future affects the past, and vice versa. Furthermore, this means that the future already exists out there somewhere, otherwise it would not be able to send us waves.

We can learn from the past by looking at the things that happened, adjust how we think about them and accept what is, rather than displace them, and then we can draw a line under the past. In this way, we will always attract only the best into our lives. To desire elements of the future in a concrete way is problematic: do we really know always what is best for us in every situation? The risk is considerable that with our limited consciousness we fetch realities into our lives that are not good for us at all. However, if we live according to the laws of nature, we are always rewarded by the Divine Presence with the best—because we are moving "here and now" and thus in the flow of natural law.

If we live at the intersection, where past and future meet, in the *here and now*, we have the opportunity to get out of the previously created world of false beliefs and limitations. When we flow in the river of life and the laws of nature, we always have access to the larger forces of the universe. Here, and only here, we determine our own destiny and can create things according to our own ideas. Because everything we think, feel and believe, consciously or unconsciously, we draw into our lives. With the alertness and the discernment of an intact mind, nourished on the pasture of the divine plan, we will hold the key to our lives in our own hands.

Our future is changing with the right vision of our past. We control and influence our environment with our beliefs much more than we think. If we want to change our loved one, we have to change our attitude and opinion. If we want harmony in the family, then we ourselves must believe that harmony takes place. If we see in others too little trust, love or energy, then it is time to start with oneself, to open one's heart and radiate confidence, love and energy. If we radiate loving energy, we will see that our fellow human beings have the choice also to react differently than in the established patterns. As you scream into the forest, it echoes back! If we change our minds about other people, they have the chance to show other sides of themselves and to change themselves.

Theatre context (1): The canon (Daniel Meyer-Dinkgräfe)

From all the numerous plays written, only a few are selected for production at all, and only a few of those "make it" to the prestigious national and international companies. Similarly, only a few written plays are selected for study and analysis in university drama / theatre studies departments. The concept usually associated with this selection is *canon*, which can be defined in the context of drama and theatre (text and performance) as a shared understanding of which dramatic texts should be preserved, which dramatic texts should be presented on stage, and which dramatic texts and performance should be studied in educational institutions (adapted from Ohmann, in Gorak 1991: 1).

Cultural historian Gombrich distinguishes three related canons: at the most rudimentary and basic level is the canon of "how to", supplying a range of useful skills. The second provides "a set of norms and practices shared by a group of artists", a "how we" paradigm of a "set of culturally preferred choices and exclusions (Gorak 1991: 92). Finally, there is the canon of excellence. The responses to works of art in this category are no longer culturally conditioned: rather, they are sublime, the "same psychological patterns that provoke the artists to creation govern the audience's initial reception and the work's lasting fame" (Gorak 1991: 113).

Although the canon underwent periodic revisions, there was little discussion until relatively recently as to *why* one would read or perform great plays: "They had, many believed, a humanizing effect on the reader [and spectator] and would develop compassionate, responsible individuals" (Orme-Johnson 1987: 324). Such certainty no longer exists, however. Gorak thus argues that Gombrich's concept of a canon of excellence tends to offend late 20th century assumptions because it suggests that creation obeys rules rather than dismantling them, because it "confers on the past the authority to regulate the present", and because it does not allow equality to all works and all cultures (Gorak 1991: 105). Such views are characteristic of the controversy over the concept of the canon which has raged over the last decades. Gorak highlights two major areas of critique: first, the canon is argued to operate "as an instrument of principled, systematic exclusion", reinforcing "ethnic and sexual assumptions, it reflects passively the ethos or ideology of a particular society of group (1991: 1). Secondly, the canon is a means to keep cultural power in the hands of a conservative minority: the scholars and critics who determine what the canon is remain in power by establishing their fields of expertise as fixed sets of orthodox values and responses, excluding texts they are not experts of. Entry to the canon thus becomes "understood as conformity with the interests of a dominant political or intellectual group (Gorak 1991: 2). In a time where culture is no longer a valued aspiration, but has become the "subject of political and ideological analysis", the canon presents "opportunities for suspicion more than grounds for belief" (Gorak 1991: 154).

Against the background of that critique, it becomes increasingly difficult to argue for intrinsic merit or genuine worth of any dramatic text or performance, whether canonised or not. Such an increase of relativity is rather problematic: both theatre as a cultural institution and theatre studies as an academic endeavour are hard-pressed by politicians and funding bodies to demonstrate far-reaching mechanisms of quality assurance and impact. At the same time, quality is extrinsically defined, preferably in small, measurable units. Intrinsic merit and genuine worth escape rational measurement and thus become suspect. Theatre and theatre studies need to redefine and revitalise their concepts of quality, merit and worth, without abandoning them in favour of small measurable units of quality.

In the context of resonance and time, the time factor plays a role not only in terms of the complexity of the energy field of a theatre play, but in still far more decisive forms. According to many traditions that describe this with words and use concepts inherent to the particular tradition, humanity is currently experiencing a massive change of the *zeitgeist*—the energy field of *time*. This means nothing else than that the energy field of *time* changes, to which even the primordial energy field of humans, in connection with their very own life plan and the divine plan, are hierarchically subordinated. Thus it is part of God's plan and purpose that people act in agreement with the respective prevailing *zeitgeist*, and that their energy field coincides as much as possible with the spirit of the time. Not only their own energy field is important, but also the energy fields that people choose to surround themselves and engage with.

The complex energy field of a play came into being in the context of the energy field characteristic of the *zeitgeist* at the time the play was written, and the energy field of the play is related, at any point in time, with the energy field of the prevailing *zeitgeist*. It may be that these energy fields match each other or not. If they fit, the piece has a high level of relevance at that given point in time, and, if corresponding energy fields are at work in transforming the play from page to stage, the play will be conducive to the life plan and divine plans of those involved in the production and reception (theatre people, readers and audience). If the energy fields of play and *zeitgeist* do not match, or not enough, then the play is not consistent with the spirit of the time, not in harmony with the energy field of the *zeitgeist*, the energy field of the natural laws that bring the *zeitgeist* into existence and determine it, and therefore is will not be beneficial to the life and divine plans of those involved in theatre production and reception.

Past civilizations have dissolved because a further evolution of the people in them under the same, unchanging conditions, was not possible. People need changing conditions in order to be able to learn. Thus even great "masters", if they are reborn among other conditions, have to learn more or sometimes they even have to begin again from scratch. Due to the diversity of energies and energy fields that mutually influence each other, new energy fields arise that produce new universes, on different terms. This could mean that well-tried things sometime come to an end and new views are required.

Consequently, in Binder's thought, the "value" of a work of art at any specific time can be determined best (and probably even only!) by investigation of the energy value. Everything has its time. Peoples' awareness, consciousness and their quality of time probably make all the difference—being faithful to the present does not imply stagnation. It is necessary that a new consciousness expresses itself here—that new plays must be adjusted to the new, present time and its challenges so that they are within the flow of time. Plays must be written with the awareness of the new time, with the finger on the pulse of the new quality of time: in this way, plays will be able to absorb the new energy in themselves and to express it accordingly. They have to be written in the light of current energy. If a play still has the "old energy", it is useless in the new time marked by radical changes since the old energy field is no longer compatible with the energy of the new—ultimately, too much old energy comes with such older plays). The following table represents an analysis carried out by Binder in October 2012. The left column provides the author or composer of canonical works of theatre and opera, the middle column provides the percentage to which the work in question was in line with the *zeitgeist*, the energy field at the time of creation, and the right column represents the energy value today.

Author / composer and work	Original value	Today's value
Aeschylus, *The Persians*	77	23
Sophocles, *Oedipus*	87	19
Euripides, *Medea*	88	17
Shakespeare, *Twelfth Night*	94	18
Shakespeare, *As You Like It*	95	19
Shakespeare, *Much Ado about Nothing*	99	16
Shakespeare, *Macbeth*	95	18
Shakespeare, *King Lear*	98	19
Shakespeare, *Hamlet*	100	17
Congreve, *The Country Wife*	99	17
Wycherley, *The Way of the World*	94	19
Goldsmith, *She Stoops to Conquer*	99	18
Goethe, *Faust I and II*	100	20
Goethe, *Iphigenie*	98	20
Schiller, *Intrigue and Love*	100	21
Schiller, *Maria Stuart*	100	22
Lessing, *Nathan the Wise*	98	20
Bulwer-Lytton, *Money*	99	19
Lorca, *Yerma*	96	20

Author / composer and work	Original value	Today's value
Pirandello, *Six Characters in Search of an Author*	93	18
Pinter, *The Caretaker*	96	17
Wesker, *Chicken Soup with Barley*	91	19
Bond, *Saved*	92	20
Kane, *Blasted*	94	17
Strauss *The Park*	100	19
Mozart, *The Marriage of Figaro*	100	16
Mozart, *Don Giovanni*	100	17
Mozart *The Magic Flute*	100	17
Verdi, *Macbeth*	97	18
Verdi, *Rigoletto*	99	17
Verdi, *Force of Destiny*	97	19
Verdi, *La Traviata*	89	18
Puccini, *Madama Butterfly*	97	17
Puccini, *La Bohème*	91	17
Puccini, *Turandot*	97	18
Puccini, *Tosca*	99	17
Wagner, *Lohengrin*	86	17
Wagner, *Tristan und Isolde*	97	18
Wagner, *Meistersinger*	93	16
Wagner, *Ring cycle*	100	17

In this selection it is interesting that even the energy field of a very blatant, *in-yer-face* play like *Blasted* by Kane originally, in 1995, when it was so controversial, was to 94% in line with the energy field of the time and even now, at 17%, has a higher value than Wagner's *Meistersinger*, and is on the same level as *Hamlet*, a play that has maintained its energy value over many centuries. It is equally noteworthy that some of the older works today, after centuries, have the same percentage, or a higher, as works of the recent past.

The result is, in effect, that creating and attending performances of opera and theatre, may do more damage than benefit in terms of the development of consciousness. To deal with the old, the past, always means that one will be overtaken by the past—and that brings with it stagnation and even shifting into reverse gear, especially in the fast-paced times we live in. Let us assume that we see a performance whose energy field is in line with the energy field of the time, and that is thus life-enhancing, to a percentage of 30. If in that scenario we are able to recognize the 30% of what is "good" about the play and its production, and if we are able to work with that material while allowing the detrimental 70% to pass through without giving it any attention, then the overall result is life-enhancing. If the spectators, or the theatre makers, do not recognise those 30%, then they harm themselves and others, in principle, since they will deal with and integrate the 70% of the material in question that is not in line with the current energy field and thus detrimental to life. The scenario with works that have an energy rating of 80% is comparable. If theatre makers or spectators do not recognize the negative 20%, that amount is also harmful. The "more" of positive energy in the case of 80% does not balance out the "less" (20%) of negative energy to create an overall positive effect. An analogy may help to illustrate this: you plant a field of wheat. The seeds are 80% wheat and 20% thistles. The thistles grow faster than the wheat and oust it. The thistles take away the light of life from the wheat, so that in the end the thistles outweigh the wheat, because they not only grow faster but they produce seed again sooner. This is the current situation, because humankind has more negative resonators in it than positive.

Furthermore, scientific study of the past, i.e., the discipline of history in the sense of the school subject, but also specifically the history of theatre or opera, in so far as they in fact deal only with the old, need to be reassessed in terms of their contribution to spiritual development. This need for reassessment is founded in the fact that these disciplines hold the consciousness of the researcher, the reader and the student always at the level of the de-energized old. To learn to recognize the good in material and not to imbibe the negative, the profiles of these professions themselves will have to change considerably. In my last book (Meyer-Dinkgräfe 2013) I demonstrated, by way of applying Schiller's idea of universal history to the history of theatre, how in each time the theatre, at its respectively highest level, expresses specific properties of pure consciousness; I also demonstrated why the respective phases of theatre history follow each other in time. Thus I described the respective value of works of theatre in its very present, showed how times have changed (different qualities of pure consciousness became topical) and new works of theatre developed accordingly. The novelty of this approach is that no one has tried to answer the question of *why* (b) follows (a): previously, theatre history merely show *that* (b) follows (a) and sought to describe both (a) and also (b) as accurately as possible. Once I have understood and explained the past in this way, I can and my readers can classify the past, cherish their respective past functions and then fully devote themselves to the present.

In terms of energy value that a new play or a new opera can reach, it depends both on the play's plot, as well as to where the individuals who wrote or edited the piece further are located with regard to their own development of consciousness. If any exceptional artist always sings in operas and productions with an energy value of up to 20%, then he/she can add of his/her own personal energy to raise the energy value of a performance. If artists want to enhance the work across time, they would have to put into it all their life force, which would eventually kill them, because their consciousness would not be sufficient to sustain such expense of energy over time. They would also have no natural support for this, especially since nature does not support the works (past) itself.

When singers sing in a language they do not understand, they will not be able to empathise emotionally or mentally with the message or the energy value of the words and cannot, therefore "stand behind" the words. They are not able to give the amount of attention / energy to the words that the words deserve and demand.

To conclude, the insights gained for the role of theatre and opera within the context of resonance and time are far-reaching and quite dramatic in the colloquial sense of the term. We realise that the value, worth, merit and quality of works of art (it is possible to generalise beyond theatre) are dependent on the time factor to a major extent. With this insight comes the recognition that a key factor in the (re-) production and reception of existing art is the ability of the producer or recipient to differentiate between the life-supporting and the destructive aspects of the work of art in question, and to express that differentiation accordingly.

Theatre context (2): Nostalgia (Daniel Meyer-Dinkgräfe)[1]

Why is it that in the relative form of the time apparent repetitions seem to be occurring again and again—why is it, that we see repeated waves of *nostalgia*? Is this because it is important to correctly identify and capture *nostalgia* and properly deal with it, and until people have learned and done that, it always comes back to them?

The statements on time in the first part of this section have shown that our main focus in life should be on the present. Many aspects of actor training are aimed at teaching the actor techniques that allow her to be in the present. Preoccupation with the past for the sake of the past was seen as one of the forms of deviation from the goal of life. The prevailing scepticism of the theatre towards *nostalgia* is thus pointing in the right direction, demonstrating that theatre must not be only a mirror of time, but must serve as signpost for the people. Examples of the *nostalgia* scepticism are the television series we referred to in Chapter One, in which detachment from history is at the centre, and the entire exile area, where people consider themselves ultimately forced to leave their home, but then long to return, full of *nostalgia*. However, if they do return, they are shocked to find that nothing is as they remembered it with their memories corrupted by *nostalgia*. In Pinter's *Birthday Party*, Goldberg, through the manipulative use of his discordant childhood memories, breaks possible expectations on the part of the reader or viewer in relation to the nostalgic component potentially inherent in such memories: the audience is brought back from the past abruptly and over again to the present.

Just as *nostalgia* generally recurs until people have solved the problems connected with it and completed affiliated tasks, also in individual life, situations will recur until the people have fully recognized, worked through and have resolved associated tasks. Susan Traherne in *Plenty* will return to the key experiences of the Second World War, and will always be moulded and influenced by them in her respective present of her daily life, until she recognizes consciously and addresses successfully the tasks contained, or hidden away, in those key experiences. In many cases, the task is to recognize the emotional wounds suffered, and to allow their healing. If the task is not recognized and the wounds are not healed, the task will appear

---

[1] See pages 169-192 for further discussion of this topic.

in another form as long as it takes until the wounds are healed. These are issues that affect the individual, and in the theatre the interests of individuals can be represented most directly, and therefore best, in constellations of a few characters. This context would explain why such constellations of friends and family are prevalent in plays which deal thematically with *nostalgia*.

The Victorian era still has a strong influence on at least the British present, as is evident from the large number of plays and television programs that deal directly or indirectly with this time. The same applies to the longing for the 1960s. The Victorian era and the specific decade of the 20th century must be understood here as examples of important phases of the past. People who lived during those times were confronted, through a whole range of situations in their lives, with tasks that they have not yet completed successfully. Therefore they are presented with the same tasks again at a later time in this, or in a next life. Theatre can take on, in this complex process, the task of confronting the theatre artists and their audience with their own tasks, through the information contained in the play and the production relating to characters and situations. According to the law of resonance, theatre producers and viewers will feel particularly attracted to the material, the plays and the productions that meet their individual needs with regard to the tasks that they have to master the most.

To conclude, the attempt of the theatre to be critical of *nostalgia*, and thus to refer to the present, can be understood further with reference to the fact that the art form of theatre is not only supposed to entertain the audience, but also to be useful to their lives (catharsis in Aristotle, restoration the golden age in the Indian *Natyashastra*)

Theatre context (3): theatre and philosophy as experience (Daniel Meyer-Dinkgräfe)

Philosophy is the love for wisdom. *Wisdom* suggests a holistic experience encompassing the faculties of intellect, emotions and tacit levels of the mind. According to this original understanding of the nature of philosophy, philosophy is practice; philosophers across history have engaged in their own approaches to discover the truth, and have sought to share their findings in their writing in the form of reasoned argument. In most accounts, there is a unified, unexpressed source of all existence, from which all manifest forms of existence emerge. Pre-Socratic Anaximander (650-545) identified the unbounded as the source and principle of all things. Anaximenes (628-585) held that all things originate in infinite air or breath. Pythagoras (570-496) explained all change, qualitative and quantitative, in terms of underlying mathematical harmonies. Heraclitus (544-484) proposed that all things change, but also that all things are one—unified by the underlying field of *logos*, which not many can experience. Parmenides (540-470) was led by a goddess on a way of truth leading to the insight (rather than speculation) that what is real is one, eternal, unchanging, indivisible: it does not come into being or cease to be. Empedocles (492-432) placed love as the all-uniting principle, Anaxagoras (500-428) explained everything in terms of mind or *nous*.

Plato (424-348) picked up on *nous* with reference to the form of the good, which is also the form of the beautiful, at the apex of the world. Knowledge of this form of the good is the greatest thing a person can attain in life (Republic 618c-e, 530e, 505a). He also attempted to discuss the means of achieving this knowledge, as experience: it involves a programme of study of mathematics and the sciences, music, gymnastics, and a form of discussion called dialectic. The final stroke of his method cannot be spoken (Letter VII 341c). In *Phaedo* he spoke of accustoming the soul to "withdraw from all contact with the body and concentrating it by itself (67b). Through regular practice of philosophy, the soul can be "struck free from the leaden weights" that "have attached to it since childhood" (Republic 519b). "The soul must be cleansed and scraped free of the barnacles which cling to it in wild profusion (Republic 611e). It must be purified (Republic 611c) so that the whole physiology is turned round to behold the light of the good (Republic 540c). Plato's technique, if there was one, has remained a secret and is lost in history.

Aristotle (382-323), the empiricist, argued for the existence of a first science which deals with being as such, one, unchanging, eternal, simple, separate from the world of change, self-sufficient, actual, indivisible, substantial, in a state of self-contentment, and self-knowing. Being as such is an experiential state which we enjoy in our best moments (Metaphysics 1072b15-1072b25).

Marcus Aurelius (121-180) believed that there is one law or intelligence which spreads everywhere and permeates everything (Meditations VII, 9, 30, VIII, 54). Becoming attuned with it, we live in accord with nature and gain perfect tranquillity of mind. To gain access to this universal spirit, we must withdraw within to our "direct mind", which is self-sufficient, invincible, and the source of goodness, and complete freedom (Meditations IX, 22; VII, 28; VIII, 48; VIII, 59).

Plotinus (205-270) wrote about the experience of a simple, unified, self-sufficient state of Being. We gain the experience, he asserted, by becoming still, at rest. It is a simplification of the soul. He said that it had happened to him many times. This state is the greatest good, the highest goal in life, described as rapture, blessedness, and the highest beauty. It is a direct experience of the "One", the source of all creation.

As a young man, Descartes (1596-1650) had a vision of seeing all the sciences all at one. The basis of all knowledge, all science, is knowledge of the self. It is the "I am". To become better acquainted with the Self, Descartes said, he shut his eyes, withdrew his senses and removed all images from his consciousness. This appears to be an essential part of his "method" of meditation. In the process, he also became aware of an infinite, eternal being which he called "God"; this afforded him the greatest joy he is capable of experiencing in this life.

As a monist, Spinoza (1632-1677) held that there is one eternal, simple, unchangeable and infinite substance, called nature or God. The material world and mind are conceived as attributes or expressions of that unity. Behind the rational deductive system of his writing is his aim, in fact, to describe a state of mind he had experienced himself, which he regarded as the high point of perfection, the highest good, in which the mind knows itself as the union of itself with the whole of nature. George Berkeley (1685-1753) wrote about gaining glimpses of the infinite eternal spirit, the all-pervading source and goal of all creation. Immanuel Kant (1724-1804) spoke of a being which is one, unchanging, self-sufficient, simple, omnipresent and in a state of beatitude. The foundation of such an idea is experience, the simplest experience possible, the experience of our own self. However, this cannot be experienced in the sense that we cannot have a sensory impression of it or form a conception of it.

Hegel (1789-1831) held that all reality is the expression of one eternal mind or consciousness which manifests according to an internal logic which we can comprehend rationally. He originally called his system the science of the experience of consciousness. The main theme of the *Phenomenology of Mind* is to identify the stages of the development of consciousness and to use this scheme to explain the forms of life that have been assumed in human history—science, religion, art, culture, philosophy etc. Johann Gottlieb Fichte (1762-1814) wrote: "I am satisfied; perfect harmony and clearness reign in my soul, and a new and more glorious spiritual existence begins for me" (Vocation of Man 145); "I rest in the most perfect tranquillity" (148); "I see everywhere only myself, and no true existence external to me" (136); and: "Upon this earth, there is no higher state than this" (114). These quotes suggest that he, too, based his philosophy on his own experience, seeking to explain it and share it with others.

Husserl (1859-1938) wrote that "I, the meditating I, reduce myself to my absolute transcendental ego through the phenomenological epoché. (Cartesian Meditations). Phenomenology was to be the discipline to study this new domain of the experience of pure transcendental consciousness. Epoché was a method of suspension of judgment in the mode of the natural standpoint, such that everything came to be understood as a phenomenon within consciousness, accessible by going within to analyse consciousness. "I experience my own conscious existence directly and truly as it itself (Paris Lectures). "We direct the glance of ... theoretical enquiry to pure consciousness in its own absolute being" (Ideas).

Over time, philosophy has become restricted to the context of intellectual reasoning, analysis and argument, devoid of the experiential component that was originally considered as an integral part of its nature. Philosophy is no longer based on practice, but theory alone, speculation. This shift of emphasis has led to philosophy losing its essential role in life, on the levels of both the individual and of society.

The debate about the relationship between philosophy and performance was spearheaded initially within PSi, TaPRA, and IFTR and, while continuing in those umbrella organisations, is now located within its own dedicated organisation, *Performance Philosophy*. That debate has at its core the restoration of practice to philosophy by means of performance.

I reviewed the history of Western philosophy as a series of attempts by philosophers not at reasoned speculations, but at sharing with their readers, in the form of reasoned argument, the essence of their own experiences. Relating my findings to the research into performance philosophy to date, I note the "four practices that deploy philosophical reflection in thinking about theatre" discussed by Hamilton (2013). They are, abbreviated and to some extent in my own terms:

(1) Philosophy illustrated through theatre;
(2) Philosophy to examine theatre;
(3) Philosophy to test the extent to which theatre is able to achieve the goals thought to be defended in the original discourse;
(4) Discussion of cultural contexts of theatre as art form and institution from the perspective of philosophy.

All these have, as Hamilton points out, the common aim of critical interpretation, and thus of finding out (more) about the meaning of theatre.

Arriving at meaning and reflecting on it constitute not only intellectual processes, but there is also a component of experience attached to (and probably even central to) them—in terms of what it is like to arrive at meaning and to reflect on meaning. Going beyond meaning and its reflection, and seeking to reach the essence of experience as such, is the implication of considering philosophy not as intellectual speculation but as based on, and relating to, experience that is within everyone's reach. The philosopher's role is that of pioneering the experience, pioneering the rendering of the experience in comprehensible words, and pioneering to write about it in such a way that the reader can relate the communication about the philosopher's experience to their own experience. Finally, the philosopher pioneers ways of enabling others to experience what the philosopher has experienced him/herself—by providing a technique that may not be secret or lost in history as that proposed by Plato.

Theatre artists engage in experiences related to their art and practice on a daily basis. Some feel inclined to write about it, and seek to pass those experiences on to others so as to enable those others to share their experiences. Examples include Artaud's experiences, which he then wrote about in terms of the language of nature, Grotowski's experiences, which he then wrote about and incorporated in his own teaching in terms of translumination, Peter Brook's experiences, which he then wrote about and incorporated in his own approaches to rehearsal in terms of total theatre, and Ariane Mnouchkine, who considers what she calls *state* in an actor essential in the actor's art—she is able to detect whether it is there or not, but she is unable, even over many years of practice, to teach it directly.

In this regard, what philosopher and theatre artist do is at least very similar: both encounter their own experiences, and, through their writing (philosophers and theatre artists) and their practice (possibly predominantly theatre artists) they seek to understand what their experiences mean, they seek to place them in the context for themselves (of the history of philosophy in the case of philosophers, in that of theatre history and philosophy in the case of theatre artists), and they seek to share their understanding of meaning and context with others (their readers or listeners in lectures), and finally they seek to enable others to encounter such experiences themselves—the tools they suggest are philosophical practice such as that proposed by Plato, with dialectic as major component, and theatre practice, for philosophers and theatre artists respectively.

To conclude: understanding this parallel, which emerges if we consider both philosophy and theatre as related to experience, contributes directly to the restoration of the experiential essence of philosophy. While philosophy as currently understood allows us develop further and deeper understanding of the texts and practices of theatre, in turn the role of theatre arts as one predominantly focused on experience is to revive our understanding and experience of the lost or forgotten experiential nature of philosophy.

Theatre context (4): simultaneity of space and time (Daniel Meyer-Dinkgräfe)

All theatre has to take *time* into consideration. On a practical level, the question arises as to how long a performance should last? How many hours can a given audience be expected to pay attention to the theatre event? Originally, *Noh* performances in Japan consisted of several plays in a row, with the comedy form of *kyogen* in between. In India, performances lasting several days were known. In the West today, attention spans are bemoaned to become shorter and shorter, due to television soap operas; thus, plays wishing to be commercially viable have to be adapted and be no more than two to two-and-a-half hours including interval(s). Subsidised companies, such as the Royal Shakespeare Company, or the Royal National Theatre London may exceed this limit, as may occasional experimental productions by acknowledged stars of the theatre, such as Peter Brook's nine-hour *Mahabharata*, or Peter Stein's 21-hour production of Goethe's *Faust*.

Time is of course not limited to the duration of a production and the commercial, socio-cultural and psychological issues associated with it. Time is an important feature of both drama (the literary text) and the performance in the theatre. Plots may progress in a linear fashion, starting at point in time (A) and moving on steadily via points (B) and (C) to the end of play at point in time (D). The time it takes spectators to watch the play is the time that is suggested to have passed in the fictional reality of the play. Other plays would still fit the category of linear, but some stages in the development are not shown on stage, but occur off-stage, and may be reported as past events on stage. Plays may reverse the sequence of events over time, beginning at a chosen point and moving back from it (as in Pinter's *Betrayal*). Some contemporary dramatists have experimented explicitly with time: in *Noises Off*, Michael Frayn juxtaposes events on stage with simultaneous events backstage, presenting us first with the on-stage scene (the play within the play), then the backstage events while the scene we had seen before on-stage takes place off-stage. The same span of time (the presentation of a scene from the play within the play on the fictional stage on the real stage) is shown twice, from different perspectives. In one of Alan Ayckbourn's plays at the Royal National Theatre, London, *House and Garden* (2000), the same fictional time span was presented simultaneously in two of the three theatre spaces in the RNT (Olivier and Lyttleton) by the same cast, presenting indoors and outdoors perspectives.

In all those cases, attempts have been made to convey the intricacies of time. However, hard as they try, Frayn or Ayckbourn have not managed to achieve the impression of complete simultaneity. Spectators intellectually *know* that this is a clever device. When they are watching the first part of Ayckbourn's *House and Garden* in the Olivier, they *know* that the situation they have seen is continued next door in the Lyttleton. Once they have seen the first part and now proceed to the Lyttleton, they can match what they see now with their memories of the performance in the Olivier. However, this matching activity is also intellectually mediated, not immediate. In Frayn's *Noises Off*, matching the events of the scene from the play within the play on stage with the events backstage is made easier by hearing at least some of the on-stage text while the same scene is repeated from the backstage perspective. However, true simultaneity is not achieved.

A look at the Vedanta model of consciousness can elucidate the specific effect of simultaneity on the stage, and show its psychological significance for the actors and the audience alike. Vedanta philosophy is concerned predominantly with consciousness, which, as subjective monism, is located at the basis of all unmanifest and manifest creation. Time fits in with this approach. The Western mind-set, in its aims for scientific objectivity, associates time with a sequential sequence of events, studied in the discipline of history. According to Vedanta, the emphasis of history is on the importance of events, not on chronology, because of the conceptualisation of time as eternal. The following passage provides a rather mind-boggling account of how time is conceptualised in Indian philosophy.

> The eternity of the eternal life of absolute Being is conceived in terms of innumerable lives of the Divine Mother, a single one of whose lives encompasses a thousand life spans of Lord Shiva. One life of Lord Shiva covers the time of a thousand life spans of Lord Vishnu. One life of Lord Vishnu equals the duration of a thousand life spans of Brahma, the Creator. A single life span of Brahma is conceived in terms of one hundred years of Brahma; each year of Brahma comprises twelve months of Brahma, and each month comprises thirty days of Brahma. One day of Brahma is called a Kalpa. One Kalpa is equal to the time of fourteen Manus. The time of one Manu is called a Manvantara. One Manvantara equals seventy-one Chaturyugis. One Chaturyugi comprises the total span of four Yugas, i.e. Sat-yuga, Treta-yuga, Dvapara-yuga, and Kali-yuga. The span of the Yugas is conceived in terms of the duration of Sat-yuga. Thus the span of Treta-yuga is equal to three quarters of that of Sat-yuga; the span of Dvapara-yuga is half of that of Sat-yuga, and the span of Kali-yuga one quarter that of Sat-yuga. The span of Kali-yuga equals 432,000 years of man's life. (Maharishi Mahesh Yogi, 1969: 253-4)

Clearly, any attempt at chronology, given this conceptualisation of time, would be counter-productive, as would any attempt to grasp this concept of time intellectually. Vedanta does not expect us to do this. Instead, it argues that human beings may experience the infinity of time (and space) in their own consciousness, in a specific state termed pure consciousness.

Usually plays are directed in such a way that there is always only one scene on the stage. Even Frayn's and Ayckbourn's attempts at simultaneity do not break this rule. The spectator's attention is allowed to focus fully on that scene. In that scene, there will be major characters carrying the scene, while other performers better be in the background physically and emotionally so as not to upstage those at the scene's centre. In contrast, for example, take the production of Mozart's opera *Marriage of Figaro* by David Freeman and the Opera Factory Zurich. Life of the house of Count Almaviva is shown throughout, breaking the boundaries of ordinary opera direction. The traditional rule is to have only the characters on the stage who have to sing something at that time. Not so in Freeman's *Figaro*. Life in the house goes on. The threads of the story come through the house. The focus of the scene is on the singers, but other characters go about their respective business at the same time. A few examples should illustrate this: already during the overture, Don Curzio enters, sits down at a table upstage right, and starts writing. Soon he is joined by Basilio. At the same time, Antonio brings parts of a wooden bed into the small area designated as Figaro's and Susanna's chamber downstage left. After that, Antonio moves to an area centre stage right that represents the garden, indicated by flowers, and starts preparing a beautiful flowerbed. Barbarina, Susanna and two maids are busy in Figaro's and Susanna's chamber, cleaning the floor. Cherubino joins them: he enjoys female company. Before the end of the overture, Figaro arrives, makes all others except Susanna leave, so that they are now ready for their opening scene. Meanwhile, Bartolo and Marcelline have also appeared, downstage right, and during Figaro's and Susanna's scene, one of the maids brings hot water for a footbath and a camomile-steambath against Marcellina's cold. Basilio moves to 'his area', indicated by a music stand, and starts composing. The maids start washing and wringing linen in the background, Basilio eavesdrops on Susanna's and Marcellina's quarrel.

Such a liveliness of parallel action is kept up throughout the production. At the same time, perception habits of the audience are provoked. Whereas the ordinary theatre experience means focusing on one central element on the stage, in Freeman's production of *Figaro*, a flood of visual input reaches the spectator. All elements of input are interesting and make much sense because they are logical elements of the interpretation that Freeman provides. The audience has to learn to focus on the main element, which is provided by the music: they have to focus on the singers, while at the same time allowing the other input not to distract but to enrich the insights gained from focusing.

Freeman carried his use of simultaneity even further in his adaptation of Mallory's *Morte d'Arthur*. The production was presented in two parts. The first half of Part I, and the second half of Part II, were presented in the traditional space of the Lyric Hammersmith, London. For the second half of Part I and the first half of Part II, the audience assembled in nearby Hammersmith Church. The space was empty (the pews had been removed), and the action took place simultaneously around five mobile pageants. Spectators had the choice to follow one storyline, or to shift between the pageants, or to stay somewhere in the space and take in just what happened to make its way towards their perception.

To conclude, simultaneity of space and time is a characteristic of pure consciousness. On this level of creation, past, present, and future coexist. If a form of theatre forces the human mind to engage in the experience of simultaneity, it trains it in functioning from that deep level. Repeated exposure to such theatre stimuli may serve in parallel to repeated exposure to pure consciousness in meditative techniques. Theatre, understood and practised in this way, may thus well serve as a means of developing higher states of consciousness.

Theatre context (5): digital performance (Steve Dixon, Kate Sicchio, Daniel Meyer-Dinkgräfe)
In their seminal book on the subject, Dixon and Smith define the term *digital performance* as follows:

> (...) broadly to include all performance works where computer technologies play a *key* role rather than a subsidiary one in content, techniques, aesthetics or delivery forms. This includes live theatre, dance, and performance art that incorporate projections that have been digitally created or manipulated, robotic and virtual reality performances; installations and theatrical works that use computer sensing / activating equipment or telematic techniques; and performative works and activities that are accessed through the computer screen, including hypertheater events, MUDs, MOOs, and virtual worlds, computer games, CD-ROMs, and performance net.art works. (2007: 3)

Dixon maintains that the application of the digital in performance, although it is historically contextualised, leads to "genuinely new stylistic and aesthetic modes, and unique and unprecedented performance experiences, genres, and ontologies" (5). Progress in this field of digital performance towards achieving such new dimensions is always dependent on the state of the art of development in technology, which seems never as advanced as necessary to accomplish ever more sophisticated creative demands. I argue that such creative demands mirror the aspirations described in terms of spiritual and religious experience in respective traditions across the world, and which are at the centre of current empirical, scientific altered states of consciousness (ASC) research.

My argument is that nearly all of digital performance seeks to achieve advances in perception and experience, for performer and spectator, which come close to, but never quite reach, perceptions and experiences conceptualised in consciousness studies as altered, possibly even higher states of consciousness. Dixon responds that there are many possible ASC, both desirable and undesirable. They relate, and exist in relation to ordinary states of consciousness. In parallel, there are many applications of the digital in performance, which, according to Dixon, have to be understood in their relevant and respective historical contexts. There are many means of triggering the experience of ASC. I argue that the digital in performance can be explored as one such trigger, and will discuss the nature of the experience enabled through digital performance in terms of ASC.

It is these developments that are central to our discussion of digital performance and consciousness. All art work, certainly all great art work, has an effect on consciousness, with a sense of altering perceptions, raising or elevating consciousness, taking us to altered states, whatever they may be. In some ways, the type of methodologies, functionalities and aesthetics that emerge from digital performance are sometimes dealing explicitly with consciousness, with philosophical ideas, which again may affect conscious perception. Examples are the treatment of the body and ideas of extending the body through space and time. This implies quantum leaps in terms of how the body might be perceived as a more fluid and less stable formation.

While some of this is covered by much critical theory today anyway, what digital performance does is to make the explicit articulation and expression of our intimate connections with nature and with other people, in terms of transcendence or theological concepts, very tangible. Digital performance thus becomes both an exploration and a celebration of this dimension.

Potentially, digital performance covers a wide range of possible experiences, but in practice, it is limited by the restrictions imposed by current development of technology. This limitation focuses current interests, for example on interactivity, or on the body rather than space and time. There is further current emphasis on the concept of identity, with evidence in relation to social media that people tend to behave in more extreme ways through the agency of, and the illusions provided by new technologies: an example are the suicide cults among young people, in Japan and elsewhere, which would not be possible without the agency of the internet.

There was a sense of opposition to what was happening in digital and cybercultures, with users losing their real and constructing virtual realities and identities, which are fully illusional. Others, in contrast, argued that the new technologies are taking users out of a virtual reality in which they were living already, in terms of a much more passive TV culture, whereas social media, for example, allow real interaction with others. Digital performance is the celebration and exploration of multiple facets of the personality or identity, of the body, of ideas of communication, and, in a major way, memory.

In relation to identity and memory, what digital performance did in terms of exploring and celebrating was indeed very childlike and playful, at the beginning of this development, by now twenty to thirty years ago. The innocent, not naïve, way of how the work went on had much to do with a re-identification with the idea of beauty, ideas of the connection of the body and the spirit, ideas that are more child-like in terms of their connection with a genuinely playful spirit or *joie de vivre* that comes from discovering new things. We are still in this period of discovery, and this is likely to go on for another thirty to fifty years before we become too cynical about the nature of the places we can still explore. Looking at the kind of work that is being done in terms of digital performance today, and in comparison with the work of twenty years ago, the current phase is more like adolescence or young adulthood than childhood. There are interesting instances of soul-searching, of teen-Angst, within postmodern and posthuman arts.

In this context, the concept of the digital double becomes important. It has its origins in older anthropological ideas and fears about shadow, doppelgänger, the uncanny, the feeling of being at once connected to and disconnected from oneself. There are also ideas from cultures without written language, about the human reflection in water. These ideas are then made material through the use of the digital double, i.e., the projected self. The video image is projected in relation to the live actor, or the myriad avatar incarnations of the body or the self as defined in digital culture and digital performance. There is of course the context of the double in the theatre, developed by Artaud. In digital performance as well, the double is the dark, animalistic, unconscious side of the self. At the same time the metaphor can refer to the elevated side of the self, the transcendent, angelic one.

The relationship of that dark side and digital performance, with regard to the degree to which any one performance enhances, purges or solely explores it, depends on the artist. It may not always be a conscious strategy, but in most cases of digital performance the aim is observation of the respective other, indeed a conscious non-observation. Digital performance artists depend on the developments in digital technology. There are, however, good examples of digital artists developing that technology further themselves.

A close consideration of the artistic trajectory and work of digital choreographer Kate Sicchio will now serve as a case study. As a teenager, Sicchio created websites and was intern with a website design company. She did this alongside dancing, and the two were relatively separate activities. She then went on to university, studying dance, and had forgotten much about the digital work. Halfway through her degree she was injured, had three knee operations, and was unable, as a result, to dance for about a year. Rather than not going to university, she filled her timetable up with multi-media classes—she was allowed to attend them because she could demonstrate she had the required skills. The Head of the Dance Department probably wanted her to leave the dance programme altogether, suggesting Sicchio do a degree half dance and half multimedia, probably implying that she had done enough of dance already and should now focus on multimedia. However, Sicchio heard that she could do dance and multimedia together. As a result came a major epiphany, and much work specifically with video. Since then all her work has involved technology.

Her fascination with the combination of dance with technology has been the extra layer, the additional set of parameters that the digital adds in particular to the visual side of the work, and she likes the resulting complexity. Many of her pieces do not use sound, apart from the sound created by the dancer in the space (such as steps, or breathing). More recently she has moved on to work that is based on technology but does not use technology. Her approach to technology has been always that of a choreographer: she even considers programming as choreography. She considers her work as choreography, which for her is different from dance. Choreography involves more organisational practices, whereas dance is specific to the body. Making this relationship more explicit, she developed a dance piece through code. The dancers have to move in relation to a fake java script. It is part of an attempt at finding different ways of choreographing.

In the context of programming, dance and choreography can be very closely related to mathematics. Sicchio relates programming to a score, with numbers in it, and the choreographic score uses similar elements. The aspect of time in dance is related to numbers, as is the frequency with which the choreographic phrases are repeated. The links to Java Script are useful here. In her PhD dissertation, Sicchio looked at geometry, in particular non-Euklidian geometry, as a way of understanding relationships in choreography: in topology, distance is not understood in terms of measures, but in terms of relations. *Choreotopology*, as she called it, describes the relationship between dancer, camera and software, projection and the overall composition they are making, not necessarily in terms of measurable distances, but in terms of existing in space that is related through movement.

Technology has a long way to develop to achieve all of Sicchio's ideas, and there are instances of long hours of programming, on occasion combined with frustrating rehearsals where a long time can be spent on achieving what may look like a minor detail. However, she acknowledges that technology has come a long way already, too, and in some cases problems arise not due to technology not being available, but due to cost issues, where artists simply cannot afford the equipment they might want to use.

Her skill as a programmer allows her to be more flexible than if she were dependent on existing programmes. She works with programming environments, such as *Isadora*, developed by a dance company, or *Processing*. In most cases she collaborates with herself. Sicchio's work is a lot about play, in so far as she likes exploring different ideas and seeing how they come together throughout the process of choreography. A playful element comes in with her intention for some of her pieces to be funny, although she does not know how many people will understand the humour. For example, she projected fake java script behind the dancers while they were executing the commands contained in the script. The joke is that it is not real java script, and those spectators familiar with java script will understand this right away—those who are not familiar with it will not. This is what makes her work childlike in a way. While twenty years ago, the approach was to see whatever was possible with technology in performance, today artists are more interested in developing methods and processes for using technology. For example, Sicchio's research has been much more in terms of methodologies, such as using topology to understand relationships. In that sense there has been an increase of intellectual activity in comparison with intuitive activity. The work of Troika Ranch is a further example. In around 1989 they developed what they called MIDI Dancers, working with sensors that could trigger sounds, making the dancers into instruments. They spent ten to fifteen years exploring how the body can create sound. Their most recent piece is about a process: they took a video of a six-minute dance piece and applied looping techniques to it, thus creating an hour-long piece. They took this piece back to the dancers and asked them to recreate it.

The interdisciplinary nature of Sicchio's work brings with it the fear of not doing the various disciplines involved sufficient justice. The demand for academic writing influences her practice: on the one hand, she engages in some practice purely for research purposes, and such practice is not intended and opened up for performance. On the other hand, there is work that is created with the intention of public performance as the outcome; in rehearsal for such performances, something unexpected or exciting might happen that she then chooses to follow up through research. Work created exclusively for a research context may not need to be at a level that others would consider "professional": the dimension of professionality comes in only when the aim of creative work is public performance.

In response to the question whether the digital dimension is predominantly pre-programmed at the expense of spontaneity, Sicchio pointed out that her work with video-tracking is very open and allows her to explore because it creates a sense of space or environment that you can move through. The camera looks for a change in pixels, and the artist can develop that in various ways. The artist has to create a relationship with the camera.

Although performance art arose in opposition to conventional theatre and conventional art, it seems to Sicchio that performance art follows the same pattern. The kind of performance art that attracts the most publicity is that which focuses on, broadly speaking, suffering, the negative, and the ugly, while the artists, and critics alike, at the same time do not own up to those descriptors, but deny them, sometimes quite vehemently. In extreme cases, behaviour is carried out, is watched, is critically discussed, is at times admired and is sold as performance art that, in different circumstances, would lead its performer(s) to be investigated with quite genuine alarm for their mental stability. There are, however, occasional instances of performance art, thankfully, in Sicchio's opinion, growing in number, which defy the current *negative* dominant mode of performance art and thus contribute seminally to its further development.

Over the years, some dance companies used to distinguish themselves in the use of technology in their work, expecting for it to develop into a genre, and into a specific movement vocabulary. Sicchio thinks that this is not going to happen, because the computer does not have a movement vocabulary and no capacity to develop one. Technology is thus likely to be assimilated, as it has been in other art disciplines as well, for example the use of video in the context of theatre.

To sum up, digital performance is related to what is cutting edge, new and original in terms of the means and tools of performance, in particular the employment of most recent developments in digital technology. Digital performance can become an exploration and celebration of making explicit some of the otherwise implicit contents and modes of consciousness. Historically, such exploration and celebration began in playful, childlike ways ("see what happens"), and has matured in the meantime to a stage of adolescence. The case study supports this position, offering insights into Sicchio's artistic trajectory and her take on the relationship between technology and dance in terms of choreography. It also confirms that technology serves as exploration, expression and celebration of not only contents of consciousness, but consciousness itself.

Intuition and *chakras*
Principles (Hans Binder)
If we focus too much on the outside, we lose ourselves in it, our mind becomes confused, we fall out of our spiritual centre, get scared, do not trust our intuition and our discernment any longer, lose our "divine reference" – all with the result that we become the toy of the powers. This is the main cause of all psychological and psychosomatic diseases.

The polarity of masculine and feminine is related to intuition as well. Men think and act differently than women, and that is because they are different. This is perfectly natural and is explained by the natural law of polarities. In all polarities there is a fundamental dichotomy that we understand as the male and female principles; these forces are in constant interaction with each other. The masculine principle is activating and the feminine principle is permitting. Both men and women need a connection both to the masculine and the feminine principles, since, as androgynous creatures, they have structured both within themselves. Here are a few examples of the characteristics of male and female principles: For the male activating principle: make, do, think, reason, fact, control, intrusion, giving, inhaling, holding, attacking, being strong, fighting, analysing, deciding, impatience, vertical and outside. For the feminine, permitting principle there are: being, non-being, feeling, heart, idea, intuition, trust, recording, receiving, exhaling, letting go, relaxing, protecting, being weak, loving, looking, letting things happen, patience, horizontal and interior. Both sides want to be lived by both men and women. They do have different access routes to the respective principles—but they need to develop both, all properties.

The feminine principle is the receiving principle, in the sense of accepting and being able to absorb. The feminine principle is directed inside: mind, emotions, creativity, gentleness, patience, discipline, heart, love, humility, and intuition are just as much their characteristics as emotionality, variability and feelings of guilt. Women collect, through their fine antennae—intuition—thought forms from the world of ideas, and men put them into practice. Hence the saying is that behind every successful man is a strong woman!

When the light of God enlivens the female principle in us, we call this moment intuition, this is moment we receive divine consciousness. Conscious creation and receiving are the cornerstones of earthly fulfilment. Both aspects want to be accepted and lived in us; we are able to express these aspects to perfection when we trust the light in us.

In relation to intuition, the *chakras* are important and in particular the sixth *chakra*. Many people consider the world of matter and the physical body as the only reality, because they alone can be perceived through the physical senses and recognized by the rational mind. In Sanskrit, the term *prana* is translated as *absolute energy*, and the Chinese call it *chi*. The level of consciousness of every life form depends on the frequencies of *prana* that they are able to absorb and store. Animals have a lower frequency than humans and spiritually more highly developed people emit higher frequencies than people whose spiritual development is still in its infancy. The human energy system is comprised of:

1 the subtle energy body
2 the *chakras*
3 the *nadis*, also known as energy channels

The *nadis* have the task of supplying the energy bodies with life energy that was previously created in the *chakras*. In the human body there are a few thousand energy channels. The most important ones are called *Ida*, *Pingala* and *Sushumna*—we know them also from acupuncture, where they are known to us as meridians.

Within the human energy system, the *chakras* serve as the receiving stations, transformers and distributors of the various frequencies of *prana*. The *chakras* draw certain energies from the subtle bodies as well as from the environment and especially from the universe, transform those energies and, in turn, pass them on via the *nadis* back to the subtle bodies. Body, soul and spirit need these energies for their preservation and development. There are ancient writings that describe a number of over 80 000 *chakras* in the human body, with the result that there is hardly a point in the human body, which is not suitable and intended for the reception, conversion and transmission of energies. However, most of these *chakras* are very small and play only a minor role in the energy system of the person. There are about forty minor *chakras*, which are of greater importance.

The most important of these are located in the spleen area, in the neck, the palms and the soles. The seven major *chakras* that lie along a vertical axis at the front centre of the body are critical to the function of the most basic and most essential areas of the human body, mind and soul.

When *kundalini* rises, its energy is transformed in each *chakra* into a different vibration that corresponds to the tasks of the respective *chakra*. This vibration is the lowest in the root *chakra* and finds its highest expression at the crown centre. The transformed vibrations are passed on to the various subtle bodies or to the physical body and perceived as feelings, thoughts and physical sensations. To what extent humans allow the operation of the *kundalini* energy within them, depends on the extent to which they have developed awareness of the various areas of life represented by the *chakras* and to what extent stress and unprocessed experiences have caused blockages in the *chakras*. The more aware a person is, the more open and active the *chakras* will be, through which in turn a greater consciousness is awakened.

In addition to the *kundalini* energy, there is another force that flows through the spinal canal to the individual *chakras*. It is the energy of pure, divine being, the unmanifested aspect of God. It enters through the crown *chakra* and causes the person to recognize the formless aspect of God's existence in the immutable and all-pervasive ground of all manifestation on all levels of life. This energy is particularly suitable to dissolve blockages in the *chakras*.

The *chakras* also take up vibrations directly from the environment, vibrations that match their respective frequencies. In this way they connect us through their various functions with the events in our environment, in nature and in the universe, by serving as aerials for the whole range of energy vibrations and information that go beyond the physical realm. They are the openings that connect us with the unlimited world of subtler energies.

Similarly, the *chakras* radiate energy directly into the environment, thus changing the atmosphere around us. Through the *chakras* we can send out healing vibrations and conscious or unconscious messages and thus influence people, situations and even matter in a positive and negative sense. To experience an inner wholeness and the power associated with it, creativity, knowledge, love and happiness, all the *chakras* must be open and work together in harmony. However, this is the case in only very few people.

Unity consciousness was lost to us when we began to rely solely on the information coming to us through the physical senses and the rational mind— at the moment, we forget about our origins and our divine basis. An apparent separation came into existence, and brought the real experience of anxiety with it. We lost the sense of inner fulfilment and security in life and began to search for them in outer areas. However, here the longing for perfect fulfilment was disappointed again and again.

This experience created fear of new disappointment. In addition, we forgot that we can never be extinguished, because death means only a change in the external form. Fear always causes a contraction and thus a spasm or blockage, which in turn enhances the feeling of separateness, and fear can continue to grow. Breaking out of this vicious circle, to win the lost unity again, is the goal of all Eastern and Western spiritual paths. The *chakras* are those operational centres in the human energy system, in which anxiety-related blockages tend to settle. Other blockages are found along the *nadis*. The effect of these contractions that have become permanent is that life energies cannot flow freely any more and cannot provide our various energy bodies with everything they need to reflect and maintain unity consciousness.

If the experience of separateness, of abandonment, of emptiness and the fear of death lead us to seek in the outer world what we can find only in the innermost core of our being, we make ourselves dependent on the love and recognition of others, on sensual pleasures, on success and material possessions. Rather than enrich our lives, those things become necessities for us which we use to fill the void. If we lose these things, we are suddenly left with nothing and the gentle feeling of fear, which accompanies almost every person, is real again before us. And of course it is people who take away from us what we need so obviously for our fulfilment and satisfaction.

Instead of loving our fellow human beings, we begin to see them as competitors or even enemies. Finally, we believe that we must protect ourselves, and must not allow certain people, or situations or information to get close to us. We withdraw our receiving antennas in order not to have to face challenges and thus cause a further contraction and blockage of our *chakras*. On the other hand, we do have to protect us from attack of so-called "energy vampires" that withdraw our energy by using "control dramas". Here dexterity is required that we spontaneously decide, following our gut feeling and supported by the tools of the ability to distinguish and of intuition, when, where and how far we "open the gates". In principle, it should be such that we are masters of each situation and decide whom we are giving energy, and when, in the forms of attention or listening, or when we want to exhaust ourselves by talking.

In connection with the intuition, the sixth *chakra* is important because it is both connected through the astrological association of Mercury (intellectual knowledge and rational thinking), Sagittarius / Jupiter (holistic thinking, knowledge of internal relationships), Aquarius / Uranus (divinely inspired thinking, greater insight, sudden insights) and Pisces / Neptune (imagination, intuition, and access to inner truths).

Theatre context (1): Intuitive collaboration (Daniel Meyer-Dinkgräfe)
The work on the showcase for *Hiranyala* can serve as a case study for the feminine principles (which includes intuition) and the masculine principles at work. Initially there was Gayathri's predominantly feminine approach. She engaged with the plot of *Hiranyala* intuitively, trusting her own training and her intuition to do justice to the text, receiving impulses and inspiration from the text, using her heart and her feeling in the creative process, allowing herself to be vulnerable in the nascent state of creation, loving the work, the character and herself, not holding on to ideas once engaged in, but remaining open to their change, allowing things to happen, relaxing into the creative process and letting go. This feminine approach was threatened when the demands of the more masculine (reason and intellect-dominated) work on her PhD became too intense.

In phase two of the project, Shrikant joined, and his approach was masculine in the sense that he brought his reason to the work, argued, presented facts, gave to the process from the reservoir of his knowledge and experience—all these both in terms of his input to the rehearsal, and also his own performance. Both were strong, demonstrating control (in a collaborative, not domineering way); he was strong, analysed the text and the performance, and made decisions.

In the performance on April 27, the two merged, creating the unity of feminine and masculine that Binder describes as the ideal state towards which all creation and all human life develop. Gayathri and Shrikant commented on that experience independent of each other.

Theatre context (2): Practice as Research (Daniel Meyer-Dinkgräfe)
Practice as Research (PaR), as defined and described by Robin Nelson

> involves a research project in which practice is a key method of inquiry and where, in respect of the arts, a practice (creative writing, dance, musical score/performance, theatre/performance, visual exhibition, film or other cultural practice) is submitted as substantial evidence of a research enquiry (2013: 8-9)

While practice may be what the artist involved in PaR is most comfortable with, in a PaR project, theory should be imbricated within practice from the start of a project, rather than starting with practice and adding theory on (32).

The relation between practice and writing about practice is important: PaR, according to Nelson, does not imply "a verbal account of the practice", and "certainly not" the requirement of a "transposition of the practice into words" (2013: 11).

Much of what happens in any arts practice is, to some extent, possibly to a very large extent, intuitive, works in terms of hunches, ideas, and relates to the concept of tacit knowledge. While Nelson acknowledges this with reference to relevant literature, he argues "against artists' claim to a special private knowledge which, based on intuition, is incommunicable other than in the art form" (58). He places "considerable emphasis" on the "processes to articulate the tacit", acknowledging that it may not "ultimately be possible to make the tacit thoroughly explicit (that is, expressed as propositional knowledge in writing), but, if practitioner-researchers wish their embodied cognitions to be better recognized, means of identifying and disseminating them must be sought" (39).

Thus for Nelson, neither theory nor practice comes, or at least should, come first, with the respective other coming second. Nelson would like to see the two as imbricated, and that means working hand in hand, closely linked, related to each other and informing each other, at all times, as a new mode of gaining knowledge, neither only theoretical nor only practical, neither starting with practice and applying theory to it nor starting with theory and exploring it in practice. This is an ideal state of affairs, the aim and goal all PaR should strive for and be measured against.

In the context of this demand for, and justification of reflection of practice, as central component of PaR, Nelson seems to be dismissing those artist-researchers who appear to resist the demand for practice imbricated with theory when he writes: "for some arts practitioners, the requirement to do a little more to articulate their research inquiry is an unwarranted imposition from beyond their culture" (4). This apparent dismissal implies the assumption that the artists concerned have a choice. I want to suggest that they may not have a choice, and now I want to explore possible reasons of why not.

First of all, we must believe artists more literally when they report that they experience the process of the creation of their art as emanating from hunches, from intuition, and that they experience further that their artistic practice is influenced by the processes of theoretical reflection. They experience the influence as inevitable. The influence of theory on practice can be perceived by the artist as good in the sense that it supports their practice, leads to new insights, and new aspects of the practice that would not have come about without reflection on it. In contrast, the influence of theory on practice can be perceived by the artist as bad in the sense that it impedes, obstructs, blocks, or changes their art in ways they do not like. In these respects, the artists who report the experience of a detrimental impact of theory on their practice really do have that experience; they do not resist this aspect of PaR for the sake of resistance, or because of political or any other reasons except for their experiences. If they thus come short of the ideal as developed by Nelson, we must not blame them as a result, and they must not feel guilty. No pressure should be exercised or felt in an attempt to achieve compliance, and supervision or mentoring must ensure to be sensitive: if the hunch, intuition comes first for an artist, this is part of the normal spectrum and the role of the supervisor or mentor in such a scenario can only be to guide the artist to reflection on their own terms, with full understanding of and empathy towards that reflection represents unfamiliar territory.

Research into *verbal overshadowing* suggests one possible reason why some, not all, artists are not comfortable with the reflective aspect of PaR, and why they are not exaggerating their reluctance about the reflexive component of PaR because such verbal reflexion does have an undeniable, and perhaps even empirically measurable detrimental impact on their creative practice. In the phenomenon of verbal overshadowing, "describing memory for nonverbal stimuli (e.g., faces, tastes, or music) interferes with subsequent recognition performance". Further, findings of a 1998 study suggest "that individuals may be especially vulnerable to verbal overshadowing when their general perceptual abilities exceed their verbal abilities" (Ryan and Schooler 1998, S105). More recent studies have broadly confirmed the findings of the initial research, and offered a range of possible explanations for the phenomenon. In some cases, studies have not been able to confirm predicted results, however, without being able to identify the reason(s).

Further potential reasons for the adverse impact of theory on practice for some artists could have to do with the concepts of sensitiser/rationaliser, or with field independence. Could it be that a structured approach to PaR is important, in which immersive creative phases, undisturbed by critical thinking, alternate with critical and reflective phases, with problems arising when such a structure is not developed in the first place, or not adhered to? Other aspects of personality such as confidence, maturity, self-assurance, being comfortable with self-exposure and vulnerability, etc., could play their roles, too. It is likely to be a complex combination.

For those who do not perceive the critical dimension as a problem, reflection allows them to make sense of the practical, immersive experience, to consider their practice in a new light, and this in turn in many cases enriches subsequent practice. With hindsight, some argue that the critically reflective phase of their PaR was less a process of rationalising but one of integrating of consciousness and unconscious contents. They consider thought to follow naturally, organically from doing and moving, as suggested by Maxine Sheets-Johnstone (1999): the boundary between verbal thought and thinking in movement might be more artificial than assumed.

Finally, if we consider theory as masculine and practice as feminine, then the state Nelson argues for, practice imbricated in theory, represents a state in which both feminine and masculine aspects, practice and theory, have been developed fully. This state of full development is the ideal of spiritual development. This unified functioning of masculine and feminine components of PaR also represents harmonious functioning of the sixth *chakra*.

Criticism
Principles (Hans Binder)
Generously give praise and recognition and be stingy with criticism. If we want to change our thinking, we must change our beliefs, redeem the parts that have been split off from our soul, and tackle our tasks. Life presents us with many obstacles. However, hurdles are nothing negative, even if we tend to regard them as such. Obstacles help us to become stronger and more powerful. Only someone who has solved many problems and crises in his life, rather than displace them, can address new challenges relatively safely, calmly and in a composed state of mind, and overcome them with ease. If we did succeed doing something, we are wonderful, great and get a boost of energy that moves us forward. And suddenly we have more potential available, because we resonate with the success of our own lives. Therefore it is good to be proud of yourself. We have perfected the self-critical look so that we do not even believe others when they praise us. We must affirm again that we are wonderful and unique. We must stand up for ourselves, with all facets of our being. We have to accept us and embrace our "Divine Self"—if we do not, who should do it, then? Our partner can do it only if we have been able to. If we are to ourselves as we are, then we have arrived at us!

We all need praise and recognition. Children must be praised all the time, because they are not yet so far developed that they can go into the observer position deliberately and from there get to the original source of their own potential. This is what we should be able to expect of adults. However, even for adults it is a question of awareness. Children must be praised, because they literally live on the energy fields of praise and recognition. However, this is recognition that comes from the outside. Adults, who are more developed, do not need recognition and praise from the outside any longer, because they have the ability to become one with their divine selves and can live the observer position.

Adults who still need the external recognition still live on the level of their egos. If we, when we are already sufficiently developed, continue to praise our fellow human beings, although they do not need this any more in the sense that children need it and less developed adults need it, then this is just an expression of love and respect. The difference is that they are no longer dependent and expect no praise from the outside because they are within themselves and know that the reward (praise / recognition) now comes from the highest Divine (in the form of natural support).

We therefore no longer live in the outside (and thus we also do no longer take in all the "crap" from the outside), but we are in the "Divine Self" (one's own divine life source from which we draw all our life force).

Applause is the artist's bread! If an artist is dependent on this applause, she is not yet at her centre and not yet in the observer position. If she accepts the applause from the observer position, she is calm and "not freaking out", whether it be through pleasure or pain— she it does not rely on this applause!

She stands in the observer position and has the overview, because she has come off the "energy field of need" and does her work—like the flower on the side of the road, the simple flowers, regardless of whether it is perceived or not!

Theatre context (Daniel Meyer-Dinkgräfe)
In Chapter Three, Brask, Youtt and I observed that critics tend to have problems with expressing their praise in as much precise detail as they are able to express negative criticism. The historical context, in terms of philosophy and religion, demonstrates why it might be difficult for critics to get out of a blame/negative mode, because blame is so deeply rooted in our culture. Binder's position confirms this argument.

Our position and argument in Chapter Three One was to raise a concern about the danger of blame becoming a popular fetish; we are not suggesting that praise might somehow be, or become, a moral imperative. Instead, we have made clear what kind of positive vocabulary is available to the critic, and pointed out what the critic might "search" for, pay attention to, and evaluate, such as the performer's aliveness and presence. Thus we do not expect critics to praise at all costs, which might involve losing some desirable distance between themselves and the performance under review, but to have at their disposal a set of criteria to be alert to, and a set of related, suitable words to make use of in expressing what they have observed and experienced, so as to share it with their readers. In line with Binder's position, the kind of criticism we would like to see is one that comes from love and respect for the actor's art and person, not one that the actor needs to bolster an underdeveloped ego.

Help for self-help
Principles (Hans Binder)
We human beings have come to earth to learn love. Love is the law of God. We live here on earth to learn love in freedom and consciousness. What do we mean by God is not a personalized form, but is a high form of energy that is alive in each cell of our existence, in any matter of our being and its manifestation in our universe. This energy is the same as the laws of nature and their correspondence. Consequently, there is no God who punishes us, we always do that ourselves with our guilt, our self-condemnation, our guilty consciences, our actions, our false beliefs and our inadequacy. If we degrade ourselves, we reduce our divinity within us. Therefore, it is of much importance that we finally get out of the habit of blaming others and take responsibility ourselves for all our actions and conduct. Everything in our lives happens in resonance with the laws of nature. They are the measure of all things. The laws of nature cannot be manipulated, as they are the source of all creation. Since the laws of nature embody the expressions and the will of God, like attracts always like—this law of nature also governs the perfect "Divine Plan." This requires and has the consequence that everything takes place in the universe in a highly precise manner.

It is only our own limitations and ideas that keep us trapped and prevent us from experiencing infinity. The true nature of human beings, our higher self, continues to urge us with increasing intensity in the direction of our original identity. We are more and more forced to reduce our activities to the essentials, as we receive less support and satisfaction from outward appearances. That is the change characteristic of this frenzied time of upheavals. Therefore, we cannot but engage in "introspection" to put our actions to the test and to think, how we can find a direction in which we can experience more satisfaction and happiness. Every disease has a cause and that cause lies hidden within ourselves. Just because we cannot find the cause in us does not mean that there is no cause. We tried for a long time to hide our causes of suffering and illness in the form of parts of the soul becoming separated and displacements, so that we are not confronted with them. However, as soon as the appropriate time comes that these shortcomings will come to light, we have no choice but act, otherwise they reflect diseases into our body, mind and soul. If we can eliminate pathogenic fault zones and dig up the roots of unhappiness through the Person Analysis, we made a very good start! This is help for self-help.

Everything is connected to everything. Therefore, the quality of the spaces where a person resides, works, lives and sleeps is very important. The environment has an effect on the people living and working in it, but it is exactly the other way around as well. The people leave their "footprint" by influencing spaces and objects with their energy patterns. These interact or resonate with existing, energetic disturbance zones, with certain objects in space and with other people and their energy fields. Thus, pathogenic energy fields are built up. The basic requirement for a person to feel comfortable in a house is always that he is in his own spiritual centre and continuous resonance with his "Divine Plan". Only then can he attract other positive situations, people and circumstances.

To achieve this goal better and with less effort, it is very useful to rid the house, the apartment, and also the workplace from exposure to radiation of any kind. If a house or apartment, as I understand and apply it, has been cleared permanently of disturbing radiation, the energy level of the house and the people increase (houses nowadays normally have no more than 11-17% of the energy potential of 100 per cent). If the house / apartment has been purified in this way, the nervous system can again recover from the stresses of the day and rejuvenate at night.

Basically, everyone is in resonance with his environment—like attracts like. This serves as a mirror for the people to see themselves in, so that they get to opportunity to change consciously. However, in this day and age, people are so overlaid with sensations, stress and pollution of all kinds, but also with environmental and radiation exposure that they are too weak to tackle and implement findings. They find their desolate situation already largely "normal", but wonder about its effects, such as burnout, depression, chronic fatigue, insomnia, headaches and back pain, all the way to organic defects, heart attacks or worse.

Since time has received a new dimension in the new age and tasks come to us more quickly, the need has emerged that people's tasks should be clearly set out to them so that they can quickly work with them. I have developed, over decades of working with the laws of nature and the study of the Veda (blueprint of life) the Detailed Person Analysis. This allows people, independent of other people, procedures, and tools, to have, for years, the benefit of being able to explore their lives, to evolve constantly and to get back to their centres.

The procedure is well structured, simple and independent of the user's formal education. Your job is simply to devote yourself with an open heart to individual points addressed in the Person Analysis in your thoughts. In that way you strengthen and expand in a positive way all determined values, which are nothing more than energy fields. However, the PA does not replace a trip to the doctor or medical practitioner. As part of the detailed PA each individual receives a survey of the individual's tasks, their parent tasks of life, their evolutionary development, as well as an analysis of all the blocks in the vertebrae, planets in the hypothalamus, *chakras*, elements, as well as their own energy and power levels. Similarly, the PA includes a large health check. Altogether, 400 different points of analysis are collected in the PA. After three months there is a free post-analysis.

Theatre context (1): a*pplied theatre (Aylwyn Walsh, Daniel Meyer-Dinkgräfe)*

Above, Binder has described the context in which he can offer his approach to helping people. Applied theatre seeks to do the same, on its own terms and in its own contexts. The term *applied theatre* was coined in an attempt to unify all the approaches that were not either aesthetic or ornamental and were instead instrumental, using theatre for certain outcomes or purposes. In this sense, the umbrella is wide, covering theatre for education, process drama within an educational context, through to social contexts of working with socially excluded people such as refugees, asylum seekers, addicts of various kinds, and people with mental health issues. Another kind of strand of work is using theatre as a means of intervention with the aim of transforming behaviour, which is in itself a problematic claim, in the rehabilitation of young people in referral units, or behavioural work in prisons.

A further strand of applied theatre is set in the context of health. Here, theatre processes and practices are used in order to engage or include the stories of those who are suffering from health conditions, or educate, inform or share their experiences of the general context of health. This could be work with staff, with specialists, with focus on an illness or health problem, which is explored through theatre processes. What unifies all the strands and contexts of applied theatre is the aspect of participation: either engaging people themselves through a theatre-related practice to present to another audience, or to do it as a process without an outside audience. The main distinction then is not ultimately whether something becomes or is performance or not, but how it has been instrumentalised for whatever the original intention was.

Thus there is, in applied theatre, a whole range of informing principles, a whole range of aesthetic and ethical questions, with the constant of participation. Another constant factor is the need for partnership: relying on expertise that is not one's own, to make use of conversations and to see what fruitful things may emerge, with the aim of change, transformation, or education. In the remainder of this section, the work of applied theatre artist and practitioner Aylwyn Walsh will serve to demonstrate issues and concerns.

Walsh encountered many of these aspects of applied theatre. As a graduate student she worked with children with learning disabilities and some physical disabilities in a South African context. The children were from the townships, without any resources at all, and Walsh engaged them in some performance-based workshops. This has links with community theatre and theatre for development. She also worked with street children, bringing them to a festival in Manchester as part of the Contacting the World festival. This serves as an interesting case study concerning the issues of ethics and participation, the extent to which we can make claims for transformation if everyone's material conditions remain the same. At the same time, Walsh started working in prisons in South Africa, which again had links with community theatre in so far as she was treating the prisoners as just another community theatre company. When she came over to the UK she worked with young asylum seekers and continued work in prison, which has become the major focus of her work in the UK for the past six years. Offshoots of this were working in the area of illegal immigration, particularly in Greece, and trying to engage socially very excluded people in activities towards social change.

The year after Walsh had brought the South African street children to the Contact the World festival, she returned to the festival as a facilitator. The structure of the festival allows for six European companies to meet and collaborate with six international companies over a period of nine months, virtually, which is quite a challenge, depending on where people come from. They also meet up in various ways and ultimately come together at the festival, in a double bill where the twinned companies present their work. As facilitator, Walsh had the opportunity of doing work in Brazil, Zambia, Poland, London, Manchester and New York. Those meetings opened up questions such as: what is it that remains the same in working with a group that you define by their age limit, as young people, and what are the cultural elements that shift that dynamic.

Whereas young people in this country have a social safety net of at least education that is supported to a certain age, and some level of social work support, in Zambia, for example, and even to some extent in Poland, young people not in education do not have any social safety net at all. The idea of having a community-based theatre project that they can be involved in, thus becomes much more important in such circumstances, and the young people tend to commit with much more vigour.

Walsh was surprised that young people in the USA are in a similar position: despite expectations of a certain level of privilege related to associations with that country, those young people excluded, for example, from education, have no safety-net to achieve reintegration. In many national contexts there is the assumption, taken for granted, that communication by email will be possible for all participants. Then there is the realisation that some participants in fact walk for an hour to find somewhere they can log on, if they know how to log on in the first place. Noel Grieg, in his book *Young People, New Theatre* (2008), the founder of this project, wrote a critical evaluation of the issues raised by this project.

It became quite clear to Walsh after having experienced three years of egocentric actor training that this could not be the basis, in the then current social and political context of South Africa, for a career. Walsh would not have been able to handle, ethically, living as a conventionally trained actor, or as a director staging conventional works, in a country where the distinction between haves and have-nots is so evident. Especially as a director, not paying attention to the specific circumstances of her audience would have been a rather blind thing for her to do. When she realised this, she also realised that engaging with those people is not merely saying "you are welcome to come to the theatre", which is what ended up happening in the National Theatre and other mainstream theatre venues, as if making free tickets available to people who have no other experience of theatre would make them go. Even if they did come, they would not experience any affinity with what is being presented, apart from being temporarily enthusiastic. Walsh instead asked herself how meaningful conversations could be achieved.

Since she has been living and working in the UK, her concerns as a slightly marginalised foreigner became relevant, and this led her to consider what position she could take in conversation with other groups that might be fruitful for both of them. The concerns with prison theatre in South Africa were rather different to the concerns here, but some of the practices employed to address those concerns might be similar.

This is how working in this field developed for Walsh. As to the question why she continues with it, there is something addictive, with all the problems that this concept entails, about creating something from scratch. The ethical issues and the gap between herself as facilitator and the people she works with in that capacity, such as mental health patients, addicts, or prisoners, can take their toll. Then it becomes necessary to find ways of working through those things, in a fruitful way, at the same time as making sure the practice is generative and interesting and valuable for the entire group.

Walsh sees her activity as a facilitator as engaging in a performance of some kind herself. In thinking about her own performance as an actor in comparison with that as a facilitator allows her to realise that she can be much more in the moment as a facilitator than as an actor. The reason is that as a facilitator she has to take into account momentary changes among members of her group. It does not always work perfectly and successfully, but the skill is necessary for her work.

Walsh encounters difficulties that she has to deal and cope with on several levels. On the one hand there is an egocentric reaction to needing to be invisible as an affected body, needing to be the person who is able to cope in every moment. Once you leave that moment, however, there seems to be quite a gap in terms of support. In a mental health context, for psychodrama or dramatherapy, facilitators get what is called supervision to help them cope with the problems of their patients or clients that they encounter in their work. Such support does not exist in other contexts of applied theatre, in particular for freelance practitioners. After working with adult male prisoners for three years, Walsh was exhausted, confused and morally her compass was clouded. This was because her everyday reality was defined by the prisoners' absolute suspicion, lack of trust, and never taking anything at face value. When this was what was happening all the time all round her, she began to question whether she had a connection to reality left, and how she could retrieve it. The freelance experience allowed her to go into the site and exit the site, but she was always alone in that. There was no sense of community to be able to share her experiences with. After three years Walsh needed a break, not working in prisons for some time, focusing on other projects instead, and allowing time to think through the experiences of the past three years, a process that is still ongoing.

In working in prison with women, the same ethical issues apply, and the institutional obstacles that need to be navigated are the same. Working with groups of women, however, is quite different from working with men, and other sets of issues arise as a result. For example, women tend to be more open, with the need to share their problems, revealing in the process information that Walsh possibly should not have access to. There is a difference between the way male and female prisoners are habituated. The men tend to demonstrate bravado and coping, and hide their emotions. Women in prison seem to be assumed to be automatically extremely emotional, and the space is open for that to happen. It is not always pretty.

For Walsh, the feelings of encouragement, satisfaction or reward when there are incidents suggesting that change has been achieved, need careful consideration on each occasion that they occur. It is natural to get enthusiastic about an amazing and well-expressed change. The question then arises, however, and this needs to be reflected on as well, if and how that change can become part of that person's everyday life. For example, it was impressive to see the changes in the street children Walsh took from the small town in South Africa they had never left before, by plane to Manchester. Their performance was very popular, they had a great response from the audience. It was delightful to watch their reactions. They were very quick to adapt to London, savvy, streetwise, and navigating difficult social interactions with ease. Walsh was feeling quite enthusiastic and proud about their achievement and her achievement. A week after their return to South Africa they had a general feedback session and one of the young men said that he liked the experience very much but he just realised how terrible his life was. Walsh was completely deflated as a result of this comment, realising that what they had aimed to be a wonderful opportunity was holding up a mirror to this man's personal circumstances which did not really have that much chance of changing. One trip abroad does not lead to another, does not lead to any further education, there is no magic wand. Thus when he went back to his own context, he had also no chance of making the kinds of friends he could make abroad. That experience was very painful for Walsh and made her realise that anything she counts as a victory in her work is at best a momentary victory, and that she cannot ever take anything for granted. Similarly, small steps ahead might have huge significance for some people in the course of time.   In a recent project on mask and face in a women's prison, one older woman who was serving a life sentence realised, as a result of the work, that she needed her personal space to maintain her face. When she had her space, she was able to cope with prison by having a certain kind of face. However, if she did not have that personal space, she felt she could not cope. As part of her sentence she was expected now to move into a dormitory with younger offenders in order to progress and perhaps ultimately be released. The project made her aware that she could not do that. It is not known how this issue resolved itself, whether the prisoner in question was able to make an argument or case and whether, or to what extent, the prison authorities were able to help.

On the other side of the coin are instances where theatre work in prisons has been used by inmates to recognise and practice the patterns of behaviour required by the authorities for them to come across as remorseful, rehabilitated and safe to be released.

The techniques of certain practitioners come up repeatedly, such as those of Boal. The choice of techniques depends on the circumstances. For the theatre in prison project Walsh did not have too much time available to work with the prisoners; she wanted to find ways to explore the idea of face and masks without having a very didactic or direct approach. The main reason for this is that she does not have a dramatherapy background: talking too much about someone's personal experience may lead to situations where the workshop leader needs to contain the situation, which is not in

Walsh's skills repertory. She used objects to create narratives, in a shared and collaborative way. Obviously in a prison context she could not ask the women to bring things with them, and had to get permission to get all kinds of objects into the prison for the purpose of the project. From those objects they went into fiction right away; the personal circumstances are in the room, they are not denied, but they are not central to the work, which is not about the prisoners as criminal women, but as people with stories. The objects helped devise, collaboratively, small scenes, and a further task was then how to connect those scenes.

They had six sessions available, with all the limitations of frustrating irregular attendance. In the end the women managed to perform a 30-minute piece to fellow inmates and staff, and were very impressed with themselves. In this context Walsh seeks to make use of whatever the women volunteering to be involved in the project bring, be it that they are shy or loudmouths or great singers, or not native speakers of English. There is thus an established canon of techniques, enhanced by techniques that each practitioner will have come across in their own work, and in each situation the practitioner selects the techniques that they consider appropriate.

When working in a prison context, Walsh is perceived as the outsider, perhaps as a do-gooder, and has learnt to work in that atmosphere. If she can work with a group for a longer period of time, as on one occasion for one project for nine months, she will no longer be an outsider at the end of that time. She has to prove herself by sharing some of the group's language, by being prepared to reveal some things about herself, and show them that yes, she is an outsider to this prison or to a group, but she has some experience in similar environments. This becomes relevant in particular in view of the mercurial, rather than fixed, atmosphere inside a prison: the atmosphere can change from one day to the next in response to events somewhere in the prison. Walsh then has to assess quickly the nature of the atmosphere and adjust her work accordingly. The prisoners will also notice any sign of weakness or insecurity immediately. She has to address challenges from the group equally immediately, both appropriately and creatively so as to allow work to progress smoothly. As a workshop leader she is considered as a person of authority, a position enhanced by the fact that she carries keys.

On the first day of working with a group of young offenders in a prison in South Africa, she had been told she would be working with "young offenders", but they were certainly not 16 but between 18-25 years old. The social worker told her that she would have a prison officer with her, which she normally does not have. The fifteen men in the group were a little bit apprehensive themselves as to what to expect. After five minutes, after the first exercise, the officer said that he had some work to do in his office and asked Walsh if she minded if he left. Had she indicated that she wanted the officer to stay, all trust would have been lost. So she thought quickly and responded that he could go because "this group is going to look after me". They immediately straightened up with pride: it was probably the first time that someone had said something like this about them. In the end it even became patronising: as they walked back along a corridor, other inmates shouted misogynistic abuse, and they would react immediately with "this is our teacher, you cannot do this"

If you can learn how to work with applied theatre, then it is only through failing spectacularly, reading about other people's failures, and learning on the job. The question arises to what extent the invention and subsequent application of a range of techniques can ever achieve a holistic impact on any context in which such techniques are applied. *Technique* always implies fragmentation, with its focus on *one*, or at best a few, but most certainly not all, or at least as many as possible, individual, isolated and thus fragmented aspects.

To achieve a holistic impact, the starting point cannot be a technique, or even a pool or arsenal of techniques. A holistic impact can be achieved only on the basis of a holistic director or workshop leader personality, who will do, spontaneously, what is needed at the moment. This is not an intellectual process, but deeply intuitive, and thus (only thus) able to integrate all aspects of the given situation that are relevant at any one time. Some of what directors or workshop leaders do in this intuitive manner may then be rationalised, reduced to, fathomed, conceptualised, made relative and comprehensible and turned from the highest possible level of individual creativity to a commercial product that can be sold at workshops and made available more widely to others.

Theatre context (2): Neuro Linguistic Programming (NLP) as an intervention against stage fright (Deborah Claire Procter, Daniel Meyer-Dinkgräfe)

In 2005, Elizabeth Valentine, Professor of Psychology at Royal Holloway, University of London, and Meyer-Dinkgräfe, received funding from the British Academy to carry out research into stage fright, comparing an approach based on South Indian Techniques (developed and taught by Sreenath Nair) with Neuro Linguistic Programming (NLP, developed and taught by Deborah Claire Procter). The scientific account of the project was published in 2006 (Valentine et al.), while the emphasis on Indian approaches to stage fright was at the centre of a 2012 publication (Meyer-Dinkgräfe et al.). In the context of this book, we focus on NLP as a help to self-help approach to combat detrimental effects of stage fright, or performance anxiety, defined as a "potentially major risk factor for any performer, across the diverse fields of the arts (musicians and actors), and sports" (Meyer-Dinkgräfe et al., 2012: 1). The context of the 2005 study is easily available open access in the 2012 publication, so that it will not be necessary to repeat any material from previous publications.

NLP looks at how we name, map and classify our experience. The key is that it is a set of tools to alert us to the fact that we create internal mental maps to perceive the world. These maps are representations of reality, full of pre-suppositions, some of which are more useful than others. One classic example is the person who says, "I'm no good at maths". On the basis of that attitude, this person, when given a mathematical problem, would spend very little time thinking it through. In comparison, a person who says "I'm good at maths" would dedicate an appropriate amount of time to solve the problem. In other words: the self-belief creates a set of behaviours that then leads to an outcome.

NLP has been called "the study of excellence" because it works with limiting self-beliefs to discover what it is that we notice or fail to notice in the construction of a sense of self. Thus in working with the actors with stage fright with an NLP model, it is important to find out the perceptions and patterns that have anchored a set of experiences known as "stage fright." This may include noticing that many actors have "stage fright" yet have successful careers, or that the sensation of a heart beating fast can be motivating, or that feeling nervous does not mean that the individual will realise their worst fear of forgetting their words.

At this point it is worth remembering the background to NLP's development. In the mid 70's at the University of California at Santa Cruz, computer programmer Richard Bandler, and linguist John Grinder set about the task of seeing if they could analyse some of the most successful therapists (including Fritz Perls, Virginia Satir and Milton Erickson) to duplicate their techniques and their results. They looked for key verbal patterns as well as non-verbal skills. What they gave birth to was a body of knowledge and methodology rather than a single technique (or as student of Erickson, Stephen Gilligan notes, a "new therapy" (2002: 54) for every client). Diagnostic categories (such as neurotic, paranoid etc.) were avoided as they were seen as having the danger of imposing a fixed model. Instead, according to NLP, clients were considered to have unique problems that they did not choose and that are outside of their conscious control. The solution was to un-cover these unconscious processes that take the form of associational strategies (e.g., "I think of acting and all I can see is a picture of myself at the time that I forgot my lines"). On the basis of their analyses of the therapists' behaviour, Bandler and Grinder realised that we are always creating "maps" of reality in a way that can be thought of as a trance. In other words, the experience of trance can be explained most simply as when attention is paid to one particular piece of information and not another (for instance, when concentrating on a task and not noticing how much time has passed, or that the doorbell is ringing). Thus in hypnosis the client listens to the voice of the therapist and not to the surroundings. In NLP this experience has been epitomised by a phrase taken from the writings of linguist Alfred Korzybski, who famously said, "The map is not the territory, and the name is not the thing named."

The idea is that as it is impossible to be aware of all the billions of pieces of information that filter through our senses, we all naturally have to select to what we pay attention, and to what we ignore, which in the case of sufferers of stage-fright, could be positive aspects of their performance experience such as Yondem (2007) suggested. Therefore the key is to move from symptomatic trance (in this case the experience named stage-fright) to a therapeutic trance (performance free of excessive stage fright). A process of noticing the patterns and thought processes behind the problem achieves this. In this process it is important to deal with paradoxical injunctions (Gilligan 2002: 21) (e.g., I want to change / I don't want to change), and allow a space to notice paradoxical patterns that may have become associated with the problem, for instance, "My mother said I could succeed as an actor, but what would I do to make a living?" Here the belief of success combined with the simultaneous expectation of failure has been fixed as an internal belief. NLP would seek to work with this kind of paradox and use similar paradoxes to achieve a therapeutic result, for instance suggesting how it can be possible both to experience nerves and achieve a great performance.

According to the way NLP conceptualises human behaviour the client is stuck in a fixed identity, in this case, "I suffer from stage fright". This statement will inevitably link to a whole set of corresponding behaviours an   d choices, such as "Because of my stage fright, I don't go to auditions", "I fall apart when a director gives me my notes", "I have trouble learning my lines", or "I blank out when the audience claps so I never really see if they enjoyed my performance or not." The role of the NLP therapist is to support the client in their quest for self-valuing. This is a problem that they did not choose or consciously control, so the therapist's role is to create spaces, "generating multiple associative pathways" that are utilized to "re-source" a client" (Gilligan 2002: 45). The technique is to search for the associations, images, words, mental pictures, internal dialogue, and feelings that are associated with the "problem", and then to identify the associations, images, words, mental pictures, internal dialogue, and feelings that can create the solution.

According to Gilligan this is a process of recontextualization, and it can be:

> associational / dissociational
> direct / indirect
> general / specific
> serious / humorous
> pacing / leading
> agreeing / disagreeing
> cryptic / straightforward
> predictable / unpredictable
> focusing / distracting (2002: 55)

With these paradoxes in mind, the approach taken for the 2005 workshop was to deliberately mix, presentation styles to create a tension between seriousness and playfulness, formality and informality, carefulness and carelessness, planned and un-planned, calculated and spontaneous. This approach gave an opportunity to imply different "models" of performance, whilst knowing that the informality would create a conflict for some participants who always like to be in control, but that so doing would also raise questions about attentiveness and carefulness (in other words, when in performance is the problem for actors with stage fright that they are caring too much about their performance? Where is the balance between vigilance in performance versus hyper-vigilance?). This work could be described as a poetic method. As Gilligan says, "A major goal of a poetic approach is to reconnect language with felt experience, and to liberate meaning from fixed assumptions." (Gilligan 1997: xviii)

In this process that drawing on Gilligan's work that he calls "to repoeticize experience" (2003: 237), NLP gives us an understanding of our habitual thought processes of "Deletion", "Distortion" and "Generalisation"; an understanding that comes from the influence that its founders received from anthropologist, Gregory Bateson, Noam Chomsky, and founder of Gestalt Therapy, Fritz Perls, who in turn were influenced by linguist Alfred Korzybski, who reminded us that we are in a constant process of constructing reality that is continually filtered through our five senses. Thus reality is shaped by what we notice and what we fail to notice. The usefulness of this in the context of resolving the issue of stage-fright, is that NLP takes, 1) the notion from behaviourism of how we can become "anchored" to our perceptions and create habitual responses, and 2) the opposite notion from systems theory that we can "reframe" our experience. Therefore in working with the actors, I sought to elicit information to ascertain how in particular they experienced, or created the "map" that led to behaviour which they labelled as "stage fright." Whilst, I worked on common factors as a group, I used a short one-to-one session to discover individual processes, in order to decipher the particular differences that would make a key difference (bearing in mind that NLP takes the theory that we all configure our realities differently).

For example, one person's particular experience of "stage fright" might stem from a separate experience of feeling belittled by a parent or teacher at a particular age. Therefore, throughout the workshop, I used more positive anchors and frames in order to replace and re-define stage fright. I encouraged the group to search for and play with new explorations and re-examinations of their stage fright. Our discussion based on NLP principles led to the idea of "standards", and created an useful new awareness that often our perceived notion is that "standards" should be high; however this "value" actually can result in raised anxiety levels. In exploring this idea someone pointed out that a Roman Army would go to war with their "standards" flying high, thus some of the group benefited from enjoying the idea and image of deliberately "lowering their standards", enabling a re-evaluation of their expectations of themselves, combined with the liberating picture of themselves like soldiers no longer at war but at peace.

The NLP sessions modelled the main aspects of the 'Milton Model' which are the patterns of speech modelled from Milton Erickson's therapeutic interventions and approaches—which were to a large degree the most fruitful of the models taken by Bandler and Grinder (Robbie 1987). In large part they emerged from Erickson's particular skill of observing the verbal patterns with which his clients described their problems. He made an art of playfully working with these speech patterns and this became one of the cornerstones of NLP because they are so effective in opening up the client's understanding of their presenting symptom, to the degree that at the time Erickson was seen as a magician operating a kind of "Sleight of Mouth." His legacy was his use of metaphor, stories, anecdotes, questions, and provocations all combined with careful observation to maintain rapport with the client. These presuppositions can be summed up as:

- *Don't know space*—let things not make complete sense to your conscious mind
- *As if*—using visualisation and imagination to create images without the issue
- *If you always do what you've done, you'll always get what you've always had*—you can create different results by changing your awareness
- *Every behaviour has a positive intention*—therefore you are not bad or wrong
- *Offering more choice expands possibilities*—you can do things differently
- *Mind and Body are part of the same cybernetic system*—therefore one affects the other

Taking into account the premise that mind and body are linked, in the exercises with the actors, I deliberately overlapped different sensory perceptions. For example, I instructed them to use images and text from magazines to create collages on a large sheet of paper, to represent in words and images what stage fright meant to them, and what the opposite (i.e., lack of stage fright) would look, sound and feel like; in this way I gave the participants the opportunity of creating a vision of themselves before and after in relation to their suffering from stage fright. After the participants had individually created these collages, we looked at all of them together; this sharing opened up new awareness and a led to a useful discussion of the particularity of the "stage fright" experience. The exercise meant that the participants were linking visual internal stimuli and external stimuli to shift their internal un-conscious representation of "stage fright". This allowed them the opportunity to look for details that could help them make a change.

This kind of activity worked on the premise fundamental to Milton Erickson's work that our unconscious mind has solutions, which it would activate if only the conscious mind would let go of its current presuppositions. The premise of Erickson's work is that a problem (in this case named "stage fright") is a kind of trance that a person has entered into, causing them to fail to notice other sensory data that is to the contrary or that could be useful (e.g., successful experiences of performing). Therefore the whole workshop was organised to allow a space for new, more useful perceptions, images, metaphors, anchors, and analogies. This included the processes of reading stories, poems, deliberate playing with perceptions (such as whether as the presenter I choose to dress formally or informally, or if I used a deliberately casual presentation style in order to "model" how a lack of over-care or over-attention can be acceptable and a part of solving "stage fright"), and the use of images to represent the possibility of a variety of conventions (such as pinning to the wall the contrasting iconic photos of the perfect elegance of Audrey Hepburn in pearls, opposite the wild energy of Albert Einstein with his tongue sticking out). All the choice of techniques in the workshop were made to encourage the participants to model a different strategy for performing, just as NLP expert Robert Dilts has come up with the different models of creativity that Mozart, Disney, and Einstein consciously and unconsciously use (1995); and in other words strategies that could have what Erickson's student Stephen Gilligan identifies as a balance of "playfulness", "tenderness" and "fierceness", where a person learns to hold their problem "not too tight and not too loose" in order to find the point of change. In the same way that balance is important for the participant, the therapist needs to maintain a relaxed and receptive state so as to be able to "sense the client's reality from multiple perspectives" (2002: 88).

Throughout the workshop these more useful perceptions verbally and non-verbally, appealing to both conscious and unconscious thought processes were modelled. Both an implicit and an explicit style of training were used to take into account that the aim of offering a model of performance that can be effective yet anxiety-free. To this end, I did not have answers but offered space and processes in which each participant could update their own perceptions in more useful ways. For example understanding that the experience of stage fright was not, as some of them believed, an indication of their deficient ability as performers. This process happened in group discussion, individual exercises, work in partners, and in written, verbal, imaginative, physical, spatial and pictorial form to take into account all sensory perception.

Participants began the process of learning how to control getting into optimum performance states with exercises like "The Circle of Excellence" which is a classic NLP exercise in which participants work in pairs and take it in turns to recall a time (or if necessary invent one) in which they experienced a state of confidence. Considering that Erickson's therapeutic model, as adopted by NLP notes that we are continually making representations and interpretations of reality, inventing a positive experience can be as effective as a similar remembered time. Equally a transferable experience can be useful, such as using the memory and image of enjoying telling a child a bedtime story. Whilst this is not an experience of performing without stage fright in a theatre, the "map" of this experience can be modelled into a strategy for having similar feelings in a performance setting. This remembered, imagined, or transferred state is represented as a space on the floor in front of them that they step into. This has the effect of fixing and physically anchoring the sensation of confidence so that it can be re-accessed at a time when there is a perceived lack of confidence. In this case as the participant steps into the space in front of them, remembering their positive experience, they squeeze their fingers together. Repeating this squeezing of fingers before performing will help them re-access the positive anchor.

Through another exercise known as *"Timeline"* they had the opportunity to see how their recollection of *past* emotions creates the problem in the present. For example, a childhood experience of feeling nervous and un-prepared could be part of what is re-triggered during an experience of stage fright, so through re-imagining the childhood memory with a more positive outcome, some of the panic is taken out of the context of performance. They experienced in another exercise how recalling the qualities and presence of a *"Trusted Advisor"* (such as a friend, family member or a detached observer) could give them the experience of a positive state; and through *"Values Elicitation"* they noticed and listed what was important to them in order to recognise that how, where, and on what, they place importance, is in turn what creates their experience. For one participant this was the self-realisation that both for an audience and as an actor, passion was more important than perfection. Such recognitions may seem obvious but can be profoundly lacking and therefore incredibly useful, for an actor who has habitually experienced stage fright. They had an opportunity to create new metaphors that in turn could create new experiences.

The details of the empirical research carried out in the project can be found in the scientific publication (Valentine et al., 2006), accessible by subscription to the journal, and the publication that focuses on the Indian component of the project (Meyer-Dinkgräfe et al., 2012). This is available online in an open access journal. Briefly,

> measures were physiological (heart rate, breathing frequency and cortisol levels in saliva, an index of stress response) and behavioural (independent experts rated the performances, the actors rated themselves before and after their performances and afterwards. The measures were taken to establish whether participating in the workshops helped the actors with their stage fright, i.e., whether they were suffering from it less after having taken the workshops. Meyer-Dinkgräfe et al., 2012, 17-18)

The project demonstrated that both NLP and the approach based on South Indian techniques can help actors cope better with excessive stage fright[2].

---

[2] See pages 213-215 for further comments by Deborah Procter on the NLP results.

Chapter Six

Feedback from contributors and discussion

In this chapter, the contributors to Chapters One to Five present their feedback to the discussion of the preceding material from the perspective of Hans Binder's thinking. In each section, the conversations cover the contributors' specific comments on the contents of their contributions in relation to Binder's approach, comments on the further thinking inspired in the contributors by reading Chapter Five, and questions seeking further clarification or voicing concerns relating to Binder's positions. Where appropriate, Binder and I respond to the comments. The material in this chapter overall was gathered by live or skype conversations (although these conversations did not necessarily take place simultaneously between participants), and the way the material is presented here reflects the format of engaged conversation.

Nostalgia

Benjamin Poore

I have been reading an article recently that made me think slightly differently about some of the things you have been talking about and that are represented in Chapter One of this book. In the article entitled *"Nostalgia is not what it used to be"*, Andrew Higson traces histories of *nostalgia* in the contexts of mainly internet cultures and film, but I think this speaks to theatre as well. He writes about heritage movies that are attempting to work against heritage, about the modern and the post-modern senses of *nostalgia*, and how they exist side by side in our culture at the moment and how different cultural products will be placed somewhere between the two. He focuses on the question of intentionality, highlighting, for instance the 2008 remake of *Brideshead Revisited*, directed by Julian Jarrold. The filmmaker's intention was to challenge our instant urge as an audience to get nostalgic about that period: however, the tropes of the heritage movie, the familiar locations, the way music is used, the ways that particular types of lengths and types of shots are held, all these work against those very intentions. This is because of the genre in which it works, which seems to go against that critique and that problematizing of the past because there are so many other heritage movies that do not bring out that questioning. The film becomes swamped, saturated by the tropes of its own genre. I feel that is a real danger with theatre as well: there are some unavoidable associations that people will have if you bring out costumes of a certain vintage, props of a certain time, all related to expectations of what kind of play they are about to enjoy. The question is how you can operate within that set of resonances that you are setting up just by putting in an old fashioned telephone or a big carved Victorian desk, or someone swishes in in period costume. Already that is setting up expectations and a field of consciousness about the particular period that the playwrights and directors are not in control of as it is something that has already been mediated by popular culture. Those resonances cannot be pinned down and cannot be controlled.

Hans Binder

I think this is the case not only because authors and directors would want to do justice to representations of the past, but truly because they cannot have all this under their control. This is because those costumes and props radiate a powerful energy field of their own accord. In addition, many people, when they get in contact with such an energy field, are reminded of the old times it represents, in which they may have been persecuted, tortured or possibly even burnt (I know of my own past that I had to endure a lot in those times and even now I have uncomfortable memories of that time—seeing costumes from those times send shivers down my spine).

Yana Meerzon

There is a big difference between TV and live performance, but I think that what we are talking about is much more applicable to live performance.

Hans Binder

A TV programme, or a film, has its own energy field, which in turn enliven all kinds of energy fields, including personal feelings, in every viewer or spectator, thus affecting mass consciousness. Often, so-called virus patterns of phantoms have been integrated, with the intent of harm, into those programmes and films, which have their intended adverse impact on viewers in their living rooms and spectators in cinemas. This is similar in live performances. Here, too, an energy field is formed, combining the energy field of the idea of the play and the energy fields of the individual actors, and drawing the spectators into it. This energy field can be very powerful.

Benjamin Poore

We are not immune to how our wider culture views a particular period just because we are sitting in a theatre. It is not as if our brains in the auditorium are lined with some substance that prevents anything from the outside filtering in and I think it would be dangerous to assume that we are so above and beyond popular culture that nothing is filtered.

Hans Binder

That is correct: such a filter does not exist, at least not automatically. However, if we bring in our consciousness and are able to act from the perspective of the observer, if we ourselves have a strong, positively polarised energy field, we have established a strong layer of protection and can differentiate between the supportive and adverse influences of the play of TV programme or film. In the observer position we remain independent of the energy field of the play, programme or film.

Daniel Meyer-Dinkgräfe

I am reminded of a project I attended in April 2013, the *Salon Project Revisited*[1]. It took place in a specially arranged space in the Barbican Centre's *Pit* theatre in London. The performance started at 6pm, finished at 10pm and the audiences were allowed in at intervals, 30 at 6pm, 30 at 6.30pm and 30 at 7.00pm and were ushered out 2 or 3 hours after they had entered. The last group to enter were the last

---

[1] Produced by *Untitled Projects*, directed by Stewart Laing. See http://theatreandconsciousness.blogs.lincoln.ac.uk/posts/ for a more detailed account of the project by Meyer-Dinkgräfe and Susie Mower.

group to leave. Shortly after booking your ticket you were approached by the company to provide your measurements and on arrival you were ushered into a changing room separated for men and women, where professional dressers and costume and make-up artists would put you into period costumes. They would add make up, style longer hair, and then you were ushered into a square space, clad in linen, lit in various ways from behind the linen screens and above with elaborate chandeliers. An elderly lady was the salonnière.

This particular event was co-sponsored by the Wellcome Trust and some scientists gave talks, in our case a male professor rattled off a list of major events or inventions of the 20th century as a prediction of the future from the perspective of New Year's Eve 1899, with the request for the spectators to boo or cheer as they saw fit. The second scientist was a very young female post-doc from Cambridge who had been doing research on the effect of stimuli of the brain on ethical behaviour. It was interesting to see how some of the people changed when they had their costumes on or the costumes brought their personality traits out more strongly than before and in public. There was an elderly couple and when the man saw his costumed wife for the first time, he yelled across the room "you could have put some socks into your bra darling", to which she responded with a kind of weary sigh that she had been through this all her life and still sticking with him. Later he talked again loudly and in public to the salonnière and said "If I promise to kill you immediately afterwards, would you consent to having sex with me straight away?" because some of what had happened in that space was a kind of reminder of how short life is and there were some noises of a bomb raid and then some vary amateurishly produced images of murder and people strewn around the place with fake blood all around them.

Hans Binder
That's precisely what I explained above: the information is inherent, to a large extent, in the costumes and the rituals, even in the quality of a past time. We are affected by them if we enter those energy fields. We pick up virus patterns or other adverse influences because the spirit of those rituals and that time are still in those objects and wants us to continue thinking about and engaging with those old times and rituals so that this negatively polarised spirit can live on and can acquire further power

Benjamin Poore

It seems from what you are saying to be almost rather than evoking a specific time and place, to be generally evoking the idea of historicity, which is interesting.

Daniel Meyer-Dinkgräfe

In a way, nobody knew quite what to do, there was not enough guidance, steering or framing for audiences to really make something of it, it was all a bit vague. There were lots of levels there that were interesting but they were not integrated well and if they were meant to be jarring, they were not specifically and precisely jarring enough.

Benjamin Poore

That is the problem with this kind of generic indeterminacy: you will notice things yourself and not be sure if those things are being signposted for your attention or just things that you have noticed.

Daniel Meyer-Dinkgräfe

… or things that simply went wrong or weren't thought about.

Hans Binder

If a play, or the general framework of something, is not structured clearly, then this means that the spectator has to invest a higher level of attention in order to be able to relate everything to a pattern they are used to. This in turn means that the spectators have to open up more in terms of energies. This is nothing else than a control drama, presented by the representatives of the dark pole in order to withdraw life energy from people, which those representatives of the dark pole use to support their own lives, the predominant purpose of which is to inflict harm on fellow-humans and the universe.

Yana Meerzon

As you know there has been a wave of interest in audience studies. In Chapter Five, you discussed Binder's ideas predominantly in the context of the written text and acting. I wonder whether what is true for actors in the context of the emotional affect of performance as emotional hangover or post-dramatic stress, and boundary blurring applies to the spectator as well.

Hans Binder

If everything in the universe can be understood as energy fields, and if spectators enter the energy field of a performance, then of course they become part of that energy field. That means that the spectators pick up all emotions inherent in that energy field of the performance, consciously or unconsciously. If they perceive the emotions consciously, they can perhaps think about those impressions later and work them through. If they pick the emotions up only indirectly, then those impressions will be stored in the unconscious (cerebellum), but they will want to come up to consciousness all the time. However, we do not allow this to happen, because we are afraid of the unknown, and we suppress them. The result is that we create layers and layers of such unconscious material that hides our true nature. In the long run this costs a lot of life energy, because we have to cover the suppressed material again and again with life energy so that it does not come to the surface. The Person Analysis I have developed allows each person working with the PA to dismantle these layers. The only way not to pick up anything when we enter an energy field is to be completely aware, within the observer position—or simply to avoid a risky energy field in the first place.

Daniel Meyer-Dinkgräfe

From a psychological perspective, the question might be addressed best with reference to the concepts of sensitizers and rationalisers, people who go very emotional very quickly when they are encountering emotionally laden material, and others who think they are cool and keep their calm and keep their distance. The question is whether rationalisers are really that cool deep down. However, for ethical reasons you could never test that empirically because you cannot subject people intentionally to material that is expected to have a negative effect on them. Not a single ethical body will approve that. You can speculate about this for a long time but you cannot even test it. You can test for a positive effect but you cannot test for a negative effect.

Hans Binder

From the perspective of natural law I can say this here: we can undergo a lot of training and invent numerous techniques that help us to create a specific energy field, a phantom. In this field we may be safe, for a certain period of time and under certain circumstances. However, if this field does not correspond to the laws of nature, it will collapse quickly. For example, as long as people still harbour negative emotions, they will "explode" as soon as they hit a corresponding resonator. If people have those negative emotions, but they have programmed themselves, with the help of a certain technique, to remain "cool", they block the positive natural law according to which they should "explode". Thus they merely manipulated the positive natural law with a cloak of energy that they created themselves. The negative emotions have not been cleared (this particular field of life was not worked with, but only manipulated). In the long run the positive natural law will not stand for this, because nature will not be manipulated.

Yana Meerzon

The *Salon Project* also reminds me of how theatre performance is shifting its focus of interest to the spectator, with the spectator becoming the protagonist of the action. In June 2013, I attended a site-specific performance, *Peter and Valerie*, that had its world premiere at the Magnetic North Theatre Festival, in Ottawa[2]. This show played for several nights during the festival for a number of exclusive audiences, a maximum of nine people during each presentation. It featured a London based performance artist *Peter* Reder and a Maltese-Canadian actor/film-maker *Valerie* Buhagiar (Toronto, Canada). They played a semi-fictional family, Peter and Valerie, who came to Ottawa to perform a ritual of mourning for their close friend Frank. According to the fictional premise, Frank passed away very suddenly and his ashes were now to be scattered in Ottawa among his close friends (Peter and Valerie) and old acquaintances, the members of the audience. The performance took place in one of Ottawa's middle-class houses in one of the city's more prestigious areas, Glebe.

At the beginning of the show, Peter personally greets every audience member at the door of his home and invites us to come to the living room. As soon as all nine spectators are seated, Valerie joins her husband to thank their old friends (us) for joining them in such a

---

[2] *Peter and Valerie* was created and performed by Peter Reder and Valerie Buhagiar: *Peter and Valerie Production* (Toronto/UK), for the Magnetic Theatre Festival, in Ottawa: June 7-15, 2013.

difficult period of their lives. Next, we find ourselves sitting together with the couple around a small coffee-table trying to reminisce about our old friend Frank, his wonderful nature and artistic gifts. The performers invite the spectators/collaborators to look at old photographs, to drink tea, and eat cookies. Then we proceed to the next room to watch an old video featuring Frank and listen to his favourite music from the I-Pod. The evening finishes with the ritual of scattering Frank's ashes in the nearby park, under the lonely tree, with us clapping to the memory of Frank, using an old British tradition of saying "good bye" to passed-away soccer players, and hence thanking the performers for an interesting theatrical evening.

Without stepping much out of his character, Peter also thanks the audience for our attention and apologizes for not inviting us into the neighbouring bar for a drink or two, something he would normally do after such a show. In Ottawa, apparently, in the Glebe area there are no Irish pubs to get a drink at such a late night hour.

This interactive performance engages and challenges a number of normative theatrical practices, turning its spectators into co-creators of the action. For example, much in line with Augusto Boal's practices of invisible theatre, *Peter and Valerie* challenges our perception of what theatrical truth is and our expectations of how theatrical illusion is created. The show begins with the hosts thanking their guests for joining them in the ritual of mourning, hence expecting us to accept the "proposed/given/fictional circumstances" of being Frank's old friends, to go along with the game and to become the active co-players, co-makers of the story.

The performers use their own names as the names of their characters, they tell us stories that happened to them in their own lives, and they share with us their own photographs and video-recordings. Peter speaks English with the British accent and Valerie speaks English with a slight Mediterranean touch, the features that reveal their geographical and cultural backgrounds, and also make the audience members believe the authenticity of the stories that these people/characters relay to us. This condition of "authenticity" makes the audience members go along with the game and accept its rules.

Thus, the successful progress of this show depends on two conditions:

1) Peter and Valerie must fulfil the dramaturgical matrix, a dramaturgical scenario of the evening, of actions and events to bring the action to its logical end; whereas

2) The audience members need to be actively involved in the proposed action, so as not to destroy the route of the story.

The performers confront their audience's knowledge of theatrical routine by evoking and relying upon our feelings of shock and pleasure, when we find ourselves in the middle of the "acting work", pretending to be the old friends of Peter and Valerie, the guests in their house.

During the night I attended the show, most of the spectators went along with Peter and Valerie's ritual. Some of us supplied extra information on Frank's life; some of us readily responded to the hosts' questions, and one of the spectators/participants even asked Peter to turn off the TV since it was disturbing her concentration and took her attention away from the grimness of the immediate action. The audience felt "safe" and engaged with the action because the performers did not violate our private space and did not ask us to reveal anything personal about ourselves. The spectators enjoyed the ambiguity of the situation, willing to improvise with the proposed turns of the scenario. For example, as the show was unfolding Valerie was behaving more and more in an unpredictable, emotional, and even rude manner. In the middle of the action, she left the living room sobbing, so one of the audience members asked Peter whether medical attention would be required, whereas another one followed Valerie to the kitchen, offering help. As we learned later, from Peter, Frank was Valerie's lover and the biological father to the couple's son (a fictional part of the play). This explained Valerie's increasingly hysterical behaviour and made Peter look like a loving and supporting husband. This twist, however, came later in the game: by the time the action started to become slightly repetitive and work on idle, the audience needed a boost of information to keep us intrigued and engaged with action.

As a result, although the spectators understood that this was a site-specific show that must unfold in the borrowed space of a private home and that the performers Peter and Valerie used certain details of their personal lives to make up a story, we still found it slightly uncomfortable to act as the uncalled-for voyeurs, who are invited to observe someone's grief. By forcing us to witness Peter and Valerie's mourning, the people who we did not really know and with who we felt no affinity, the performance violated our sense of psychological privacy. It made the spectator's experience one of discomfort, and evoked our feelings of *nostalgia* and anxiety at the same time.

Hence this production presented a clear example of post-dramatic theatrical techniques that seek more active theatre audiences and try to shift the focus of a theatrical encounter from actors as the only doers of the action to spectators. Imposing on us the function of active co-creators of *Peter and Valerie*, the performance team expected their audience to experience in ways analogous to the actors' work transformation. The spectators were to undergo a similar process of turning into a character as the actors, to engage our imagination and even physicality to "become" Frank's friends for the 60 minutes duration of this production. This way, the staging of *Peter and Valerie* became more about the spectators' psycho-physical, sensorial experiences, not actors' techniques of character execution or dramatic coherence.

Such psycho-physical engagement of the audience with the performative action is the central element to the practices of interactive audio/video installations and performance art today. As DiBenedetto writes, instead of seeking our intellectual involvement with a theatrical production, post-dramatic theatre engages with "physiology and neurology of the human body as a receiver of outside stimuli" (2010: 1). It repeatedly investigates how theatrical lighting, sound, acting techniques and other material mechanisms of production "can assist the artist in using sensorial stimuli to compose a live theatrical event and create an in-between state of experience and awareness" (2010: 1). The artistic premise of *Peter and Valerie* was to make the audience members re-connect with their own bodies, memories, and other psycho-somatic experiences "inside out", to exchange our positions of passive spectators with the actors and become the co-creators and co-performers of the action.

For me, as an experienced theatre-goer, the most interesting part of this theatrical experiment was the close proximity between the actors and the audience in which this semi-fictional action unfolded. The space of a living room with people sitting next to each other on a sofa and a love-seat created a high voltage of interpersonal energy. It accentuated the feelings of danger and unpredictability, the sensations that bring us pleasure in watching a theatrical event live. This stage-audience close proximity also put the acting team into extremely demanding working conditions. It forced them to act as naturally as possible and be as concentrated as they could in order to sustain this sense of authenticity of the action. In watching/participating in the show *Peter and Valerie*, the spectators became the active players of the proposed action, Ranciere's "emancipated spectator", who challenges the habitual theatrical binary "between viewing and acting" (2009: 13).[3] Our will for and necessity of emancipation instigated by the performative situation changed our psycho-physical and sensorial experience and so took us beyond our normative position of receivers/transmitters/senders of energy in theatre (Ranciere 2009: 14). The audience members who participated in the action and thus changed (even if just slightly) its course, became the co-creators of a new theatrical community, the goal that defines today's theatre experiment. As Ranciere writes, "the precise aim of the [contemporary, experimental - YM] performance is to abolish this [stage-audience – YM] exteriority in various ways; by placing the spectators on the stage and the performers in the auditorium, by abolishing the difference between the two; by transferring the performance to other sites; by identifying it with taking possession of the street, the town or life" (2009: 15). By making a spectator an active maker of theatrical meaning and action, today's theatre avant-garde, similarly to the 1930s theories of Artaud or the 1960s experiments of Living Theater ensemble, seeks the return of the older performative forms, such as ritual and communion, with actors and spectators creating a consolidated, collective body of energy arising in a theatre auditorium. By placing the actors and the spectators in an arm-length proximity to each other, and by forcing us to participate actively in the course of its action, *Peter and Valerie* challenged the

---

[3] [The spectator's emancipation "begins when we understand that viewing is also an action that confirms or transforms this distribution of positions. The spectator also acts [...] she observes, selects, compares, interprets. She links what she sees to a host of other things that she has seen on other stages, in other kinds of place. She composes her own poem with the elements of the poem before her. She participates in the performance by refashioning it in her own way – by drawing back, for example, from the vital energy that it is supposed to transmit in order to make it a pure image and associate this image with a story which she has read or dreamt, experienced or invented. They are thus both distant spectators and interpreters of the spectacle offered to them" (Ranciere 2009: 13)]

stage-audience binary similarly to the previous theatrical experiments but on a smaller, private scale of our experience. By reminding its spectators of a ritual-like nature of our everyday life, based on acts of constant imitation, this production engaged with our (adults') *nostalgia* for the freedom of gaming and mimicry that characterizes our childhood experiences of cognition and play.

At the same time, I found this objective a bit too ambitious and partly naïve, since no interactive, game-based theatre experience depends on the spectators' will only. From the Greek theatre practices to those of Meyerhold and Artaud, theatre audiences functioned as the objects of artistic experiment and the subjects of emotional manipulation—hence the targets of the theatre makers' artistic intentionality. I expected a similar master-plan devised by the *Peter and Valerie's* production's team to condition their experiment. However, when I asked Peter and Valerie[4], how would they behave if even a single audience member rejected their invitation for this theatrical game and refused to answer their questions, thus slowing down the action or completely destroying the proposed circumstances, their carefully constructed illusion to manipulate our responses, the performers replied that they did not really anticipate such a situation, since they expected the audience members to be civilized and to respect the hospitality of their guests. In case someone would categorically decline the game, Peter and Valerie would adjust their behaviour by employing their theatrical training and thus would try to bring the story back to its original route. This way, in other words, the creators of the performance remain in control of its action, allowing spectators only the minimum of freedom, making sure that the show keeps up with its dramaturgical canvas and can be successfully terminated within the given time-limit.

Hans Binder
To me this sounds like a dislocation towards the spectator, perhaps manipulation, if the spectators are drawn into the play unwillingly.

Benjamin Poore
I, too, have been in situations when you are crowded in a small room sharing the space with the actor who then has no stage left to exit so

---

[4] Talk back with the University of Ottawa theater students, Friday 11, June 2013.

they must choose whether they are going to leave the room still in character or whether they are going to make that switch and play along with the audience to say sorry, I now have to become myself again. It doesn't really solve the riddle of the enigma of the spectator to turn them into a participant, that does something different. That is not going to enlighten spectatorship as a process, it's going to change it.

There would be some historians of theatre that might argue that the sense of theatre as a ritual still existed in western theatre up until the point where say Irving insisted on having the auditorium in darkness and rather than you responding to it in the moment, as it may have been earlier in the 19th century, it becomes something you sit back and detach from and watch from a slightly more "cool" vantage point. I wonder if there are degrees of ritual quality even in what you might consider the paradigm of the proscenium arch theatre. I think there maybe history within that where it was more of a ritual that involved everybody and had become less so, it is more like something in a gallery that you are invited to look at with a separation of "here's the frame, and here is you, here's the completed art object".

I was in the Wilton's Music Hall, the only surviving completely intact grand music hall in the world, watching a modern performance of something that was set in the 1880s and thinking about how that space was designed for a very different kind of performance. Even in the most audience-friendly interactive performances that we can devise and present today and utilising that space, it is still not using it in the same ritualised sense of the audience and performers and the acts together forging a night's entertainment. It is still not reaching back enough to what the building was designed for even though they are trying all the tricks of moving people in to the left and right, down the aisles, it is still a facing forward kind of show instead of what the building seems to suggest, which is something more like 360 degrees.

We were talking about performances that evoke the music hall and evoke the sense of camaraderie and the community that existed there, and the more you revisit those things with a level of irony, the more one is separated/alienated from that sense of community and ritual which one is actually evoking. If you pile layer and layer of irony, ironic *nostalgia*, it actually takes you further and further away from the thing that you are evoking.

Yana Meerzon
The question is, who brings that irony? The people who create the performances or us who watch them?

Benjamin Poore
Is it inherent in the performance or a mode of reading or a mode of creating? Daniel, you write that "The statements on time in the first part of this section have shown that our main focus in life should be on the present" (124). In response to this, I do not see that that necessarily translates into theatre.

Hans Binder
In my opinion, theatre should have a future-oriented, visionary plot. What is the point of hanging on to the past, nourished, as it is, by lack of consciousness? If theatre is not moulded by consciousness and if it does not go ahead of the people in order to spurn them on and to lead them into consciousness—what then is the purpose of theatre in these new times? Is it meant to hold people back within the past through old, contaminated energy fields? That should not be the case, in my opinion. Theatre has a global responsibility for the new world, in which humans are liberated from the scourge of the past. Theatre has the power and thus the responsibility to be path-breaking for a new "fiction", to show to people, in a playful and creative manner, the direction in which the new consciousness can move.

Benjamin Poore
Most performances, while they live and breathe in the present, are the result of extensive rehearsal, which is a focus on the future. As a theatre historian, my focus is on rediscovering the past.

Daniel Meyer-Dinkgräfe
You bring out a very interesting point about theatre and theatre scholarship here: the art form itself, and scholarship in relation to it, are related to past, present and future in very intricate ways. When I refer to the first part of this section, I refer to the ideas Binder has developed on the relation of past, present and future (115-117), with an emphasis on the need to be in the present and not seek to explore the past or wonder about the future.

Hans Binder
Precisely. Theatre should not put questions in an ignorant way like the masses, but should be ground-breaking, with consciousness and creativity, in our search for new ways of life, instead of continuing to enliven the old, dusty past, which brought us much calamity, war, manipulation and strife. Let us be glad to be allowed to finally let go of those old patterns!

Daniel Meyer-Dinkgräfe
Nostalgia is a prominent mode of existence, in all the facets we discussed in Chapter One of this book that focuses on the past, and one of the questions we raised in our discussion is that of the value of *nostalgia* for human life.

Hans Binder
A little bit of *nostalgia* can earth or ground us a little and can give us a bit of security, but a little bit too much of *nostalgia* binds us to the past.

Daniel Meyer-Dinkgräfe
Binder's position to the effect that emphasis should be more on the present than on the past provides an answer to that question, and in the section in Chapter Five of the book (124-125) on *nostalgia* I relate Binder's position to the threads and outcomes of our discussion of *nostalgia* in Chapter One.

Benjamin Poore
I'm not convinced that the examples that I have contributed to the discussion in Part One are fully representative of what prevails in theatre more broadly. It may, therefore, not be possible to claim, as straightforwardly as you do, that there is a "prevailing scepticism of the theatre towards *nostalgia*" (124). The examples I gave were Beresford and Hare, for instance; both might be said to be writing in the realist tradition. Thus the plays' response to *nostalgia* might predictably be that it interferes with and retards the personally, socially and politically progressive.

Hans Binder
But they are not writing for a new world order. If theatre succeeded to say good-bye to the old thinking, in order to become "godfather" of a new world order, in which consciousness is endowed with new ideas so as to allow war, ignorance, social injustice in all areas to become issues of the past, then theatre can become a major pillar of life also in that new era.

Benjamin Poore
Daniel, you write that the spiritual context provided by Binder, "If the task is not recognized and the wounds are not healed, the task will appear in another form as long as it takes until the wounds are healed", can explain why constellations of "friends and family are prevalent in plays which deal thematically with *nostalgia*" (125). However, there are other competing explanations for this perceived pattern. For example, one of the tenets of naturalism was to investigate the influence of environment and heredity on human behaviour, and so the family became the theatrical mainstay of naturalism. Many of the assumptions of naturalism still dominate the English-speaking theatre, of course. Families, by their nature, generate memories, lore, *nostalgia*, and repeated patterns created by the interaction of nature and nurture. In addition, of course, much western drama is given its shape by repeated action, which is a storytelling tool that helps us make sense of experience. So I think there are formal and cultural-historical reasons for the exploration of memory and *nostalgia*, as well as a psychological or spiritual interpretation of the characters' behaviour.

Hans Binder
Heredity implies a karmic connection that takes us back invariably into duality. Every generation is influenced by the genes of the previous generation. It is part of the duty and the universal quest of people who develop their consciousness to dissolve any patterns that seek to bind us to old patterns. In my own case, for example, my task was to dissolve our family karma, so that our offspring, but even our parents and grandparents were freed from these fetters. If this were not the case as a principle, everything in the universe would become rigid, without evolution.

Daniel Meyer-Dinkgräfe

Benjamin, your historical perspective complements my argument well. My earlier argument (125) is to correlate real life conditions with life depicted in theatre. Independent of cultural and historical contexts, in spiritual terms as developed by Binder, people encounter tasks on their paths of spiritual development, and in many cases those tasks take the shape of having to face challenging situations that allow them to recognise and transform, and thus heal, emotional wounds. Theatre represents real life on stage, no more so than in realism and naturalism. Spiritual development is an individual rather than a social issue. For spiritual development, it is essential for the individual to be as much in the present as possible. In this context, a clinging to the past, characteristic of *nostalgia*, would be detrimental to spiritual development as it would keep the individual in the past and not allow her to be in the present to the extent necessary to recognise and transform the wound that challenging situations in the present invite the individual to address. Many plays that deal with *nostalgia* directly or indirectly are critical of *nostalgia* because it keeps the characters in the past, often a faulty memory of the past, and does not allow them to deal with the present, let alone the future. In addition, many plays that deal with *nostalgia* focus on constellations of only a few characters, often friends or members of a family. There is thus a correlation between the insight that spiritual development is a matter for an individual rather than a larger group of people, and that in drama it is easier to present the concerns of an individual within a smaller constellation of characters, in a play with two or three characters, rather than a play with more characters. These two further correlate with the observation that *nostalgia* is considered, from the spiritual perspective by Binder at the core of this book, as detrimental to spiritual development, and a tendency to regard *nostalgia* as problematic central to many plays that deal with *nostalgia*.

Hans Binder

This is how I see it, as well.

Benjamin Poore

I do not think that the examples I gave justify as a general inter-pretation your argument that "people who lived during those times were confronted, though a whole range of situations in their lives, with tasks that they have not yet completed successfully. Therefore they are presented with the same tasks again at a later time in this, or in a next life." (125)

For a start, I think that the Victorians and the 1960s are periods of history that have been commodified and retold through so many media channels that even those who lived through the periods concerned will have had their memories distorted by the weight of interpretation, evaluation and representation of the period. This was true of the end of the 1960s, which was mythologising the demise of the decade of 'peace and love' before it was over, and true of the Victorians, who were talking about how history would remember them for decades before Victoria actually died, and fell into a fresh pattern of introspection and retrospection in 1901 when she did die.

Where this statement does make sense to me is in interpreting the fictional world of the 'supernatural realism' plays that I discuss in chapter 6 of my book, and which I mentioned in our discussion, but it only makes sense as one reading of what the hauntings by Victorians in these plays mean. On the other hand, the plays could just as easily be saying, 'people got murdered then, people get murdered now. Past and present are the same. Men will abuse women whenever they can'. Plays like *It's A Great Big Shame* seem to me to have a narrative of repetition which does not end in positivity, healing or emotional closure.

Hans Binder
Spiritual development progresses from incarnation to incarnation. Even if we deviate from our life plan, the "straight motorway", because we have to learn something here and here along the way, our consciousness will grow despite, or actually because of those detours. We deal with some tasks in one incarnation, while we are not able to deal with others because we do not recognise them or only suppress them—it is those that we will encounter in the next incarnation. But altogether our consciousness develops further from incarnation to incarnation.

Daniel Meyer-Dinkgräfe
Benjamin, the respective positions do not rule each other out, they are not incompatible. The statement you quote relates to Binder's position on wounds and how to deal with them. To start with, we are talking

about real people, not characters in a play. A person has encountered a situation in her life that she could not deal with; a wound is created, and the person possibly shuts that wound out, stores it away somewhere assumed safe, because it is just too much for the moment, for survival. However, the wound yearns for healing and contributes to the creation of situations in the person's life that would allow such transformation and healing. If the person does not take up this opportunity, a further opportunity will arise. This applies not only for that current life, but, in view of the assumption of reincarnation, across many lives.

Binder further argues that people are attracted to the things that provide them with opportunities for transforming and healing their wounds. One scenario, among many, is thus that the person who is attracted to the theatre as an artist, a spectator or a scholar, will find, in their encounter with the art form of the theatre, including the contents of the plays, triggers to enable them to deal with one or more of their own wounds. If theatre plays dealing with the 1960s or with the Victorians were particularly popular at any one period of time, this can mean, within the scenario just outlined, that those plays contain a good number of such triggers for the people who are the potential spectators of such plays, for example. Dramatists may be writing their specific plays because the writing process contains the triggers they need to deal with their own wounds.

This perspective is then complemented by the historical details that you developed in your book and in our discussion presented in Chapter One of this book. In graphical terms, the spiritual perspective could be drawn as an outer circle in which the broad historical perspective forms the next circle, all the way down to the circumstances of one individual.

What I am doing in Chapter Five, (124-125) is really to confirm from Hans Binder's perspective that the attempt of theatre to be critical of *nostalgia* which we found is there throughout, and thus to refer to the present can be understood further with reference to the fact that the art form of theatre is not only to entertain the audience but also to be useful to their lives. Trying to be in the present and *nostalgia* is something that draws us back to the past and therefore theatre has been critical of *nostalgia* and in that sense, theatre is something that seems to be emphasising the need to be in the present, which *nostalgia* isn't. So in a way, this debate that I offer in the second part goes someway in further answering our question that we propose in the first chapter on *nostalgia*, whether *nostalgia* is something good or bad in very broad terms. That was one of the questions. We come to the conclusion that a lot of theatre in dealing with *nostalgia* seems to be critical of it. Criticism is then enhanced by the perspective of looking at *nostalgia* again from Hans Binder's point of view.

Hans Binder

Life is about larger perspectives, about natural law on a large scale. One of the principles of life suggested by Maharishi Mahesh Yogi was "highest first". He wanted to say: don't spend too much time with the small detail, but open your focus to the bigger picture, the more important things in life—with that emphasis, the answers to the questions of detail will come automatically.

Yana Meerzon

Nostalgia can be an atmosphere, it can be an energy field that can be exchanged in the theatre, and maybe that is exactly the answer to why certain performances are successful today: they are generating a *nostalgia* field for the audience. *Nostalgia* can be a negative or positive feeling. *Nostalgia* can be very pleasurable. We can say that performance does it on purpose; it stimulates this field of energy. Robert Wilson creations are beautiful, very abstract, they are very "cold". He does not look for emotional attachment from the audience, what he wants us to do is to admire the tableaux vivantes.

What I find fascinating is that there are not many acting teachers who actually sensibly use their spiritual side. To my knowledge Michael Chekhov was one among not many. He discusses the actor's everyday "I", her higher "I" and the "I" of the character. During the acting process, all three come together. What is interesting about the higher "I" and the related consciousness is that it has this creative power to give the actor the sense of being above his/her acting moments and allows the actor to observe himself/herself on stage. There was a lot of discussion of energy exchange and the notion of radiation and the notion of atmosphere. This all resonates much with what Hans Binder says.

Daniel Meyer-Dinkgräfe
In recent years, more about the spiritual dimension of Stanislavski's approach has come to light in the new translation of his work, especially the influence of Indian philosophy on his thinking. With Chekhov it has been there all along, with influences from theosophy, anthroposophy and Steiner.

Yana Meerzon
I wonder to what extent the reader needs to be too much of a specialist in the areas that Binder is writing about. When I read Hans Binder's statements, it feels like you either believe it or you don't. In a way I say "wow this is really interesting" I totally believe in that, but I don't know how you prove his observations—and whether you actually need to do it.

Daniel Meyer-Dinkgräfe
I think that all of this is such that it could be put to scientific empirical test. The question is if you find a scientist who is interested in it and who will have the time to spend time and money on it. That is I think the challenge—not the possibility whether this can be dealt with in scientific empirical terms or not. If you find a scientist who is open enough and prepared to spend their limited time on this rather than the thing they have trained to be doing or they feel is more likely to get funding, or is more likely to get them kudos in their own community.

Hans Binder
Awareness lifts the veil—when that has happened, then you will simply *know*—what are scientific approaches compared to that? Only consciousness ultimately *knows*. I think that in the end consciousness alone is able to decide what endures and what is, in the long run, right and important for people and the universe. Science has had a lot of time already to show where people have their problems, and we all know the problematic results of this endeavour. On the other hand, the kinds of results that science has been able to develop so far are related to the level to which humankind has been able to develop its consciousness. This is a statement of fact, not a value judgment.

Benjamin Poore
Also, like Yana, I have concerns that the Hans Binder material on energy fields and *Zeitgeist* is not academically explicable or defensible, and I cannot conceive of how a numerical figure for a play like Bulwer Lytton's *Money*, for example, is arrived at, based on what assumptions about canonicity, what instances of performance, for example?

Hans Binder
A lot of training in relation to radiesthesia and methods for the development of consciousness. Insights into the world of the laws of nature. Life in the present, in the here and now, and not in the past. Knowledge gained in many previous incarnations came back to the surface. I analyse energy fields of people, plays and productions.

Daniel Meyer-Dinkgräfe
This is without doubt the most challenging aspect of Binder's thinking. We have to go back to the understanding that everything in the universe is ultimately an energy field, from the large, overarching systems such as galaxies, to the very minute occurrences on the subatomic levels. We experience life in terms of time and space, and those dimensions also exist as energy fields. However, while time passes in so far as our experience of time tells us that it passes, the energy fields related to time continue to exist. Therefore, it is possible to experience the energy field of any single event or occurrence or item at any point on the spectrum we describe as time and history. The ability to perceive those energy fields is in principle open to every human being, but so far not many have been able to develop this ability. Hans Binder is among them, he can experience the energy fields and translates that experience in terms of a percentage scale from 0-100, which is something we can relate to even if do not have developed the ability to experience the energy fields for ourselves in the way Binder does. Where we are able to perceive energy fields, that experience is vague and such that many people would possibly even deny it, or at least struggle to explain it: for example the experience of *atmosphere*, the way it feels when we enter a room where a tense discussion with a lot of fighting has been taking place. In the case of the energy value of a work of art, the implications of original value and today's value is the extent to which the energy field of a given

work, is in line and expresses the *Zeitgeist* of the time we are looking at it, so either the original value when it was originally written/performed or today's value. *Zeitgeist* in this context is also not an intellectual concept derived by adding up a limited number of well-defined parameters, but is as well an energy field, the energy field created by a vast number of components or contributing factors that exist at any one time period as we define it. It is difficult to develop a critical position to something that is completely new, and presented to the wider public here for the first time. I present this experience as axiomatic and try to tease out the implications.

Hans Binder
Every person is on her or his own individual path of development, which will bring her/him to knowledge one day. Some have only just started on that path, some are more advanced, but every person will reach the goal in due course. The Personal Analysis adds turbo speed.

Yana Meerzon
How do you measure that? And: are there differences with regard to the language a piece has been written in, and whether it is read or spoken by a native speaker of that language? Also, isn't there a difference between the text as written, and a performance of the play?

Daniel Meyer-Dinkgräfe
In this case he is talking about the actual text as written and the opera as composed, i.e., is the combination of libretto & score. I have asked him on occasion about the specific full productions so I asked him about the *Hedda Gabler* production by Thomas Ostermeyer in Berlin when it was performed in 2006; he gave me a percentage value for that. I saw *Tristan und Isolde* production in Minden in September 2012 and he gave me for that production a specific percentage number. The ones in this book, pages 122 onwards, that is the actual text as written or the opera as composed with libretto and score.

Hans Binder
Language can change, exchange or misunderstand much. However, if you are able to sense an energy field, the linguistic differences of different countries are not that important any longer, you will be able to sense the energy value independent of them. For example, many

people say something that is different from what they are really thinking of what they have already done in secret. If you are able to sense the energy field, you sense the truth.

Coping with demanding roles
Daniel Meyer-Dinkgräfe
Nicola Tiggeler has developed a range of approaches to be able to cope with the demanding role of Barbara von Heidenreich in the long-running tele novela *Sturm der Liebe*. It would of course be inappropriate to comment in this public forum on the extent of success she has had with this. From Binder's perspective, there are a number of areas in the Person Analysis that would be particularly relevant to Tiggeler's case: the stability of one's own energy field, which psychology would perhaps relate to field independence. The ability to close off one's own energy centres (*chakras*) to others for purposes of self-protection is equally important. Related to this is the extent to which we open up towards other people in the context of energies— here, any value above 50% is problematic

Hans Binder
In our time it has become common to evaluate and assign everything that is in any way relate to us. Thus we associate a clear and well-structured view with the terms "positive or negative" and derive clear judgments from them. Depending on whether positive or negative, we feel different emotions that affect us in the totality of body, mind and soul in ways that should not be underestimated. By "positive" we understand and we feel a good, conducive, pleasant, benevolent and increasing energy field, and by "negative" the exact opposite. We respond to "negative" with decreasing energy, discomfort and destructive thinking. Why is that? Actually, the terms "positive and negative" represent only polarities, i.e., opposites, without which there would be no evolution in the universe; thus they are a necessity of life.

Here are some further examples of polarities: positive and negative, good and evil, light and dark, up and down, fast and slow, and hot and cold, and so on. Only polarities produce the necessary "friction" that allows a field of tension to build. Let us take electricity as an example: only when we bring a positive and a negative pole together, a mutual field of tension is created, an energy field which we call electricity. Another example: for us living beings on earth, it is only possible to move because we have integrated resonators for an electric and magnetic fluid in our nervous system. These electric and magnetic fluids, however, need a daily charge, a voltage so that they have permanent power and can carry out their services. The perfect divine nature has set life up in such a way that every morning, at an early hour, from the East electric power and from the North magnetic energy enters our atmosphere. In this way, the electric and magnetic fluids are rebuilt; they find a resonance within us and thus recharge the "batteries" of our nervous system.

If everything can be understood in terms of necessary polarities, then why have "positive and negative" developed such a distinct position in our consciousness and in society? The reason is that this very polarity is being used by diverse powers for their very own purposes. Over a long time, a large amount of attention and energy have been projected into the energy field of "positive" and "negative", thus allowing two very powerful energy fields to form. These in turn has become deeply ingrained in our subconscious.

Added to this is that the "negatively charged energy field" has been used to control us and generate fear in us. It is the "playing field" of the "dark pole". If we allow ourselves to enter this playing field, the dark pole will take control of us quickly, will superimpose our consciousness, turn us and overlay us—thus enforcing power over us. Once we engage with the dark pole, our life is drained away from us. In such a state we are no longer able to think and act neutrally or impartially, because we are influenced and occupied by the negative energy field.

However, if we engage with the good, positive energy field of the love of the heart, and the universal love of God, our consciousness will remain pure and clear, and our inner light will shine more and more. We will be able to see and perceive universal contexts increasingly clearly. The more we are able to be in the position of an observer, which is equivalent to the inner source of life, the more energy, equanimity and heart energy will we be able to radiate. We are in the observer position, and thus we can act while at the same time remaining "separate from the action", impartial and neutral. In this way we can eliminate any kind of harmful emotions at source. The more we delve into the positive energy field, the more support from nature we will experience; thus it will be just this that helps us to cope with our tasks in life and our life goal—the liberation from death and rebirth.

Intuitive Collaboration
Gayathri Ganapathy

Regarding the chapter about Spirituality and Subjectivity—we have spoken about the male and female bodies and how they come together in the performance. I was thinking we could include that bit and take it further as the kind of research that can be looked into, or how we can introduce it as a concept to students at an Under Grad level. It can come across as a concept of gender differences in cross cultural studies or just cross cultural studies as a research practice. Alternatively, cross cultural studies as a module for students at an undergraduate level so there are more options created for people to pursue this and take it forward. Right now we all know we are stuck even if we are trying to do it, it does go as far as a certain point and then it becomes difficult to carry it further – why is that? If the solution to that is to make it available first to Performance Studies students so they get exposure and they practice it and take it forward, that is one of the options. It needs to start at the elementary level so an introduction of maybe a module for cross cultural collaboration work in the new semester maybe a start of a solution.

The philosophical dimension you bring to the discussion with reference to Hans Binder makes sense. I remember a friend of mine telling me about a South African stand-up comedian who was talking about the differences between men and women and how they think – it was called Defending the Cavemen. The attitude has penetrated into who we are today, during the comedy scene, men just needed food so they hunted, women gather information and everything else that needs to be done. Male stand-up comedians have spoken about it in a jovial fashion but I think there is a lot of truth in the fact that they put across. Yes the material makes a lot of sense, there is a lot of difference in the way they think and that is the way that we have approached *Hiranyala*. I was representing the woman, the female body and I would agree to the logic that the man explains but from outset she is always intuitive.

Theatre Criticism

Harry Youtt

Nostalgia of exile really segues well to the second chapter which is in effect bringing three cultures together to deal with the post-nostalgic event of what you describe of the exile in the first chapter. I don't know anything about the three histories but in effect the original text is German-based, with your mother, and all of these elements find themselves in a country not of their origination. That in a very broad sense is the reference back to the exile that you defined in the first chapter. It seems to me that the segue to the third chapter which we all collaborated on, is to the whole question of "what is nostalgic about the critical theatre experience?" The one non-nostalgic element is the performance and the escape from *nostalgia* is by avoiding the performer and talking about the text. The segue from the *nostalgia* of exile to the second chapter and then picking up the nostalgic comparative of the third chapter is an interesting concept.

Per Brask

In the case of the revival of Edson's *Wit*, we show, in our chapter, an example of criticism where one performer, Cynthia Nixon, is being compared to previous performers' portrayal of the role, and we also have the example of the *Death of a Salesman* in which so much of the production is in homage to the original production of the play, especially with regard to the set design. This, to me, suggests the presence of *nostalgia* in at least some productions and some reviews of productions. I think in the later chapters of your book and in your case studies there is this sense of reverberations from the past into the present into the future and also from the present into the past. In terms of the effects of the past, this may create a sense of *nostalgia*, a longing for the way things used to be. I think this line goes through the book if we focus on the theme of *nostalgia*.

Harry Youtt

There is the segue between the first three chapters and the rest of the book that I was searching for.

Per Brask

I think the Hans Binder material is also very interesting. I don't have a problem with the fact that you can look at a play and its importance to the Zeitgeist in its own time and its lesser importance to the Zeitgeist in the present. What I have a problem with is the ability to assign percentages to it. I think there may be ways in which you could produce Goethe's *Faust* and deal with it in contemporary terms, for example, as a vehicle for looking at scientism and the thirst for control of the universe that the play suggests is out of sync with reality. That subject is also mirrored in the play *The Physicists* by Dürrenmatt: it is the same sort of theme; an overreach on the part of a certain kind of rationality; an overreach undone by those realities that are the mysteries of life, that is of "how do you actually live and act in the now in order to create the future".

Many of Hans Binder's comments are suggestive of an update of a kind of Goethian humanism. If you look at Goethe's studies in morphology and including his sense of the spirituality of nature, and if you look at somebody like Rupert Sheldrake's studies in morphology there is a sort of contemporary sense that some of the things that appear to have been experienced and written about are becoming relevant again. I find Hans Binder's sense of the interconnectedness of energy fields interesting, that all things and all products of the human mind, and all human beings are nested in various energy fields. That rings a bell with regards to Daniel Siegel who talks about interpersonal neurobiology and energy patterns, the energy pattern of the mind, the energy pattern of relationships and the energy pattern of the body intertwined as a whole, but you separate it into strands so you can talk about them. That research I find very interesting, it is not the same as what Hans Binder is talking about but there are parallels. Daniel Siegel is at UCLA where he runs a program on interpersonal neurobiology. He is an interesting researcher from a scientific viewpoint who comes to some observations that seem to agree with what Hans Binder is talking about in terms of energy fields and the impact that the relationships of people have on the individual mind as well as on groups of people. This extends our responsibility beyond the individual to deal with both our new relationships, old relationships and also our relationship to the planet that we live on. What I found interesting in terms of one of your discussions in terms of theatre practice is when you talk about the kinds of energy fields a playwright is engaged in when writing a play, that the process is affected by the entirety of the playwright's relationships and that can affect what happens to the audience, the exchange between artists and audience. In fact this is not a relationship with only has one direction, it has several directions that go back and forth, each influencing the other across time. The whole idea of nestedness that Hans Binder describes and that you describe is where we go back to what Harry said earlier about *nostalgia*: this is where *nostalgia* can become both disadvantageous as well as advantageous. Sometimes it is good to forget, sometimes it is absolutely essential to remember but it all depends on the extent to which what you engage in the past and how you engage with the past. That seems to be me to bind both sections together.

Harry Youtt

My problem with *nostalgia* is that it is so comprehensive. As I think of *nostalgia* in the broadest possible way, *nostalgia* defines theatre, so that it is almost impossible to say good *nostalgia*, bad *nostalgia*—it's all *nostalgia*. I have a great difficulty getting away from that notion. What I see as the complexities of *nostalgia* could easily comprise an entire book. Relatively short coverage doesn't comprehensively deal with the term and the concept. And the first chapter seems to flit from thing to thing. And yet Binder's discussion and Per's suggestions to relate all of the aspects of the book to each other, with a kind of *nostalgia* base, is attractive to me.

Per Brask

I think that another point is that the art form of theatre itself is nostalgic in this overly technological society that we live in, in the sense that it harks back to a time when it was necessary for people to come together and be face to face when stories were told. That is no longer necessary – though I personally believe it is necessary. In terms of the delivery of stories, in terms of the telling of stories, it is no longer the main vehicle. Even though theatre now involves much technology, at least it still requires the presence by both performer and audience member and it's the interactions between those sets of presence that defines theatre as increasingly unique in our culture.

Daniel Meyer-Dinkgräfe

Does that then mean by implication that a movement of theatre away from the actual presence of actors and performers and audience in the same space, in virtual theatres for example, is a movement away from *nostalgia*?

Per Brask
It may be a movement away from *nostalgia* but it is also in the same breath, a movement away from necessary encounters - actual social interaction amongst actual living human beings is a fundamental aspect of our mental health.

Daniel Meyer-Dinkgräfe
I am asking because I have recently found out about a company called *Zoo Indigo*, based in Nottingham. For one piece, *Under the Covers*, the two women performers who are the core of the company, Rosie Garton and Ildiko Rippel, came on stage and said that they were both young mothers and couldn't find babysitters. They connected up their babies via infrared camera from their homes, they then switched on the relevant screens and told the audience if they saw their babies move and stir to please interrupt the performance or engage themselves in calming the babies down and make cooing noises to comfort them. In another performance, *Blueprint* , Garton and Rippel were joined by another two female performers, and all four interacted with their mothers via Skype. The mothers were at home, showed the audience their homes, then the daughters played their mothers live on stage while the mothers watched, and related stories from their mothers' lives which the mothers watched or the mothers told stories from their own lives from the distance or told something about the daughters' lives.

Per Brask
I like the first one a lot. The reason the first one appeals to me the strongest is that it puts an onus on the audience for a certain kind of alertness as well as the two live performers, one I think could inspire an engagement and a sense of responsibility for the audience in a nearly mediated encounter.

Harry Youtt
That certainly is one of the nearest things to a complete departure from *nostalgia*, but at the same time there is the classical theatre experience in that there are people sitting in an audience, watching a

stage performance no matter how much verisimilitude you add. The principal departure is from the stage to the video screen; however, even then there is the metaphor of the audience sitting in a theatre seat looking at what is happening on screen as well as what is happening on stage.

Per Brask

It reminds me of a philosopher, Colin McGinn, who wrote a book about watching movies, *The Power of Movies*, suggesting that the state you are in when watching movies is not dissimilar to the state you are in during lucid dreaming. I think he is right about this, the level of alertness to life and presence in a live theatre is different from that, I don't think you enter that state as easily when you are watching live theatre. Christopher Hampton made fun of this in his play *Tales from Hollywood* in the scene when Brecht comes out and places a green rug on the floor and a parasol, and a sign above with the words "Brecht's garden". Horvath then comments something to the effect that Brecht always wanted people to know they were in the theatre, but I never understood why he thought that they thought that they were somewhere else. In the theatre you are always completely aware that you are in the theatre, but in a cinema you can be wrapped up in a movie and experience an alpha state close to lucid dreaming.

Harry Youtt

Coming back, Daniel, to the two examples you were talking about, I find the distinction between the two examples really interesting. On the one hand I am assuming that the babies at home was a mimetic kind of setting, as I can't imagine two actors leaving their babies at home.

Daniel Meyer-Dinkgräfe

Their husbands were with them.

Harry Youtt

But the other example was not mimetic in the sense that the mothers were reacting on stage (via Skype) to the performance on stage. Again the performance was mimetic but the reaction was not.

Daniel Meyer-Dinkgräfe
One of the performers, Rippel, is trying to theorise at least the presence of the babies in terms of the non-performer.

Harry Youtt
Again giving the audience in effect a role: the role of cooing the interrupting baby back to sleep is an interesting theatrical experience.

Per Brask
It is putting the audience on the alert that I find particularly interesting.

Harry Youtt
Let me now come directly to what we did in our Chapter Three and one of the things I didn't pay enough attention to is the whole question of the word "praise": its evolution from a theological concept to a critical concept is really fascinating to me. What is the etymology of praise and how did it evolve from worship to an expression of personal approval? Again I remember when we were in the process of entering that phase of the draft; as I read it again I thought it was the whole core of an interesting development. It is an evocative concept in our cultural evolution when we turn from praise as something that people give to a deity, to a term that is ordinarily used in admiring a performer's work.

Daniel Meyer-Dinkgräfe
This becomes especially interesting when we think about the assumed origins of the theatre in the context of religion and ritual.

Per Brask
There's an interesting connection between our chapter, Daniel's case studies in the last section of the book, Hans Binder's term of "God's Helpers" and what Daniel is writing about when he writes about the levels and fields of energies that a playwright may be involved in. To me what it reveals is an underlying virtues ethics, i.e., it is not just what is being said, it's also about who is saying it, the trustworthiness of the speaker, the critic, the playwright and the actor. The trustworthiness of the critic requires a set of virtues just like the trustworthiness of the playwright, of the actor, and of the director.

Trustworthiness can be founded only upon a certain set of virtues: for example, in a film or TV series, there can be moments when you know that you are being toyed with: the film is withholding information merely to toy with you, not in order to explore a character. This is one of those moments when you say you no longer trust this filmmaker. I think there is a connection between what Hans Binder is talking about and the kinds of requirements of the person who engages in the art and who engages in the criticism.

Harry Youtt
This is something I have talked about briefly at the conference a couple of weeks ago[5]. On the one hand we get the sense of being toyed with, especially when we are expecting more verisimilitude than is being delivered. But at the same time part of the experience, actually or figuratively, of entering the theatre, is our suspension of what Richard Gerrig talks about as the *anomaly of suspense*. We are willing to watch the same play numerous times and become similarly and emotionally involved with it even if we know what's coming because of the *anomaly of suspense*, an experience that happens when we sit down in that seat and watch the curtain rise. That is also part of the really fascinating phenomenon of the theatrical experience.

Per Brask
We also know that there are times when you know you are being toyed with, just to be toyed with.

Hans Binder
Everything is related to everything else. Every now and then, even people who live predominantly in the head have moments of inspiration in which they can see energy fields or parts from within them.

Harry Youtt
when you go to the theatre to watch a performance for the second time you know you are being toyed with every time, to a certain extent, but you are willing to be toyed with in exactly the same way—because

---

[5] Youtt is referring to his keynote presentation at the 5th International Consciousness, Theatre, Literature and the Arts, Lincoln, 15-17 June 2013.

you know it is going to effect the same response on your part, even though you know exactly what is coming.

Per Brask
Daniel, I would like to say that I find your book to be very adventurous and very daring. I really have to commend you for putting this forward in an academic context because you are touching upon, particularly in the last part of the book, ways of thinking, ways of knowing, ways of experiencing that in most academic contexts would be seen as a taboo and I think what you are doing here is a great service to opening up, talking about spirituality in a theatre context and I think that is really, really good. I know you have done that in so many other books but I am sensing a radical turn here in your inclusion of Hans Binder in your discussions.

Harry Youtt
I agree, it is truly courageous work.

Hans Binder
I agree as well. But what would be the point, for consciousness and the universe, if you keep turning, with your ways of thinking, in the circles formed by those who have always seen everything as others do? Would that be the way of creating a new age of developed consciousness?

Daniel Meyer-Dinkgräfe
It takes the debate further to what was in the last book (2013).

Per Brask
It seems to me that you are taking a leap here. It has been present in your previous books, this commitment to a spiritual way of understanding consciousness, it has always been there, but the previous books have been more expositional than this one. In particular the last section of the book takes the leap into "but what if we actually took all of this seriously, where would it bring us in terms of our discussion about the life of the spirit and the life of the theatre".

Harry Youtt
Speaking of Binder I wasn't entirely clear about whether Binder is anchored in the Vedanta model of consciousness. Or do you place him there?

Daniel Meyer-Dinkgräfe
I think to some extent some of this thinking has affinity with it but I think he has read far more widely and experienced far more widely, and found his own kind of terminology as a result of that which I try to translate literally (as he doesn't speak any English). There are parallels and links with the Vedic context but it is not exclusively the Vedic model of consciousness that he is working with as I have done in my past two books.

Harry Youtt
That explains why Vedic concepts were not identified in the context of his text. I am not suggesting they should be. If you were to add anything it would be a summary of what you just said, somewhere along the line.

Per Brask
Am I right in detecting an inspiration from Goethe's esoteric writings?

Hans Binder
Actually, I have not read much in this incarnation, especially not these authors that you and others have mentioned—I did not have the time for that especially over the last few years. I can explain it in terms of memories, of relevations of consciousness

Per Brask
I felt that in the relationship to the kind of morphology of energies. I also detect some Spinoza in there in terms of the relationship between the human being and the universe. Then there is the connection to other philosophers and the relationship between the individual and "Nature" so I sort of see him as someone who has evolved with his thinking of his own terminology based on a variety of inspirations. Goethe did plant studies for example where he talks about how plants grow etc. – he has quite a substantial well thought-out worldview, a kind of spiritual humanism which is interesting. I don't know if

Rupert Sheldrake the biologist picked something up from there but he talks greatly about morphology.

Harry Youtt
I don't think Sheldrake talks about Goethe?

Per Brask
I haven't read enough of him to be aware if he has but I don't think he has from what I have read. Daniel, you mentioned Binder's person analysis; do you think you should write more about that? It may be applicable to fictional characters as well as living persons and could prove useful in various ways.

Daniel Meyer-Dinkgräfe
I can give you some of the headings: evolutionary position; energy exchange; current life energy; flow of energy through the body; energy level; immune system; stability of the energy field and appropriate balance of energies; flow of energy between yourself and others; being able to close one's energy centres in relation to others for self-protection; getting the energy that one needs for life from outside through control drama or from one's own divine source; the senses; the qualities of our heart; goodness; patience; compassion, selflessness, unconditional qualities, being happy, gratitude, being well-meaning towards others, inner self-expression, self-love, naturalness, gentleness, wrong pride or wrong ambition, humility, naiveté, sadness within the soul, giving, taking, receiving, the various elements (fire, water, air, earth and ether and the elements of metal and love)

Per Brask
As you hit on some of those categories particularly about energies and internal energies, that is the kind of thing that I could see could be helpful in an actor preparation. You have written about that yourself in terms of getting ready and in terms of cool down, ways in which energies can be used in the wind up process as well as the cool down process and what is necessary in order rid oneself of associations. Some of those terminologies can really be helpful in terms of understanding a character, understanding what a character's energy

exchange is with another character. I can imagine a number of actors who would click into that kind of exploration of a character.

Hans Binder

The Person Analysis is not a tool to analyse a character in drama or literature. Rather, it consists of the individual energy fields of a living human being with the purpose of showing up those fields and the extent to which they are developed. The PA is thus a tool for each individual to work with on their own.

Digital Performance
Steve Dixon

You have represented some points in our discussion far better than I remember them. A lot of the points are good ones. I was also interested in certain themes you were bringing up like *nostalgia*. This really interested and excited me. I think that *nostalgia* has never been bigger and part of a more complex and sometimes rather paradoxical sense of ideas of time and our consciousness of where we are, both as conscious or spiritual beings but also within critical ideas of temporality as well in that sense of how time may have changed and how time may have changed in relation to technology.

In my book we have a whole section regarding time and we talk quite a bit about it there, but this idea of *nostalgia* that you are working on, there are some nice ideas coming through there. I think *nostalgia* is interesting as a concept as in simplistic terms it has both positive and negative connotations, in terms of the *nostalgia* as that yearning, that lyrical wonder for the past but also that sense of regret and mourning the past. George Steiner wrote very eloquently about this sense of *nostalgia*, that kind of mourning and melancholy of *nostalgia* whereby we squandered the Utopia. There is both this wonderful thing of this Proustian value of *nostalgia*, that sense of recapturing a lost past, a romanticised past and the joyous attributes of that and the joy of memory whilst also a sense of mourning and melancholy for one's present. Also in some ways if one is living in the past, that can't be a good thing. Equally within that there are spiritual dimensions to the past in that sometimes when one remembers a past event or looks back, not nostalgically, it is because of a sense of the altered state of consciousness that comes in line with that. I often have *nostalgia* for childhood holidays where I have never been as alive and felt something for the first time in the same way that Proust talks about those memories. Our search of *nostalgia* is a great reference point for that, although of course in some ways it is the tragedy of Proust's life, he was always caught in that. I think in terms of one's spiritual consciousness, ironically one thinks of one's past or one's future i.e., death being the gateway through so many traditions/ cultures and religious ideas, so that the problem of never being able to stand in the present and always being in the past or future really resonates in terms of consciousness, philosophy, and spirituality.

The other thing I have spoken about in the past is the idea of the extra-temporal, being able to step outside of time which is an area of theatre which is very interesting. I have just been to Brazil and saw a Robert Wilson piece in Portuguese, Susan Sontag's adaptation of Ibsen's *The Lady from the Sea*. In some ways it was one of those ironies. Because it was in Portuguese and I couldn't understand a word of it, it was actually better as I was able to luxuriate in the sonic values of the words, in the wonderful soundscapes and wonderful visuals that any of Robert Wilson's productions has. Because of his use of slow motion and heavy stylisations, he is able to really play with time and that sense of placing oneself outside of time, not in a negative post-modern sense, but the more primitive idea of cyclical time is really interesting within the theatre generally.

A lot of your ideas in your book started to excite that. I think equally the kind of explicitly spiritual areas in your book and the ideas of the *chakras* and *yogic* practices I find very exciting in terms of the whole sense of theatre as ritual, developing out of ritual and in a sense such values become perhaps increasingly poor. I am talking more in terms of avant-garde theatre/experimental theatre. I think there is increasingly an interest in those altered states, in altering perceptions in audiences or the experiential perception and consciousness by way of that. Equally, in terms of self-help, which is closer to the section on practice as research, and again without being too obvious in this and on reflection of my own practices of research and that of colleagues and friends, I think in some ways performance is about self-revelation, that one is constantly trying to reveal oneself as the other rather than the object or subject. A certain sense within practice and research, and within ideas of authenticity which I am increasingly interested in, as a changing meaning, as a problem of authenticity is something I think people are more and more conscious of.

In relation to the *chakras*, I have a couple of colleagues here, one is an American voice teacher, teaching acting here, he is a specialist in Fitzmaurice technique. He is African American and collaborating with a woman from South East Asia who is an expert in Kalarippayattu, the martial art. They have just been awarded some internal funding to look at combining Kalarippayattu and Fitzmaurice techniques and working with professional actors in workshop situations to bring those two together as a new sort of acting methodology and again in terms of opening new channels and work which has a more spiritual "objective". It is really interesting as this is about the currency of these issues you are talking about – now what you have been talking about over the years regarding consciousness is coming of age.

Also in terms of digital culture and ideas of memory/*nostalgia* but also about amnesia, and certain selective consciousness, I think while the computer is this fantastic *nostalgia* machine and an archive of our thoughts and acts and consciousness, it is also a huge amnesia machine where our consciousness can swim in half-formed ideas and half-truths and also where we can erase inconvenient parts of our consciousness or loose ourselves in a technology bubble. The computer can be a spiritual machine but it can also be the exact opposite.

Working here at LASALLE College of the Arts, Singapore, and working on our strategic plan, one of the values of the current strategic plan it about the communication of truth beyond words, quite an amazing thing to see in the values of an institution. Those ideas of truth, whether it is self-revelation or revelation in relation to research, not on oneself but working on those old traditions of pre-expressivity in terms of trying to become some sort of channel for certain creative spiritual forces.

Daniel Meyer-Dinkgräfe
Do you think it is also culture-specific, do you think it works in Singapore because of the higher levels of Buddhism for example?

Steve Dixon
Very possibly but it was written by my predecessor, an Englishman from the UK. There are many religions in Singapore which is growing

constantly. We are in part of the world here where truth is not seen in relative post-modern terms or as a compromise concept.

Kate Sicchio

The thing about time is really interesting. For me in some of the things in my work, especially in the digital play with the idea of time, there is the idea of real time, and how it allows for things to happen pretty much simultaneously— if there is a slight delay, usually we can't detect it. We perceive as well as make the work up to create things in different spaces, all happening at the same time. As a result, there is a shift in awareness, due to the aspect of simultaneity. The other dimension is the ability to capture something, then to manipulate it and by doing so to manipulate time as well, doing something in real time, then looping and distorting it.

Daniel Meyer-Dinkgräfe

Why is simultaneity so attractive?

Kate Sicchio

You link the action to the video projection because it is happening at the same time so the link becomes more apparent and they become more united in composition. Time has come up a lot in my work particularly with this idea of topology because it is the relationships in time that is defining space rather than the measurement defining space.

What Binder has to say about the echo wave is something that really comes up a lot in digital performance: it is either this that just happened or even real time has a latency of whatever point, whatever seconds so it is technically the past reoccurring. I am not quite sure on how you would present a future wave. I made a piece two years ago. There is an actual culture in South America that say the future is behind us because you can't see it and the past is in front of us as you can see it, and even their gestures have developed that way. I have used that as a starting point for a piece with the idea that perhaps the past is in front of us and then I made these screens out of shark tooth mesh so basically you can project on them and if you back light someone behind the screen you can see them and the projection in front of them. I used that for this idea of the past is actually being projected in front of the person.

Daniel Meyer-Dinkgräfe
Did it work?

Kate Sicchio
Yes it did. There was one section in particular where I keep gesturing forwards and it is making this big abstract blue pattern on the screen in front of me. So it is this idea that this gesture that just happened is in front of me as the performer.

Daniel Meyer-Dinkgräfe
How did the audience react to that?

Kate Sicchio
I think people were really interested in it as the idea of the projection in front of the person.

Daniel Meyer-Dinkgräfe
Were they thinking about how you achieved it technically or were they interested in the actual experience they had as a result of what you did?

Kate Sicchio
A lot of people talked about it from a technical point of view. I think people liked it because it was this abstract thing happening from my gesture; it almost looked like a painting. No one really discussed what they thought it meant because it was very abstract, they liked the aesthetic of it as well as the technical aspect.

Daniel Meyer-Dinkgräfe
Do you feel that when you have an audience of colleagues, they talk about other things than those members of the audience who are not dancers, practitioners, choreographers themselves but "only" spectators?

Kate Sicchio
Definitely, I find dance colleagues in particular get very upset if they think the body is not showcased enough, if they feel they are not watching the dancers enough and are watching the screen, whereas colleagues in media are much happier watching the screen. A more

general audience can enjoy either, a lot of them become more engrossed with the screen as they are used to being in cinema mode, but some of them have really surprising comments.

Daniel Meyer-Dinkgräfe
Could it be that specialists lose something because they are looking in specialists' terms?

Kate Sicchio
I think so, particularly the dance people.

Daniel Meyer-Dinkgräfe
I am reminded of a performance I saw many years ago, it was very powerful and lively in my memory. It was *The Labyrintth: Ariadne's Thread*, a performance where we were lead into a space and had to take off shoes, watches, glasses and things like that and led into a dark space with a mirror held so we could see into the mirror and then a reflection from the ceiling. The mirror was then taken away from us and we were led just in pitch black darkness by the performers in the space following with our hands and guided by smells, gentle touches. In between there were themed spaces, on one occasion it was a girl in a school room playing ball, there was a woman in a bridal outfit showing very old yellow black and white photos and a gypsy doing a circle around a fire. What was for most people, especially the drama students, the climax of the whole thing was you were looking at yourself in the mirror then suddenly your face changed into a minotaur. I still don't know how it was done but for many people in the audience, they felt a major kind of spiritual transformatory experience when their face changed into that of the minotaur.

Kate Sicchio
I think the other thing that struck me was that the awareness you have to have of all the different layers happening when making the work in digital performance is a different kind of awareness from non-digital performance. This is particularly the case when I put myself into the work. Then I not only think about how I do certain movements with the body and they will be read in a certain way by the audience—at the same time I have to consider that the camera will have to see this in a certain way, to make a certain effect happen on the screen. These

are different levels of awareness, relating to being in the work and making it.

Applied Theatre
Aylwyn Walsh

I had about six intersecting responses that seemed to have emerged from reading back the interview material, and looking at some of the others as well. I thought one of the differences I would highlight a bit more was the idea of collaborations and partnerships that need to be seen as counter balances to the isolation that I talked about. That takes a lot of time to develop resources in terms of funding but when it happens can make the work much less isolating. Thinking about really what is exciting at the moment is the commitment to aesthetic innovation seen as counter balance to the pressure of demonstrating impact which has given some applied theatre a bit of a bad name. There is a commitment to developing and celebrating diverse ways of knowing, so instead of being aesthetic innovation in terms of the product which some of the other contributors were talking about, it's about process much more and so in this kind of way the practitioners would seek to unfix canonical ways of presenting work in this final product format. The idea on that is really about collaborative practice. Something I have realised through this conference[6] which was very encouraging is that the "field" is contested and at the same time emergent, so as it is battling it's developing this kind of tension which I think is productive. For a couple of years there was a dogmatic approach to work and I mention Boal in the interview and where people would just latch on to someone like that, where they have a defined practice and "this is it, this is what we are going to do" without really being critical or innovating enough in a context specific way. Now I think that is being destabilised a little bit more, or people are getting a little bit more confident and saying "how can I use my own aesthetic input in the process instead of relying on someone else's ideas"?

   Then also in connection with that, thinking about the scholarship that is happening which tends to be more focussed on so called failure, I noticed myself reflecting on the struggle and difficulty

---

[6] This material was recorded at the Annual Conference of the International Federation for Theatre Research (IFTR), Barcelona, July 2013.

in the interview, that actually the critical evaluation of what might be perceived to be failure is also very useful. Of course from a scholar's perspective, what the final product of failure may look like and what it means for those people might be very different to what it means when a piece of theatre doesn't get a great review or a full house. Therefore implications and ethics become very, very important and the fact that you can really learn something about the process and the potential through looking at those failures. I think people were discouraged from doing that for quite a long time so I won't be too critical of that but the really interesting work is going to begin to come out now.

I had one more thought that might connect with some of the other contributions which is the idea of facilitation or collaboration in process being about presence and being with others and how spectatorship and participation are not separate things but it is that performance and presence that defines those kinds of projects. It becomes very difficult to define in words what that feels like although in several case studies there is mention of feeling like family, which is not unproblematic in itself but a kind of gathering and a bond of care that is forged and if that is questioned as well, that is valuable. I think that this presence is particularly meaningful when looking at changing the dynamic, the relationships or the definitions of who is vulnerable and marginalised.

From memory what I would say is that I think as an explanation the Binder material was helpful. I think it would be difficult to apply spirituality as a label as there are so many competing narratives that are on top of this kind of work. But in terms of how a lot of these projects get evaluated, most of the emphasis is on the extent of certain kind of awakening of an individual moment of transformation and how that then relates to wider practices or potentially issues of spiritual development as an individual or as a make shift community of sorts.

The next point was that how do we then take those small and individual moments of awakening, realisation, integration and belonging. If we have a critical mass of disaffected youth who felt able to understand, how does that belonging in this workshop transfer to a wider belonging in the community which at the same time could be a wider belonging in the world? The implications of the work I think sometimes get lost because of the instrumental approach "ok we have done it now, this is the final celebration and that's it!", but the spiritual steps are the steps that take longer, that is where the most fruitful thinking can be done around connecting these ideas.

Neuro Linguistic Programming
Deborah Claire Procter
I would like to bring in some more material from the 2012 study here, to reflect on the differences between the South Indian approach and NLP, and bring that difference into perspective.

> An obvious limitation of the study was the small sample size permitted by the logistics and budget, and unequal numbers of men and women. However, it was considered more important to balance motivational factors. As one of the participants commented in the General Feedback, it would have been desirable to have had a larger audience to maximise performance anxiety. The performance situation was more akin to an audition than a public performance. However, for professionals this may be an even more daunting experience. The workshops were relatively short and only immediate results are reported here. Participants judged the likely benefits on both performance and on anxiety to be greater in the long-term than in the short-term. This was also supported by some of the comments: "In the short term I do not feel my performance anxiety is lower as a result of a week of workshops – if anything I would think the readings will be higher." (NLP: in fact, this participant's heart rate and behavioural ratings showed an improvement but the self-ratings showed a decline.) "I expected to be less nervous before the second performance but was more nervous. However, I feel that this is perhaps due to increased expectations of myself." (NLP: In general, this was borne out by the results for this participant.) It is undoubtedly the case that many of the participants gained substantially from the opportunity provided to interact with like-minded people, perhaps with similar problems, and a relatively closed environment, whether this was the workshops or the town and environs of Aberystwyth. The group lived, worked and 'played' together for a week. Close and positive relationships were formed. The group 'gelled' and bonded in a remarkable way. As many of them commented, it is likely that this week will have far-reaching effects on many of the participants, some as yet unknown, or unpredicted, such as one participant who felt a break through with a related problem of writers-block, or a first year drama student who reported feeling more relaxed about the prospect of entering the second year. These non-specific effects seemed to apply particularly to members of the NLP workshop, where the exercises were more general and less specifically focused on acting per se, as many of their comments in the general feedback indicated:
>
> - It was very useful in terms of working with other people with similar problems.

- The week was certainly helpful but often in unexpected ways.
- Opportunity to interact with like-minded people in a sheltered environment.
- Opportunity to work with some interesting people.
- Bonding with others [as one of the most useful aspects of the workshop].
- Pleased I attended. Definitely learned 'stuff', although not quite sure what yet. (Meyer-Dinkgräfe et al., 2012: 21-22)

SIT is offering a consolidated practice (taught model) and NLP is individual answers. Both have a different kind of validity. One model comes from a more Eastern tradition of master-pupil, the other from a Western philosophical tradition that the individual can be their own master. For me this is the interesting aspect of the study – that the two models both have their own validity, each bringing different benefits and disadvantages. Being a practitioner of martial arts myself, I do not see the separation. Or for me it's a circle of mind and body. NLP helped my martial art practice including helping my body to be more relaxed and more flexible—e.g., anxiety stops the body's ability to be pliable. So in my opinion there is definitely room for a new study where groups take both sessions—in other words, it's not an either / or scenario.

Mark Hewitt, one of the participants of the 2005, commented on his participation in the NLP workshop as follows in 2010:

> Deborah's playfully radical approach to [group coaching] using intuition and metaphor helped open up dimensions of self that were latent but comparatively unrealised. Her work infused me with the confidence to explore imagination and visualisation in ways that I had always previously held back from, (Lord knows why). The processes she facilitated for the group I was working with were loose, open-ended and fun, as well as genuinely revealing.

He added this in 2013:

> I feel that since that time (11 years ago) my artistic practice has gone on from strength to strength. I was always willing to take risks but often lacked the confidence or composure under stress to back up the bravado. Not that there haven't been dodgy moments inbetween time, but the more one does the more confident one becomes. I very rarely these days use the NLP exercises to which we were introduced; it's more that I've absorbed the broad principles into my psyche and ways

of working. There are things I do now and ways of being that I recognise can be traced back to the sessions in Aberystwyth.

Summary and Outlook

In this book we have taken the discussion of the subjective dimension of theatre, its spiritual context, its relation to consciousness and natural law, further than ever before, thanks to the context provided by the thinking of Hans Binder. I have sought to present relevant aspects of Binder's approach as precisely as possible, then to take Binder's approach for granted and to tease out, in my own writing, the implications of that approach to the issues of theatre I discussed with colleagues, at length in Chapters One, Two and Three, and in the form of shorter case studies, also in conversation with colleagues, in Chapter Five. Contributors to Chapters One to Five then had the opportunity of commenting on the material presents in those chapters, particularly the application of Binder's approach to issues in drama and theatre in Chapter Five, with responses by Binder and myself, edited to appear as an engaged discussion of a ground-breaking position and its implications.

In that discussion in Chapter Six, Youtt and Brask observed the overarching theme of *nostalgia* across all chapters. In view of that observation, it is possible to conclude that the outcome of the material presented in this book is an overarching emphasis on the importance of living in the present and the concomitant need to abandon obsolete but still powerful patterns of the past. In this context, theatre, according to Binder, has a global responsibility for the new world in which humans are liberated from the scourge of the past. Theatre has the power and thus the responsibility to be path-breaking for a new "fiction", to show to people, in a playful and creative manner, the direction in which the new consciousness can move.

Bibliography

Aciman, André. 1996. *Out of Egypt: A Memoir*. Riverhead.

——. 1997. Letters of Transit: Reflections on Exile, Identity, Language and Loss. The New Press.

——. 2000. *False Papers*. New York: Farrar, Straus and Giroux.

——. 2011. *Alibis: Essays on Elsewhere*. New York: Farrar, Straus and Giroux.

Aguirre, Carmen. 2010. *The Refugee Hotel*. Vancouver: Talonbooks.

Alexander, Charles N. and Robert W. Boyer. 1989. Seven States of Consciousness: Unfolding the Full Potential of the Cosmic Psyche in Individual Life through Maharishi's Vedic Psychology". *Modern Science and Vedic Science* 2 (4): 324-371.

Apter, Terri. 2009. The Science of Praise. *Psychology Today* 26 May. http://www.psychologytoday.com/blog/domestic-intelligence/200905/the-science-praise (accessed May 3, 2012).

Ardal, Maja. 2009. *You Fancy Yourself*. Toronto: Playwrights Canada Press.

Atkinson, Kate. 2000. *Abandonment*. London: Nick Hern.

Ayckbourn, Alan. 2000. *House and* Garden. London: Faber and Faber.

Bakich, Olga. 2000. Emigre Identity: The Case of Harbin. *The South Atlantic Quarterly* 99 (1): 51-73.

——. 2002. *Harbin Russian Imprints: Bibliography As History, 1898-1961: Materials for a Definitive Bibliography*. New York: Norman Ross

Bartlett, Mike. 2010. *Love Love Love*. London: Methuen Drama.

Basu, Paul. 2006. *Highland Homecomings: Genealogy and Heritage Tourism in the Scottish Diaspora*. London: Routledge.

Bean, Richard. 2005. *Harvest*. London: Oberon.

Beckett, Samuel. 1971. *Warten auf Godot. En attendant Godot. Waiting for Godot*. Frankfurt am Main: suhrkamp.

Behan, Brendan. 1956. *The Quare Fellow*. London: Methuen.

Beresford, Stephen. 2012. *The Last of the Haussmans*. London: Nick Hern.

Beumers, Birgit and Mark Lipovetsky. 2009. Performing Violence Literary and Theatrical Experiments of New Russian Drama. Bristol: Intellect. http://www.intellectbooks.co.uk/books/view-Book,id=4654/

Billington, Michael. 1993. *One Night Stands. A Critic's View of British Theatre from 1971 to 1991*. London: Nick Hern.

——. 2010. "Pygmalion". *The Guardian*, July 20. http://www.guardian.co.uk/stage/2010/jul/20/pygmalion-review (accessed August 20, 2010).

Blackburn, Simon (ed.). 2005. *The Oxford Dictionary of Philosophy*. Oxford: Oxford University Press.

Bloch, Susana, Pedro Orthous and Guy Santibañez. 1987. Effector Patterns of Basic Emotions: A Psychophysiological Method for Training Actors. *Journal of Social and Biological Structures* Jan.: 1-19.

Boym, Svetlana. 2001. *The Future of Nostalgia*. New York: Basic Books.

Brantley, Ben. 2012. American Dreamer, Ambushed by the Territory. *New York Times*, March 15.

http://theater.nytimes.com/2012/03/16/theater/reviews/death-of-a-salesman-with-philip-seymour-hoffman.html?pagewanted=print (accessed May 3, 2012).

Brodsky, Joseph. 1989. *Marbles*. New York: Farrar, Strauss, Giroux.

Brown, Scott. 2012. Theater Review: Mike Nichols' Staggering New *Death of a Salesman* Goes Back to the Source. *Vulture*, March 15. http://www.vulture.com/2012/03/mike-nichols-new-death-of-a-salesman-review.html (accessed May 3, 2012).

Bulgakov, Mikhail. *1969. Flight*. New York: Grove.

Butterworth, Jez. 2009. *Jerusalem*. London: Nick Hern.

Bye, Daniel. 2007. Blog entry, July 24. http://unknownpersonsunknown.blogspot.com/2007/07/sub-post.html (accessed May 3, 2012).

Carlson, Marvin. 2003. *The Haunted Stage: Theatre as Memory Machine*. Ann Arbor: The University of Michigan Press

Chan, Marty. 2001. *Mom, Dad, I'm Living with a White Girl*. Toronto: Playwrights Canada Press.

Croggon, Alison. 2007. Blog entry, July 24. http://unknownpersonsunknown.blogspot.com/2007/07/sub-post.html (accessed May 3, 2012)

Derrida, Jacques. 2006. *Spectres of Marx: The State of the Debt, the Work of Mourning and the New International*. London: Routledge.

Di Benedetto, Steve. 2010. *The Provocation of the Senses in Contemporary Theatre*. New York: Routledge.

Dieckman, Suzanne Burgoyne. 1991. A Crucible for Actors: Questions of Directorial Ethics. *Theatre Topics*, 1 (1): 1-12.

Dilts, Robert W. 1995. *Strategies of Genius*. Capitola: Meta Publishers

Dixon, Steve. *Digital Performance. A History of New Media in Theater, Dance, Performance Art, and Installation*. Cambridge, Mass.: MIT Press.

Dweck, Carol S. 2006. *Mindset: The New Psychology of Success*. New York: Ransom.

Edson, Margaret. 1999. *Wit*. New York: Dramatists Play Service.

F., Alex. 2007. Blog entry, July 24. http://unknownpersonsunknown.blogspot.com/2007/07/sub-post.html (accessed May 3, 2012)

Falkenhagen, Carola. 2012. Personal communication, Email.

Fensham, Rachel. 2009. *To Watch Theatre*. Frankfurt: Peter Lang.

Foer, Jonathan Safran. 2002. *Everything is Illuminated*. Boston: Houghton Mifflin.

Frangione. Lucia. 2011. *Paradise Garden*. Vancouver: Talonbooks.

Gable, Shelly L., and Jonathan Haidt. 2005. What (and Why) Is Positive Psychology. *Review of General Psychology* 9 (2): 103-110.

Gale, Lorena. 2000. *Je me souviens*. Vancouver: Talonbooks.

Gee, Shirley. 1987. *Ask for the Moon*. London: Faber and Faber.

Geer, Richard Owen. 1993. Dealing with Emotional Hangover: Cool-down and the Performance Cycle in Acting. *Theatre Topics* 3(2): 147-158.

Gilligan, Stephen. 1997. The Courage to Love: Principles and practices of self-relations psychotherapy. New York: W.W. Norton.

——. 2002. *The Legacy of Milton H. Erickson: Selected Papers of Stephen Gilligan.* Phoenix, Arizona: Zeig, Tucker, & Theisen.

Glowacki, Janusz. 1986. *Hunting Cockroaches.* New York: Theatre Communications Group.

——. 1997. *Antigone in New York.* London: French.

Gorak, Jan. *The Making of the Modern Canon. Genesis and Crisis of a Literary Idea.* London and Atlantic Highlands, NJ: Athlone, 1991.

Grieg, Noel. 2008. *Young People, New Theatre.* London: Routledge.

Groot, Jerome de. 2008. *Consuming Histories.* London: Routledge.

Hadamovsky, Carolin. 2012. Personal communication, Email.

Hamilton, James. Performance and Philosophy. Unpublished conference presentation, *What is Performance Philosophy: Staging a New Field.* University of Surrey, 11-13 April 2013.

Hampton, Christopher. 1983 *Tales from Hollywood.* London: Faber and Faber.

Hansberry, Lorraine. 1959. *A Raisin in the Sun.* New York: Random House.

Hare, David. 1998. *The Judas Kiss.* New York: Grove.

——. 2000. *Plenty.* London: Faber and Faber.

——. 2009. *The Power of Yes.* London: Faber and Faber.

Hepper, E. G., Ritchie, T. D., Sedikides, C., & Wildschut, T. 2012. Odyssey's end: Lay conceptions of *nostalgia* reflect its original Homeric meaning. *Emotion 12*: 102-119.

Higson, Andrew 2013. Nostalgia is not what it used to be: : heritage films, nostalgia websites and contemporary consumers. *Consumption, Markets and Culture*

Hirsch, Marianne. 2008. The Generation of Postmemory. *Poetics Today* 29 (1): 103–28.

——. "Past Lives: Postmemories in Exile". Exile and Creativity: Signposts, Travelers,Outsiders, Backward Glances. Ed. Suleiman, Susan Rubin. Durham and London: Duke University Press. 1998. 418–47.

——. Family Frames: Photography, Narrative, and Postmemory. Cambridge: HarvardUniversity Press. 1997.

Holdsworth, Amy. 2011. *Television, Memory and Nostalgia.* Basingstoke: Palgrave Macmillan.

Hwang, David Henry. 1996. *Trying to Find Chinatown.* New York: Dramatists Play Service.

Kaufman, Moisés. 1998. *Gross Indecency: The Three Trials of Oscar Wilde.* New York: Vintage.

Lahr, John. 2012a. Boldfaced Bard: Shakespeare's scandal sheet. *The New Yorker,* January 30. http://www.newyorker.com/arts/critics/theatre/2012/01/30/120130crth_theatre_lahr (accessed May 3, 2012).

——. 2012b. News from Nowhere: Tales of blighted lives by Margaret Edson and Daniel Talbott. *The New Yorker,* February 6. http://www.newyorker.com/arts/critics/theatre/2012/02/06/120206crth_theatre_lahr#ixzz1thoGjJed (accessed May 2, 2012).

——. 2012c. Lives in Limbo: Illusions and delusions in Arthur Miller and Tennessee Williams. *The New Yorker,* March 26. http://www.newyorker.com/arts/critics/theatre/2012/03/26/120326crth_theatre_lahr?currentPage=all. (accessed May 2, 2012).

Letts, Quentin. 2010. Gurning, gawping, brainless laughter. July 28.
    http://www.dailymail.co.uk/tvshowbiz/reviews/article-1298230/The-Prince-
    Homburg-Gurning-gawping-brainless-laughter.html#ixzz0xdC3ieuc.
    (accessed August 25, 2010).
Listerud, Paige. 2010. Review: *The Emigrants.*
    http://chicagotheaterbeat.com/2010/02/06/the-emigrants/)
Littlewood, Joan. 1969. *O What a Lovely War*. London: Methuen.
Mac Liammóir, Micheál. 1963. *The Importance of Being Oscar*. Dublin: Dolmen
    Press.
McGinn, Colin. 2005. *The Power of Movies: How Screen and Mind Interact*. New
    York: Pantheon.
Maharishi Mahesh Yogi. 1969. *On the Bhagavad-Gita. A New Translation and
    Commentary, Chapters 1 – 6*. Harmondsworth: Penguin.
Mandiela, Ahdri Zhina. 2012. *Who Knew Grannie: A Dub Aria*. Toronto: Playwrights
    Canada Press.
Maxwell, Dominic. 2008. Whatever Happened to the Cotton Dress Girl? at the New
    End Theatre, NW3. *The Times*, June 17.
    http://entertainment.timesonline.co.uk/tol/arts_and_entertainment/stage/theatr
    e/article4168201.ece (accessed August 15, 2010).
Meerzon, Yana. 2005. Interpreting Diaspora: from Accented Character to Accented
    Audience. *New England Theatre Journal* 16: 71-97.
——. 2007. The Ideal City: Heterotopia or Panopticon? On Joseph Brodsky's Play
    Marbles and Its Fictional Spaces *Modern Drama* 50 (2): 184-209.
——. 2009. The Exilic Teens: On the Intracultural Encounters in Wajdi Mouawad's
    Theatre. *Theatre Research in Canada*. 30 (1): 99-128.
——. 2010a. Searching for poetry: on improvisation and collective collaboration in
    the theatre of Wajdi Mouawad. *Canadian Theatre Review* 143: 29-34.
——. 2010b. On Theatre and Exile: Toward a Definition of Exilic Theatre as a Form
    of Glocalization. In *The Local Meets the Global in Performance*. Eds. Koski,
    Pirkko & Sihra, Melissa. Newcastle: Cambridge Scholars Publishing, 113-
    129.
——. 2011. Theatre in Exile: Defining the Field as Performing Odyssey, *Critical
    Stages* Vol. 5: December
    http://www.criticalstages.org/criticalstages5/entry/Theatre-in-Exile-Defining-
    the-Field-as-Performing-Odyssey?category=2
——. 2012. *Performing Exile – Performing Self: Drama, Theatre, Film*. International
    Performance Series; Eds. Janelle Reinelt, Brian Singleton. Houndmills,
    Basingstoke, Hampshire: Palgrave Macmillan.
——. 2013. Staging Memory in Wajdi Mouawad's *Incendies*: Archaeological Site or
    Poetic Venue?, *Theatre Research in Canada* 34 (1): 12-37.
Meerzon, Yana and Silvija Jestrovic (eds.) 2009. *Performance, Exile and 'America'*.
    Houndmills, Basingstoke, Hampshire: Palgrave Macmillan
Meyer-Dinkgräfe, Daniel. 2002. Brook and the Freedom of Intercultural Theatre' in
    David Bradby and Maria M. Delgado (eds.), *The Paris Jigsaw.
    Internationalism and the city's stages*. Manchester: Manchester UP, 71-82.
——. 2006. Cold Dark Soft Matter Research and Atmosphere in the Theatre". *Body
    Space Technology* Volume 6, 2006. Online at
    http://people.brunel.ac.uk/bst/vol0601/home.html

——. 2013. *Theatre, Oper and Consciousness: History and Current Debates.* Amsterdam: Rodopi.

Meyer-Dinkgräfe, Daniel, Sreenath Nair and Deborah Claire Procter. 2012. Performance anxiety in actors: symptoms, explanations and an Indian approach to treatment. *Canadian Journal of Practice-Based Research in Theatre* 4 (1): 1-28.

Miller, Arthur. 1996. *Death of a Salesman.* Harmondsworth: Penguin.

Moscowitch, Hannah. 2009. *East of Berlin.* Toronto: Playwrights Canada Press.

Mrozek, Slavomir. 1984. *The Emigrants.* London: French.

Nabokov, Vladimir. 1985. *The Man from the USSR.* London: Weidenfeld and Nicolson.

Nelson, Robin. 2013. 2013 *Practice as Research in the Arts, Principles, Protocols, Pedagogies, Resistances.* Basingstoke: Palgrave MacMillan.

Norris, Bruce. 2011. *Clybourne Park.* London: Faber and Faber.

Orme-Johnson, Rhoda. 1987. A Unified Field Theory of Literature, *Modern Science and Vedic Science* 1 (3): 323-373.

Osborne, John. 1967. *Inadmissible Evidence.* London: Faber and Faber.

Pinero, Arthur Wing. 1894. *The Second Mrs Tanqueray.* Boston: W.H.Baker

Pinter, Harold. 1991. *The Birthday Party.* London: Faber and Faber.

——. 1998. *Betrayal.* London: Faber and Faber.

Plater, Alan. 1969. *Close the Coalhouse Door.* London: Methuen.

——. 2000. *Close the Coalhouse Door.* Newcastle upon Tyne: Bloodaxe.

Poore, Benjamin. 2012. *Heritage, nostalgia and modern British theatre: staging the Victorians.* Basingstoke: Palgrave Macmillan.

Prebble, Lucy. 2009. *Enron.* London: Methuen.

Priestley, J.B. 1947. *An Inspector Calls.* Oxford: Heinemann Eductional.

——. 1932. *Dangerous Corner.* London: French.

——. 1938. *Time and the Conways.* London: Harper&Bros.

——. 1938. *I Have Been Here Before.* London: Harper&Bros.

Rancière, Jacques. 2009. *The Emancipated Spectator*, trans. Gregory Elliot. London, New York: Verso.

Reynolds, Simon. 2012. *Retromania: Pop Culture's Addition to its own Past.* London: Faber and Faber.

Rich, Frank. 1998. *Hot Seat.* New York: Knopf.

Robbie, Eric.1987. Neuro Linguistic Programming. In *Innovative Therapies in Britain*, eds. John Rowan and Windy Dryden, 251-279. Milton Keynes: Open University Press.

Rossi, Vittorio. 1998. *Paradise by the River.* Burnaby: Talonbooks.

——. 2009. *The Carpenter.* Vancouver: Talonbooks.

Rubin, Don (ed.) 1994. *The World Encyclopedia of Contemporary Theatre. Volume 1: Europe.* London: Routledge.

Russell, Willy. *Educating Rita.* 1990. London: Longman

Ryan, Robert S. and Jonathan W. Schooler. 1998. Whom Do Words Hurt? Individual Differences in Susceptibility to Verbal Overshadowing. *Applied Cognitive Psychology* 12: S105-S125.

Schwarz, Bernd. 2012. Personal communication, Email.

Seton, Mark Cariston. 2006. 'Post-Dramatic' Stress: Negotiating Vulnerability for Performance. *Being There.* Sydney: University of Sydney.

Sheets-Johnstone, Maxine, 1999, *The Primacy of Movement*, Philadelphia: John Benjamins.

Sherman, Jason. 2006. *After the Cherry Orchard*. Toronto: Playwrights Canada Press.

Sherriff, R.C. 2000. *Journey's End*. London: Penguin.

Stafford, Nick, and Michael Morpurgo. 2007. War Horse. London: Faber and Faber.

Stern, Susan L. 1980. Drama in Second Language Learning from a Psycholinguistic Perspective, *Language Learning* 3:1 (1980).

Valentine, Elizabeth, Daniel Meyer-Dinkgräfe, Veronika Acs, David Wasley. 2006. Exploratory Investigation of South Indian Techniques and Neurolinguistic Programming as Methods of Reducing Stage Fright in Actors. *Medical Problems of Performing Artists* 21 (3): 126-136. Wardle, Irving. 1992. *Theatre Criticism*. London: Routledge.

Wesker, Arnold. 1965. *Chicken Soup with Barley*. London: Longmans.

Wildschut, Tim, Constantine Sedikides and Jamie Arndt. 2006. Nostalgia: Content, Triggers, Functions. *Journal of Personality and Social Psychology* 91:5, 975–993.

Williams, Garrath. Praise and Blame. *Internet Encyclopedia of Philosophy*. http://www.iep.utm.edu/praise/ (accessed August 29, 2010).

Williams, Tennessee. 1979. *Vieux Carré*. New York: New Directions.

——. 1997. *The Notebook of Trigorin*. New York: New Directions.

Wilson, August. 2007. *Fences*. New York: Theatre Communications Group.

Yondem, Z.D. 2007. Performance anxiety, dysfunctional attitudes and gender in university music students. *Social Behaviour and Personality* 35(10): 1415-1426.

Contributors

Per Brask is a Professor in the Department of Theatre and Film at the University of Winnipeg where he has taught since1982. He has published poetry, short stories, drama, translations, interviews and essays in a wide variety of journals. Recent books include *We Are Here,* a collection of poems by the Danish poet Niels Hav (ed. and trans. with Patrick Friesen, Book Thug, 2006), *Copenhagen* a collection of short stories by the Danish writer Katrine Marie Guldager (trans., Book Thug, 2009), *Performing Consciousness* (ed. with Daniel Meyer-Dinkgräfe, Cambridge Scholars Publishing, 2010), and *A Spectator*, a collection of his ekphrastic poems (Fictive Press, 2012). Per Brask has served as dramaturg on countless plays.

Steve Dixon is a world-renowned academic, researcher and interdisciplinary artist with a distinguished career in both higher education leadership and the professional creative industries. He is President of Lasalle College of the Arts, Singapore, one of Asia's foremost arts and design institutions. He has an accomplished record as a strategic and visionary leader, prior to Lasalle as Head of the School of Arts, then as Pro Vice-Chancellor at Brunel University, London. Following a successful career as an actor and award-winning director of film, theatre and digital media productions, Steve established an international reputation for his research in the use of media and computing technologies in the performing arts. His 800-page book Digital Performance: A History of New Media in Theater, Dance, Performance Art and Installation (MIT Press 2007) won two international book awards. He is co-founder/Advisory Editor of the International Journal of Performing Arts and Digital Media. His recent practice-as-research includes an Internet film, Soapopolis (2011, starring Rik Mayall), two collaborations with media artist Paul Sermon, and two one-man multimedia theatre productions: Chameleons 5: Brain Holiday (2011) and an interpretation of T.S. Eliot's The Waste Land (2013). He has been a UK Arts and Humanities Research Council panel member (Music and Performing

Arts), a QAA quality assessor, and has worked in advisory capacities for the Higher Education Funding Council for England and the UK Parliament. He holds a higher Doctorate (Doctor of Letters) and is a Fellow of the RSA (Royal Society for the Arts, Manufactures & Commerce).

Gayathri Ganapathy holds a BA in Psychology, Literature and Sociology from Jyoti Nivas College, Bangalore, India and an MSc in Clinical Psychology from Montfort College, Bangalore, India. She is a trained Bharat Natyam dancer and has been pursuing this art form for the past 18 years. Apart from this she has trained in Bollywood, contemporary and hip hop dance styles. She is currently pursuing research for her PhD on *Dance Movement Training and its Impact of Cognitive Processes and Motor Skills* in the Lincoln School of Psychology, University of Lincoln.

Dr. Yana Meerzon is an Associate Professor, Department of Theatre, University of Ottawa. Her research interests are in theater and drama theory, theater of exile, and Russian theatre and drama. Her articles appeared in New England Theatre Journal, Slavic and East European Journal, Semiotica, Modern Drama, Theatre Research in Canada, Journal of Dramatic Theory and Criticism, Canadian Theatre Review, and L'Annuaire théâtral. She published *The Path of a Character: Michael Chekhov's Inspired Acting and Theatre Semiotics* in 2005. Her book on theatre of exile *Performing Exile – Performing Self: Drama, Theatre, Film* was published by Palgrave, in the series Studies in International Performance, in 2012. She has co-edited two volumes on a similar subject: *Performance, Exile and 'America'* (with Dr. Silvija Jestrovic, Warwick University) Palgrave, 2009; and *Adapting Chekhov: The Text and Its Mutations* (with Dr. J. Douglas Clayton, University of Ottawa) Routledge, 2012.

Daniel Meyer-Dinkgräfe studied English and Philosophy at the Universität Düsseldorf, Germany. In 1994 he obtained his Ph.D. at the Department of Drama, Theatre and Media Arts, Royal Holloway, University of London. From 1994 to 2007, he was a Lecturer and Senior Lecturer in the Department of Theatre, Film and Television Studies, University of Wales Aberystwyth. Since October 2007 he has been Professor of Drama at the Lincoln School of Performing Arts,

University of Lincoln. He has numerous publications on the topic of Theatre and Consciousness to his credit, including *Theatre and Consciousness: Explanatory Scope and Future Potential* (Intellect, 2005) and is founding editor of the peer-reviewed web-journal *Consciousness, Literature and the Arts* and the book series of the same title with Rodopi.

Benjamin Poore is Lecturer in Theatre in the Department of Theatre, Film and Television at the University of York, UK. His main research interests are connected with the fields of Neo-Victorianism and Adaptation Studies. His first book, *Heritage, Nostalgia and Modern British Theatre: Staging the Victorians* (Palgrave, 2012) was an account of the British preoccupation with the Victorian period, as reflected in plays staged since the ending of theatrical pre-censorship in 1968. Benjamin's other publications include articles and book chapters on stage and screen adaptations of Dracula, Sikes and Nancy, and Queen Victoria. His most recent work has considered the cultural afterlives of Sherlock Holmes and Professor Moriarty.

Deborah Claire Procter (Wales) works independently making performances that are a hybrid of live art, dance and theatre. On graduating from Exeter University, she acted with Theatre Alibi, receiving through them extensive training with Gardzienice Theatre Association in the U.K. and Poland. She completed her Masters in Fine Arts at the University of Wales (Cardiff), and in 2005 received the Creative Wales Award. Performing in numerous prestigious venues such as the Ferens (Hull), Spacex (Exeter), Hemsley Theatre (Madison - USA), and Museum Theatre (Madras); in 2004 she began making videos, one of which showed at the "Dance on Screen Festival" at The Place, London. Since 1995 she has trained intensively in NLP including with leading practitioners Stephen Gilligan, and NLP co-founder John Grinder. She teaches voice, performance and NLP as a part-time and guest lecturer in many institutions such as University of Glamorgan, University of Wales, Cardiff, and University of Baroda (India). Following a travel grant from the British Council she began collaborating with Argentinean composer Oscar Edelstein on a number of pieces of musical theatre such as *Insanas, Rivers and Mirrors* and *La Grilla Acústica*, as well as being a guest vocalist with Edelstein's ensemble, Ensamble Nacional del Sur (ENS).

Kate Sicchio is a multiplicity. She is a choreographer, media artist, and performer. She works at the interface of choreography and technology. Her work includes performances, installations, web and video projects and has been shown in Philadelphia, New York City, Canada, Germany, Australia and the UK at venues such as Banff New Media Institute, WAX Brooklyn and Arnolfini. She has presented work at many conferences and symposia including ISEA, ACM Creativity and Cognition, DRHA, CORD, and SDHS. She has given artist talks at Times Up Linz, Dorkbot and Moves Festival. Her PhD focused on the use of real-time video systems within live choreography and the conceptual framework of 'choreotopolgy' a way to describe this work. Her research has been published by Leonardo Almanac, Performance Research Journal and Learning Performance Quarterly. Kate Sicchio has had extensive teaching experience within higher education. She has taught contemporary dance, choreography, and interactive performance technology to both undergraduate and masters level students. She is a visiting lecturer at University of Malta. She is currently Senior Lecturer in Dance at University of Lincoln, Lincoln UK.

Shrikant Subramaniam is an enthusiastic and motivated professional specialising in Indian Classical Dance (Bharata Natyam), Theatre Studies and Dance anthropology with experience in teaching, performing and research. Shrikant has performed extensively in India and abroad and has worked extensively as a freelance dancer, choreographer, story teller, yoga instructor in some of the reputed dance companies and theatre companies in the UK. After working as the dance and education officer of a reputed South Asian Arts Organisation *Manasamitra* (www.manasamitra.com) based in the West Yorkshire region of the UK, Shrikant now works as Artistic Associate (Dance) for *Kalasangam*, based in Bradford, UK.

Nicola Tiggeler was born in Hannover, Germany. Her mother was a violinist, her father opera director, and at the age of four she knew she wanted to be an opera singer. At the age of eight she sang her first role at the Staatsoper Hannover. After the Abitur in Salem she studied singing at the Hochschule für Musik in Hamburg, graduating in 1986 with a diploma in opera singing and as a singing teacher. She sang at the opera in Hannover as Cherubino in Mozart's *The Marriage of Figaro*, followed by six seasons at the Städtischen Bühnen Augsburg, her work ranging from opera to operetta, musical and theatre, with 120 performances per year. In Augsburg he met her husband, Timothy Peach. She moved into film and television when, at her first casting, she was chosen to be the girlfriend of the new actor cast in a long-running series as private investigator. Since then she has worked predominantly for TV, playing lawyers, society ladies, lovers, abandoned wives, divorced women, single women, working women, and especially mothers of all kinds. In particular, since 2006 she has been playing arch-villainess Barbara von Heidenberg in the German soap opera *Sturm der Liebe* in more than 500 episodes, returning from apparent death three times, most recently in October 2013. She is living with her family in Munich, from where she also works as a voice coach as an authorised Linklater teacher.

Aylwyn Walsh is a performance maker/ scholar working on the arts and social change. Her work is concerned with exploring the intersections of interdisciplinary methodologies. She is currently completing research on women's prisons in the UK. Aylwyn lectures at the University of Lincoln and is artistic director of Ministry of Untold Stories. Recent publications have included work on arts in healthcare for the *Journal for Applied Arts and Health*; on street art in *Journal of Arts and Communities*. She has published in *Contemporary Theatre Review* and *Research in Drama Education*. She co-edited *Remapping Crisis: A Guide to Athens*, published by Zero Books, 2013.

Harry Youtt. Since 1990, Harry has been an instructor in the UCLA (Ext) Writers' Program. He was granted the distinction of being a co-recipient of the Writers' Program's Outstanding Instructor in Creative Writing Award for 2004. In 2012 he was the recipient of a Distinguished Instructor Award from the UCLA Extension. For several years, Harry was an instructor in the Digital Arts Program at the University of California at Irvine, teaching courses in writing for convergent media and information design. Harry is also the creator and writer of the critically acclaimed ABC Television pilot season website for David E. Kelley's episodic television series: *The Practice*. He has also been deeply involved in development of practical applications, particularly in higher education, for the internet and the World Wide Web. He has presented papers on internet and broadcast communication theory in the United Kingdom, Ireland, Canada and Mexico, as well as the United States. He co-developed UCLA Extension's original on-line courseware system, in which he taught the first writing courses. He also worked with UCLA to perfect its live two-way interactive video conference course delivery system, and he taught its first on-line live interactive video courses in creative writing. Harry is a fiction writer and poet whose recent collections of poetry include: *What My Father Didn't Know I Learned from Him, Outbound for Elsewhere, I'll Always Be from Lorain*, and *Even the Autumn Leaves..* His poetry has appeared in *Passager, California State Poetry Quarterly, Squaw Valley Review, Raging Dove*, and *Bardsong*, among other venues. His short fiction and non-fiction appear in numerous other publications. He is a member of the Squaw Valley Community of Writers. He has also conducted periodic poetry readings in Ireland and Wales, as well as in the United States. He served for two years as the Poet in Residence at the Philosophical Research Society in Los Angeles, and for several years he conducted poetry workshops at the Dylan Thomas Centre in Swansea, Wales. For a short time during the late 1990's, Harry served as principal drama critic for a Los Angeles-area weekly newspaper.

Index

Lightning Source UK Ltd.
Milton Keynes UK
UKOW05f0241281113

221989UK00002B/163/P